INTELLECTUS: ORIGINS DISCOVERED

INTELLECTUS: ORIGINS DISCOVERED

CHRONICLES OF AN URBAN ELEMENTAL™ BOOK 5

AUBURN TEMPEST
MICHAEL ANDERLE

DISRUPTIVE IMAGINATION®

DON'T MISS OUR NEW RELEASES

Join the LMBPN email list to be notified of new releases and special promotions (which happen often) by following this link:

http://lmbpn.com/email/

This book is a work of fiction. All of the characters, organizations, and events portrayed in this novel are either products of the author's imagination or are used fictitiously. Sometimes both.

Copyright © 2023 LMBPN Publishing
Cover by Fantasy Book Design
Cover copyright © LMBPN Publishing
A Michael Anderle Production

LMBPN Publishing supports the right to free expression and the value of copyright. The purpose of copyright is to encourage writers and artists to produce the creative works that enrich our culture.

The distribution of this book without permission is a theft of the author's intellectual property. If you would like permission to use material from the book (other than for review purposes), please contact support@lmbpn.com. Thank you for your support of the author's rights.

LMBPN Publishing
PMB 196, 2540 South Maryland Pkwy
Las Vegas, NV 89109

Version 1.00, September 2023
eBook ISBN: 979-8-88541-329-9
Print ISBN: 979-8-88878-632-1

THE INTELLECTUS: ORIGINS DISCOVERED TEAM

Thanks to our JIT Team:

Dave Hicks
Daryl McDaniel
James Caplan
Dorothy Lloyd
Diane L. Smith
Jan Hunnicutt

Editor
SkyFyre Editing Team

CHAPTER ONE

The autumn air is as crisp and sweet as the apples we picked. The afternoon sun shines golden across the pumpkin fields and the corn stalk maze. It's a perfect day to visit *Verger Labonté*, the Labonté Orchard.

"Not too much longer," Charlie calls to Micah, Anna, and Sammy. "It's getting cold, guys."

"Cold?" I laugh.

Charlie makes a face at me. "For normal people, yeah, it's getting cold."

I think about that objectively. They all have rosy cheeks and are bundled in bulky cable knit sweaters, puffy vests, and scarves.

I'm toasty warm in only a long-sleeved jersey.

Maybe I'm not the best judge of the temperature anymore. Since Azland unlocked my fire elemental powers, I run hotter than everyone.

Well, except Gareth.

I smile at my broody boyfriend, and the fire within me burns even hotter. There's nothing I love more than spending time with my siblings, and it's even more perfect today because Gareth agreed to join us.

Things with him have been going great...well, when it's only us, that is. Anna and Micah seem fine with me dating a demon hybrid, but Charlie and Kenzie are quietly cautious. Briar and Zephyr are vocally concerned. Azland is silently simmering.

I'm not sure he's entitled to an opinion, but he has one anyway. He lived in the path of destruction when the Poreskoro swept through the elemental kingdoms with their demon armies and consumed everything in their way.

He's understandably bitter. I think he's also genuinely worried. Me spending time alone with the enemy who possesses the ability to devour my elemental powers is dangerous in their eyes.

I can't help how they feel.

All I can do is show them the Gareth I know and care for. The man who would rather die than consume me.

"We aren't leaving yet, are we?" Anna asks.

"Soon, buddy," Charlie replies.

"We can't leave until we pick our pumpkins," Micah gripes. "Anna, Sammy, and I are going to have a carving competition."

"We're not even cold," Sammy adds.

Anna nods. "I read somewhere that it's good for us to race in this weather. It's supposed to strengthen our immune systems or something."

Micah nods, taking his cue. "Yeah, you wouldn't want to stunt our health potential, would you, Charlie?"

Charlie arches a brow and laughs. "Seriously? You two are too much."

Micah bats his eyes. "You know you lurve us."

Charlie shoos them away. "Go have fun. I'll buy some hot ciders to warm us all up."

The beauty of teenagers is that you don't have to tell them twice to have fun. They bolt through the crowd before Charlie can check that I'll monitor them.

When we arrive at the ticket vendor for the pumpkin patch, I flash the vendor a warm smile. She's a weathered old girl but has a kind face and an amiable smile.

"*Bonjour, madam.* How much for the entry into the pumpkin patch?"

"It's free to go in. It's the pumpkins you pay for. It's five dollars for a small and eight dollars for a large. The sizes are marked with colored stickers."

"Wonderful. Thank you." I wave my brothers over to join us and usher the kids through the slatted wooden gate. "Remember, guys. Careful where you walk. There are enough vines and pumpkins around here that you can break your neck. Then Charlie will wring mine."

The kids snort and rush off, laughing.

"I think it's even busier than last year." Kenzie tugs Tad behind her. "If that's possible."

"I heard Old Man Labonté is thinking of selling," Briar replies. "This might be our last year coming here."

That news hits me hard. "Selling? Labonté Orchard is a keystone to autumn in Montréal. They can't sell. Where will we get our pumpkins?"

Zephyr chuckles. "At one of the twenty other pumpkin patches around the city?"

"Or the supermarket?" Briar adds.

I hiss. "Supermarket pumpkins? Shame on you, Briar Gagne. No. We're going to be hauling our butts out to farm fields every autumn until our children's children are too old to pick pumpkins."

Gareth's eyebrows arch. "Wow. I didn't realize you're so serious about pumpkins."

"It's not about the pumpkins. *Maman* and Papa brought us every year, and we loved it. It's about building family memories."

I know Gareth doesn't have great childhood memories, but hopefully, we can help him by building new ones. "On your marks, people. Let the pumpkin hunt begin."

We all spread out with our plus ones, searching for the prize-winning pumpkin. Gareth and I head to the left. Tad and Kenzie take the row straight ahead. Hannah and Briar wander off to the right. And Zephyr…

He's wandered along the fence line with Onyx on his leash and is flirting hard with the brunette we saw at the beer nut hut earlier.

Labonté Orchard has something for everyone.

Row by row, we tromp through the culverts of dirt in search of this season's best.

"Why can't we pick from the perfectly good ones at the market store by the front gate?" Sammy asks.

I laugh. "Picking them from the field is much better."

"It's certainly dirtier." Micah frowns at all the dirt near his white sneakers. "I wore the wrong shoes."

I feel for the kid. He's sixteen and has gotten attached to Sammy—the little pink-haired faery I placed with Charlie a few months back. He's crushing hard on her and always trying to impress.

The thing is, Micah is impressive in every way. He just hasn't learned that yet because of his rough beginnings.

"It's less about the pumpkin itself," I tell them. "It's about the experience. Walking through the field, getting a little dirty, and finding the one pumpkin that calls to you—that's the adventure. Be the Michelangelo of produce. Every pumpkin has a personality yearning to be let out. It's your job to see it and free it."

Sammy mulls it over, then grins. "All right, l can do that."

Anna grins, her eyes sparkling. "I love that. I want to be the Michaelangelo of the pumpkin patch."

"It's a little-known fact that Michelangelo used to carve pumpkins in his spare time," Micah offers.

I side-eye the kid and take the bait. "Oh yeah? Why was that?"

"Because he wanted his masterpieces to be truly *gourd-geous!*"

I groan but can't help laughing. "Go find a pumpkin, dork. You need to redeem yourself after that one."

With that, everyone scatters again.

Gareth and I meander through the rows, the scent of earth and ripe pumpkins thick in the air. As we wander, I watch him. He's a hard one to figure out. He looks as comfortable in a field in jeans as he does swinging a hammer as he does dressed up and going to dinner.

He catches me looking and flashes me a crooked smile. "Something on your mind, spitfire?"

"Still trying to unravel the mystery of my man."

He chuckles. "There's no mystery. You know all my deepest and darkest."

I like that. Likely more than I should.

We continue and pass Briar squatting to examine a particularly funky-shaped pumpkin. Hannah is laughing. She hasn't experienced his sympathy for the underdog before.

He might have grown into a big, burly bear since we were kids, but he's still an orphaned softie at heart.

"Going for the Charlie Brown Christmas tree vibe again this year, B?" I ask.

He flashes me a middle finger salute. "There's nothing wrong with this pumpkin."

Kenzie snorts. "Or at least there won't be once you access your earthly mojo and fix it, right?"

Briar picks up his mutant pumpkin, brushing off dirt. "Don't listen to her, buddy. You're perfect just the way you are. No fixing necessary."

I continue my search, scanning the rows for my pick. Suddenly, I spot it—a plump, round pumpkin with a slight curve to its stem. It's a quirky little guy but has the hallmarks of all the great pumpkins.

Even in shape. No flat side. Graceful lines.

"I found a perfect Ernie." I crouch, inspecting my pick and the row of pumpkins Briar led me to. "Actually, there are a few perfect Ernies on this row."

Running my hand over the round, plump surface of the one calling to me, I assess the bumps and grooves that make it unique.

It's perfect.

Gareth watches me curiously, amused by my enthusiasm. "What makes a pumpkin an Ernie? Help a guy out who's trying to understand the method behind his girlfriend's pumpkin madness."

I straighten with my find, brushing him off. "An Ernie has to have a certain roundness to it like it's been well-fed and happy in the pumpkin patch. It's very different from a Bert."

He chuckles. "Ah…I'm seeing the methodology now. I take it a good Bert is more oblong and tall?"

"Exactly. But shape is only part of it. A perfect pumpkin also needs a good, sturdy stem so you can carry it. And of course, it has to have a certain charm that calls to you."

"Of course." Gareth grins. "You've really thought this through, haven't you?"

I nod, completely serious. "It's a very important decision. The fate of the Gagne Halloween reputation depends on it."

He laughs again and examines the pumpkins, trying to find one that meets my criteria. As he does, my insides warm, and it has nothing to do with my fire powers.

"Here he is." Gareth holds up a pumpkin that's nearly as broody and dark as he is. It has deep grooves, a twisted stem, and a few rough bits that add to its imperfect character. "I think it suits me."

He's not wrong. I nod. "Not bad for a first-timer, but it's no Ernie."

Gareth smirks, lifting his pumpkin. "We'll see whose pumpkin is better once they're carved. This fella is going to be *gourd*-geous. Just like Micah said."

"Excellent. It's catching on," Micah shouts from two rows over.

I groan. "Don't encourage him."

Still, I accept his challenge with a grin, and we wait while everyone else makes their selections.

Once everyone has their respective pumpkins cradled in their arms, we head back to the gate and settle up with the old girl in the booth.

Then we're off to find Zephyr, Charlie, and Azland.

After securing our pumpkins in the back of Briar's truck, Gareth heads over to his truck to let Jinx out of the cab. When we arrived an hour ago, Gareth's hellhound conveyed to him she had no interest in joining us.

It seems she's changed her mind.

With her head up, Onyx's mother comes almost up to my armpits. Her ebony coat is long and wiry, sticking up in every direction the same as Onyx's. To say she's intimidating is the understatement of the century—which is fine because it keeps the dog people from coming over to ask if they can pet her.

Well, that and her demon dog ability to repel people.

Gareth's brooding expression as he leads her toward the apple orchard makes me chuckle. He's not the apple-picking type, but he's trying.

Kenzie comes over with Onyx bouncing energetically at the end of his leash. My boy is having a blast. "Hey, baby. Did you have fun with Zephyr?"

Kenzie laughs as she gives me the leash. "Zephyr's exact words were 'best chick magnet evah.'"

I roll my eyes. "No doubt."

Gareth and I walk the dogs through the orchard. Children run around us, laughing and playing. Their parents stick close, most of them giving us wary glances and keeping their kids away from our hounds.

They're in no danger as long as they don't suddenly go demon and attack us. Then they'd be in big trouble.

After we've picked a decent amount of apples, we buy little bags of food for the petting zoo and send the kids in to have fun.

"You're not coming?" Anna asks.

I gesture at the two hellhounds. "Not this year. These two could make normal goats into fainting goats."

Micah snorts. "Ohmygoodness, could we try that? Fainting goats are hilarious."

"What are fainting goats?" Sammy asks.

Micah's face lights up as he pulls his phone out of his back pocket. "Prepare to pee your pants."

As the two walk off, we follow the outside of the fence and end up at the beer nut hut. "Two large bags, please," I request.

When the brunette hands them over, I settle up, and the two of us claim a picnic table off to the side.

"You really get off on days like this, don't you?" Gareth palms a handful of nuts and pops them into his mouth.

"Yeah. I love family days." I watch the kids giggling as they feed the chickens and Zephyr playing with one of the goats. "I think working as a cop and now an enforcer of the empowered world, I see a lot of dark and dangerous. There's something about a family day that reminds me why it's all worth it."

He leans back, watching them as if considering that. "I suppose that's true, given the family you have."

Yeah, his family mostly sucks.

While I'm not a huge fan of Rance, Gareth's oldest sibling has a code he lives by, which I can respect.

I'd never go as far as saying he's a good guy, but if your father is a king of hell, the odds aren't good that you'll grow up without a few dark habits.

Gareth draws me out of my mental musings and snorts. "Your brother will get you kicked out before you get to the corn maze."

I glance around to see what he means and roll my eyes. Zephyr is in the pen, playing with one of the goat kids. "Z, boundaries! Get your butt out of the goat corral. You're setting a poor example."

Zephyr pouts. "Don't worry, little guy. I'll come back and visit you again before we go."

As Zephyr reluctantly leaves the pen, I shake my head. "You're now an enforcer for the Guild of the Laurentians, remember?"

Zephyr grins, unbothered by my chastisement. "Life's too short not to enjoy the little things, right?"

As much as I should, I can't argue with that.

CHAPTER TWO

The live band's upbeat music fills the air as I make my way to the grilling area. Burgers and dogs never smelled so good. While I'm in line, my gaze drifts to Gareth. He's watching the band, his fingers tapping out the rhythm against the denim of his thigh.

He's relaxed and enjoying himself.

I take that as a major win.

I'm halfway through my second sausage dog when the gang returns, red-faced and laughing. I finish chewing and swallow. "How did bobbing for apples go?"

"Amazing." Kenzie grins from ear to ear.

"She totally cheated," Micah claims. "The rest of us are all dunking our heads like ducks in a pond, trying to grab hold of a honey crisp, and Kenzie's all 'la-ti-da,' barely puts her mouth into the water and comes up with a giant."

I stifle my laugh and peg my sister with a look. "Did you use your powers to bring the apple to your mouth?"

Kenzie shrugs. "There were no rules against it."

Micah throws up his arms. "The rules against it are implied."

Kenzie giggles unrepentantly. "I'll remember that for next year. Promise."

I laugh and point at Sammy and Anna. "Hey, why aren't you two red in the cheeks? Did you not partake in the bobbing fun?"

Anna blinks at me. "Do you know how many strangers had their spit and eye gunk in that water? Gross. Yeah no, not interested."

"Eye gunk?" Briar makes a face. "You're the one who's gross."

Anna waves away his comment. "Are you ready for the corn maze? It's the last thing on our list, and Charlie's crock pot zuppa Toscana awaits."

I pop the last bite of my barbequed sausage dog into my mouth and wipe my fingers. "Yep. Give me two minutes to run to the little girl's trailer and wash up."

Briar and Hannah exchange a look before nodding. "We're going to grab a drink. Then we'll head over," Briar confirms.

"I'll text Zephyr and tell him where we're heading," Tad replies. "Let's say we meet up in five?"

Micah checks in with the girls. "Sounds good. We're going to study the map. Fastest through wins. And no cheating." He points two fingers toward his eyes and swings them around toward Kenzie.

Kenzie laughs. "How can I cheat in a corn maze? I'm a water girl."

I take a couple of minutes in the portable bathroom trailer to refresh and get ready for the last event of the Gagne fall festival day.

Gareth is leaning up against the trailer's wall when I exit, and he seems to have gathered quite a group of female fans while I was inside.

"Doesn't that get old?" I giggle.

"Doesn't what get old?"

"Girls staring at you."

He looks at me and glances around. "No one is staring at me."

I snort. "Are you telling me you honestly didn't notice a half-dozen women undressing you with their eyes?"

He looks around again and shrugs. "I guess not. Honestly, I know what I am, and nine and a half times out of ten, the surrounding women are human. I guess I've never considered them an option."

I slide my arm into his. "Their loss is my gain."

We head over to the maze's entrance, and Briar tilts his head toward the two cruisers parked on the edge of the field. "What's that about?"

I glance around to double-check that the kids aren't within earshot. "Marx knows we come here most years and mentioned a couple of people have been reported missing in the maze over the past two weeks."

"You're just telling us now?"

I shake my head. "I told him we'd have a run-through and see if we notice anything. This is what we do, right? We are protectors of the people. Guardians against the whacked and weird?"

Kenzie laughs. "Speaking of whacked and weird. Why is our brother carrying a goat?"

I wait until Zephyr gets closer and peg him with a look. "Did you steal a goat?"

He grins as the goat *bleats* softly in his arms. "This is Dude. He's my partner for this adventure."

I blink. "Does anyone else see the irony in the fact that we're about to investigate missing people and one of us kidnapped a goat?"

"*Kid*-napped." Micah snorts. "Good one, Jules. Get it? A baby goat is a kid."

I roll my eyes and meet Gareth's gaze. "Do you see what I'm dealing with here?"

"What did you mean missing people?" Anna asks.

I draw a deep breath. "Likely people who got drunk or

ditched their friends. Just to be safe, stay together in there. Okay?"

Charlie flashes me a stink-eye and waves my words away. "You know how Jules gets. She sees mystery and mayhem behind every corner. We're here to have fun. Focus on that."

There's no need to worry because the teens have already lost interest. They're plotting their route through the maze using the map posted at the entrance.

I meet Charlie's gaze. "You okay?"

"Of course. Why wouldn't I be?"

Since we rescued Payton, another magic elemental, a few weeks ago, Azland has been acting weird.

He lived with the assumption that he was the last of his kind for the past twenty-five years. Finding out there is another, and she's a pretty blonde, has thrown him for a bit of a loop.

"Just checking in. Are you and Azland having fun?"

She laughs. "Stop your worrying. I'm a big girl. Azland and I are living in the moment. Yes, for the moment, we're having fun."

Zephyr's goat lets out a long *bleat,* and we all stiffen and look around.

"You're seriously going to get us kicked out of here." I smack his arm.

"Then let's get this race started and stop standing around waiting to get caught." He tucks the little goat into his coat.

"Okay, we're ready," Micah shouts.

Briar grins. "Excellent. Let's make things a little more interesting by adding a challenge."

Zephyr glances at him sidelong. "What are you thinking, brother?"

Briar scans the map of the maze. "The first one to take a load off at this seating area in the center of the maze wins."

"What do we win?" Micah asks.

Briar scratches his cheek, looking around. "Bragging rights and royal carte blanche."

"Well now, things just got interesting," Zephyr remarks.

Charlie rolls her eyes. "For you. Whenever you guys offer royal carte blanche, it's a royal pain in my butt."

Briar pushes out his bottom lip. "Come on, Charlie. Play with us. You don't want to ruin our fun, do you?"

No. She doesn't. "Fine, royal carte blanche."

"Yes!" Micah and Anna hiss, pumping their arms.

"What does that mean?" Sammy asks.

Micah grins. "It means that for an entire day, we get to be the king—"

"Or queen," Anna adds.

"Or queen," Micah agrees. "Everyone must serve us and do our bidding. If we want to go to the zoo and be carried in a litter and fanned as we walk, they have to do it."

"And if we want our entire apartment cleaned and our closet reorganized, it must be done," Kenzie adds.

"So, why does Charlie hate it so much?" Gareth asks.

I chuckle. "Because it usually involves her cooking favorite meals and baking desserts all day."

"Which she loves," Briar adds. "Don't buy into her feigned annoyance. She loves seeing what we come up with when we play this."

Charlie frowns. "No live lobster. I don't care who wins. I'm not going through that again. Or eel. That was almost as upsetting as the screaming shells."

Briar nods. "Fine. Nothing upsetting. Is everyone in agreement?"

When no one objects, he points at the entrance. "Pair up. Kids together. No powers or cheating with phones or anything. This is a straight race to the center based on instinct and sense of direction."

"Agreed." Micah gets his hands up to keep us from passing him. "See you in the center, suckers."

The kids are the first to rush off, but that doesn't worry me. Anna and Micah have the worst sense of direction imaginable.

Kenzie and Tad will probably end up making out somewhere.

Zephyr has a goat as a partner.

Briar and Hannah are the ones we need to beat.

Although, we've never played against Azland. He might be good. He seems to have a natural navigation system...or at least he did when he was our dog.

Jogging through the cornstalks with Gareth and the dogs is surprisingly fun. We laugh as we hit dead ends and backtrack, trying to remember which turns we've already taken. Since it's the end of the season, the corn rises at least four or five feet over our heads.

"Would lifting you to peek over the top be cheating?" Gareth asks.

"I don't think so. Although I'm not sure, even then, if I'll be able to see."

Abandoning that idea for the moment, the two of us rush off. Onyx thinks this is the most fun ever and his butt wags madly as we maneuver the field.

The atmosphere is lively in here, with children running ahead of their parents and teenagers racing around, oblivious to the other people around them.

Gareth and I navigate the twists and turns, enjoying ourselves. "I think if we keep edging northeast, we'll be in good shape."

I check the sky and head off again.

Onyx drops his head and growls as we delve deeper into the maze. It's the first time he hasn't been all in and having a ball. "What's up, buddy?"

I gently tug his leash and pat my leg to encourage him, and he goes another ten feet before he sits, refusing to move.

He's not alone this time. Jinx sits and drops her head. A menacing growl rumbles out of her chest.

I exchange a worried glance with Gareth. "What do you think is up with them?"

He meets Jinx's gaze, and his eyes flash scarlet. "She says there's dark magic in the air. They don't like the energy of it."

I close my mouth before bugs fly in. "Okay, we're going to circle back to you mind-speaking with your hound and not sharing that little tidbit before now. First, tell me what kind of energy is upsetting them. Like demon evil energy? Or like a Goblet of Fire keystone and Voldemort waiting in the cemetery kind of evil energy?"

Gareth blinks. "I don't even know what those words mean. Are you speaking pop culture again?"

I giggle. "Oh, sorry. Yeah. Never mind."

Gareth's expression grows serious. "I don't like there being a darkness in a place with so many innocents."

"Me either. Maybe this is part of the problem Marx is trying to figure out. Maybe there's a minotaur in this maze or something."

When his eyebrow arches like I'm a fruity nut bar, I laugh. "Or some kind of modern cornstalk stalker. Yeah…a cornstalker! Do you think that's a thing?"

He grunts and says something in his demon language I don't understand. Jinx and Onyx do because they both stand and we move again.

"All good?" I ask.

"Not in the slightest, but they trust us."

That's reassuring. I'm never sure if Jinx likes me or will consider me a threat to her relationship with Gareth and eat me while I sleep.

As we continue deeper into the maze, the children's laughter fades, replaced by an eerie hiss of wind wrestling through the surrounding stalks.

The air feels heavy and oppressive as if something unseen is trying to suffocate us.

"Okay, this is officially creepy." I pull my phone out to text the family chat group and tell them I want them out of the maze. "No signal."

I hold it up higher, tilting it this way and that, seeing if I can get any bars. "Am I the only one who feels like we're about to be the victims in a bloody murder scene in a horror movie?"

Gareth chuckles. "I've never been a victim in my entire life. I won't start now."

No. I don't suppose he will.

He winks at me with a reassuring smile. "Don't worry, spitfire. Your big, powerful man will protect you. I'm here."

I snort, the tension of the moment broken. "Thanks, I needed that."

He grins. "I thought you'd enjoy that one."

I did. Gareth is all kinds of powerful and can beat the snot out of the scariest of beasts, but the day I tremble in the corner while my boyfriend—or anyone—swoops in to fend off the bad guys is the day the earth opens and swallows me whole.

Not going to happen.

Gareth frowns as he turns his head and closes his eyes. "I think there's a repulsion spell at work, too."

"To keep people away from what?" I ask as we walk again.

"I'm guessing the big bad whatever."

"So whoever or whatever is behind this stomach-curdling energy wants to be left alone?"

"Maybe."

"People have gone missing."

"Maybe it's a selection process?"

"Or the cornstalker doesn't feed often?"

Gareth curses as we hit another dead end, and we have to turn back. "There's no such thing as a cornstalker."

The maze seems to grow darker and more ominous with every step we take, the feeling of danger growing heavier.

As we round a blind corner in the middle of the maze, the dogs vocalize in an endless, vicious snarl.

"There!" Charlie and Azland grin at us with triumphant looks as they race the last steps to the seating area set up under a metal gazebo.

Charlie sees me and laughs. "Close, but not close enough, you two. You snooze. You lose."

She drops backward to sit on a bench, and I race to stop her. "Charlie, no!"

Gareth's heavy footfalls are behind me as a wave of dark magical energy hits us like a tsunami.

The force behind the wave is overwhelming. It knocks me back, sending me into Gareth's chest, then scrambling across the grass and dirt of the cornfield.

The air crackles with power, and the energy invades my system, coursing through my veins and setting my nerves on fire.

The champagne swirls of sunset spin out of focus and in the next moment, I sprawl on my back, looking up into a turbulent navy sky.

It takes a moment for the centrifuge in my cranium to settle, then I struggle to get to my feet. "Gareth? Are you okay?"

He's kneeling on one knee and rubs his head. "I think so. I'm most worried about Charlie. That was powerful—maybe too powerful for a human."

I see the concern etched into his features and follow his gaze to where Charlie is out cold next to a dazed-looking Azland.

With my pulse thrumming in my ears, I reach the bench and drop to check on Charlie.

She's horribly pale, but her sallow complexion might have more to do with the weird lighting of this place than her current state.

Azland probes his head. "What the hell was that? It feels like someone blendered my brains."

It really does.

Gareth helps Charlie sit up and settles her back onto the bench.

"What happened?" She looks around. "More importantly, where are we?"

Gareth is standing rigidly stiff next to me, his eyes glowing scarlet. Jinx is in about the same mood, and the two scan our surroundings.

I straighten to stand beside him and curse. "Toto, I don't think we're in Kansas anymore."

CHAPTER THREE

Gareth, Charlie, Azland, and I take a moment to digest our strange surroundings. The twisted trees of the orchard. The eerie mist hanging about a foot off the rocky ground. The muted blue haze that makes the world look bleached of color.

Jinx growls, her eyes glowing with flickering flames as her body expands in height and breadth. It's crazy. It's like she's super-sizing from a massive dog to the size of a small horse. She turns to look at Gareth and bares her fangs as she snarls.

Gareth strokes a hand down her back and picks up Onyx. "Okay, girl. I've got him."

My mind blanks out. *Holy hell dog.* "Wait. Is Onyx going to get that big?"

Gareth meets my gaze. "Likely bigger. Onyx is male and has an incredible bloodline."

That shorts out my mind.

"Where the hell are we?" Charlie asks.

Gareth shakes his head. "Not in hell, but other than that, I have no idea."

Azland frowns at Gareth. "Is this your doing?"

Where I'm surprised and disappointed by the question,

Gareth doesn't miss a beat. How often must accusations like that be flung at you before they faze you?

"Why would I bring us to a place like this?"

"Why does a Poreskoro do anything? To delight in another person's fear? To exploit vulnerability?"

"Enough, Azland," I snap. "Why would you put this on Gareth? Couldn't you feel the dark foreboding? All competitiveness aside, why would you allow Charlie to go deeper into such dark energy?"

"What dark energy?"

I look from him to Charlie. "Surely you felt it. The cloying dread? The malignant darkness?"

The two of them stare at me blank-faced.

"I get Charlie might not have sensed it, but I find it strange that a magic elemental couldn't feel it."

"Unless the darkness drew them in instead of repelling them like it did to us." Gareth strokes a hand down Onyx's neck and ruffles his ears.

Jinx is still growling, casting wary glances back to Gareth and Onyx before scanning the area.

It's unnerving that a hellhound is anxious about the safety of her pup. It makes me wonder what we're about to find ourselves facing.

Gareth straightens, scowling at the creepy orchard. "We need to figure out what's going on and how to get back."

I check my phone, not expecting any love, but I'm still disappointed we can't phone a friend and fast-track our return home. As I move to catch a signal, the thick carpet of leaves blanketing the ground muffles my footsteps.

"This place is terrifying." Charlie scowls at the crooked shadows stretching across the uneven ground. "I half expect a headless horseman to come clopping out from behind a tree."

Yeah, there is an Ichabod Crane feeling to this place.

I flex my fingers, feeling the warmth of my fire element

tingling in my fingertips. "Since no one is rolling out the red carpet as our welcoming committee, I guess we'll need to explore and figure things out on our own."

"What we seek is that way." Azland points.

I arch a brow. "First, don't say shit like that. Second, what do you mean, 'what we seek?' Are you talking about the way home? Can you feel a portal?"

"No. I feel magical energy. Only it's not an evil repulsion like you mentioned. It's a call. It's a plea."

I stare at Gareth. "How concerned should we be that Azland is tapping into the energy and acting weird?"

"He's not acting weird." Charlie shoots me a look.

I lean close as we walk. "He's following the magical call of a creepy orchard realm and thinks it's asking us for help. You don't think that's weird?"

"Every bit of this is weird. Don't put it all on Azland."

I grunt. "Oh, I'm not. This freak show has plenty of weird to go around."

Azland snaps out of whatever freaky trance he's been under and shakes his head. "There's a tree in the center of the orchard. It's the power that brought us here, but not the malevolence we feel."

"Or that's what the evil tree wants you to think," I add. "You never can tell with psychotic plants."

Gareth chuckles. "Dealt with a lot of treacherous trees in your lifetime, have you?"

"Oh, sure. Treacherous trees, baneful bushes, and a few shady shrubs."

Charlie huffs and shakes her head. "Not now, Jules. Seriously, can we focus on getting home to the kids and not turn it into a joke?"

Gareth frowns, but I raise a hand. "It's fine. Charlie doesn't thrive on humor to handle stressful situations. S'all good. I can tone it down."

Gareth doesn't seem pleased about that but doesn't fight me on it, either.

It's fine. Charlie doesn't laugh in the face of danger. She hunkers down and raises the shields. It's one of the few things we've truly fought about.

She hated it when I became a cop.

Azland leads the way along a meandering dirt path that looks silvery blue in the distorted light. As we walk, my head is on a swivel, taking everything in.

It's as if the trees are alive, their branches reaching out to us like gnarled fingers, trying to ensnare us in their grasp. Shadows dance at the edge of my vision, and I can't shake the feeling that something is following us.

After years on the force and now with my elemental powers unlocked, my instincts are sharp, and I don't question them.

Whoever or whatever is following us, they aren't a figment of my imagination. They're out there. I'd say something, so we're all on the same page, except it wouldn't do Charlie any good.

She doesn't want to be anywhere on this page.

Not that I need to say anything. Azland seems to be plugged into the magic of this place, and if Gareth hasn't sensed the eyes on him, Jinx has and expressed her concerns about it.

Jinx's hackles are raised, and she's glaring scarlet toward whoever dares to stalk us. Whether she's holding them at bay or not, I'm not sure. If *I* were the stalker staring down a homicidal hellhound, I would give her a wide berth.

"Charlie, are you okay?" I glance at her sidelong, studying her as we walk.

She offers a shaky smile. "Sorry about before. I'm not used to this kind of thing, you know?"

"Don't worry about it. I get it. Just know that the three of us kick ass and we're certainly not going to let anything happen to you. We've got you."

Azland reaches back to take her hand and laces their fingers together. When he's pulled her tight to his side, he stops and points. The enchanted tree stands tall, its twisted branches reaching for the hazy blue sky.

I breathe deep, my lungs filling with the damp scent of earth and decay. "I take it we have arrived?"

Azland nods. "We're in the orchard's heart. This is the tree that brought us here."

"The *tree* brought us here?"

"Not the tree, exactly." A man pushes off the broad trunk. His untamed hair is an amalgamation of branches and leaves in a range of greens. "As the Keeper of the Orchard, I am the intention, while Aetherbough is the source of the orchard's power."

His presence is shocking. If he hadn't moved, I'm not sure we would've seen him standing there.

Gareth hands Charlie a squirming Onyx and frees his hands. I call a flame whip to my palm, ready to defend in case the Keeper of the Orchard gets any big ideas.

"Why have you brought us here?" Gareth snaps.

The Keeper of the Orchard straightens. His skin is more like bark, rough and dappled with hues of rich earth and aged wood. It's etched with a pattern reminiscent of tree rings, and I wonder if they're a testament to the years he's spent among the trees.

His gaze is severe. "We seek one with the strength and courage to face the ancient evil plaguing our home. We believe you are the ones we have been waiting for."

His hand slices through the air as he gestures at the forest, and dozens of smaller fae creatures emerge from the shadows.

Beings with globe eyes and clothes made of woven plant fibers come forward. They are small, shy, and adorned with ornaments of berries and seeds. It's unsettling how perfectly they blend in with the orchard's colors and textures.

A halfling wearing a cloak of leaves moves to stand beside the Keeper's leg. The fabric of his cloak shifts from vibrant greens to rich golds and reds, as if in sync with the changing of the seasons.

I exchange wary glances with Gareth and Azland. They have more experience than I do with fae creatures, but one thing I've learned is their appearance is rarely indicative of the power they possess.

Others step forward, their frail forms shimmering in the hazy mist. It's difficult to discern their true appearance, but part of me wonders if that's intentional.

The Keeper of the Orchard bows his head, his gaze never wavering from our group. "You won't need weapons against us, fire female. We pose no threat to you or yours."

I frown. "Other than portaling us here against our will to pit us against an ancient evil you don't want to deal with yourselves."

He shakes his head, disturbing a couple of moths from the thicket of his hair. They flutter up in disjointed flight and settle back into place once more. "It's not that we don't want to deal with our enemy. It's that we aren't capable of dealing with him."

"What makes you think we are?"

The Keeper's gaze locks with mine, and I swear I can feel him as if he's boring into my soul. "Your powers are strong, stronger than any we have encountered. You can save our orchard."

"And if we don't, we die? Is that what happened to the others you've brought here to fight your enemy?"

The tree man shrugs his branches. "I can't say for certain, but they didn't return. We assume they are lost to the evil."

"But you don't know?"

"How could we know?"

I blink. "By checking on them? They could be hurt. You kidnap people and shove them into your issue, and you don't follow up?"

He doesn't seem affected by my words. "You will defeat the ancient evil plaguing our orchard. We believe you are strong enough."

Gareth steps in front of me, his eyes narrowed. "What do we

gain in this arrangement? Why should we help you battle a foe that has done us no wrong?"

The Keeper inclines his head. "With our gratitude comes our assurance that you will return to your world unharmed."

Gareth's eyes haven't stopped glowing since we arrived in this clearing. Even without hellfire burning in his retinas, it would still be easy to tell that he wants to burn this tree man to the ground.

"Very well." He straightens to his full height. "We will face your foe and remove the danger to your orchard. You will return us and any others we find to the time and place you found us. In the future, you will cease taking innocents from their lives to bring them here for your purposes."

Something in the precision of his words makes my skin tingle. Fae are very literal beings. They can also be very deceitful and self-serving.

Still, I trust Gareth.

After a tense moment, our host nods. "Very well."

Gareth doesn't look happy, but he's reining it in. "Very well. We'll help you in exchange for your promise to fulfill your end of the bargain. But know this. If you betray us, we will not hesitate to destroy this orchard, your people, and everything you hold dear."

The Keeper's eyes flash dangerously, but he inclines his head again, sealing the agreement. "We will honor our word. May our alliance prove fruitful."

With the bargain struck, the Keeper gestures for me, Gareth, Charlie, and Azland to follow him along a wide path leading off to the left of the way we used to get here. "You must hurry. The evil grows stronger by the day. I fear we might run out of time."

Rude. They're blackmailing us into fighting their fight, and they have the nerve to tell us to hurry?

It hasn't slipped my attention that Gareth unclipped both dogs from their leashes and let them walk freely at our sides. I'm unsure what to make of that but don't want to bring it up in mixed company.

As we make our way through the twisted, misty forest, I marvel at how the glowing fruit on the trees casts a strange, ethereal light. That's where the strange silver-blue lighting is coming from.

While Gareth, Azland, and I are resolved to tackle the task at hand, Charlie is clearly on edge. She clings to Azland's arm, her gaze darting from shadow to shadow.

Gareth occasionally murmurs quiet reassurances to Jinx and Onyx. While he can speak telepathically to her, I don't think he has that ability with her pup.

I wonder if that's my honor.

It makes sense that maybe a hellhound can speak to the person with whom it shares a blood bond. In that case, that would be me with Onyx and him with Jinx.

How freaking cool is that?

As we continue deeper into the orchard, the shadows seem darker, the mist thicker, and the air more oppressive. I can tell we're getting closer to the source of the ancient evil by the way the contents of my stomach are curdling.

"This is as far as I take you," the Keeper states. "I must return to the heart of the orchard to be with Aetherbough. I wish you well."

He hustles off like a ferret scurrying back to his hole, and I shake my head. "Him wishing us well has nothing to do with us and everything to do with what he expects us to do for him."

Gareth chuckles, but there's no humor in it. "Welcome to the self-serving nature of the fae. Their enchanting allure only serves to mask their masterful manipulations."

Azland pegs Gareth with a look. "Says the fae prince."

"Half fae," Gareth corrects.

Azland scoffs. "I'm willing to bet that's the better side of the two when considering your gene pool."

The flames in Gareth's eyes leap higher as he steps forward. "Oh, you don't want to go splashing in my gene pool, magic man."

I step in between them and wave my hand to get their attention. "Okeedokie. On that note, how about we deal with the ancient evil turning my bowels to acid? Then you can continue your pissing match back at the fire station. Sound good? I thought so too."

Pointing the way, I grab a couple of broken branches off the ground, call flame to my hand, and make torches.

Boys.

CHAPTER FOUR

The flames of torchlight flicker orange against the muted blue haze of the fae orchard. It casts eerie shadows on the trees and the ground around us. When Charlie shivers, I let a bit of my core temperature free and dispel the cold seeping into her bones.

She meets my gaze and puts on a brave face. "You're a handy girl to have around."

"That's me. I'm all the rage at bonfires, death pyres, and burning man festivals."

She chuckles. "I'll keep that in mind."

Jinx and Onyx have been jogging around us, crisscrossing the area with their noses to the ground. I don't want to know what they're on the trail of because given the dank scent of death building in the air, it can't possibly be good.

When Jinx sits ahead of us, I slow. "Gareth? What did she find?"

Gareth jogs past us and waves to signal Azland to take the rear. I stop with Charlie and give him a moment to investigate. "It's a body...or it was."

"What does that mean?" I leave Charlie with Azland and stride to join him. When I see the mangled corpse, my morbid side is thoroughly intrigued. "What the hell can do this? It's bizarre."

"What's bizarre?" Charlie snaps, glancing over from where she stands with Azland.

"Well, normally I get a good idea about a person based on the rate of decay, what bugs are present and in what stages of life, and the state of the tissue. These bodies are keeping their secrets."

Charlie groans and closes her eyes. "Not everyone hangs out at the morgue for fun, Jules. What are you trying to say?"

"I'm saying that whatever killed them seems to have sucked their energy and vitality dry. They're withered and drained. It's hard to explain beyond that. Luc would think this is so cool."

"It's not cool," Gareth says. "A few weeks ago, this was a thirty-something male. Now he's desiccated, and his life force has fed that evil entity we sense."

Pulling out my phone, I take a couple of pictures.

"What are you doing?" Charlie looks appalled.

I shrug. "We knew we'd probably come across the other people the fae sent here to take care of their enemy. It's important to catalog the ones we find so I can report back."

Charlie meets my gaze. "Do you seriously not see how disturbing that is?"

"It's closure for families. No matter how bad the news is, it's better than not knowing. Trust me, Charlie. I know of what I speak."

She stares at me for a long time before sighing and closing her eyes. "Fine. Do what you need to do. Then can we get out of here? I'm not like you. I don't enjoy being near dead bodies, or worse, the beast that made them dead."

Fair enough. "That's fine. Azland can guide you past the body. Hold on to his arm and close your eyes. We'll let you know when the coast is clear."

As we continue deeper into the grove, more bodies appear,

each desiccated like the last. I take a few pictures of each, knowing they'll be important when we get back. There's no way we can bring all these bodies home, so recording them is the best I can do.

"They're not all human." Gareth crouches in front of the next victim Jinx discovered. "The Keeper of the Orchard must've taken some of them from other portal locations."

I hustle over to see what he's talking about. "Well, I suppose we should be grateful he didn't only target Montréal pumpkin seekers."

"I suppose so."

The farther we go, the more I feel a growing unease in the pit of my stomach. There are more dead than I expected. "If the ancient evil has drained and fed on this many victims, how strong will it be?"

Gareth frowns. "It's hard to say. That depends on what kind of being it is, how large, how long it's been since its last feedings...but certainly stronger than it would've been without feeding."

"So, in a twisted way, the Keeper of the Orchard has been sustaining his enemy in his attempts to destroy it?"

"You could look at it like that."

Finally, after what seems like hours, the dogs lead us to a hidden grove within the orchard. The air here feels heavy, saturated with a darkness that sends shivers down my spine.

The grove's trees differ from those in the orchard, their bark blackened and twisted like tortured souls. In the center of the clearing stands a massive tree with its heart hollowed out.

Charlie whimpers. I don't blame her. It's as if that tree is pulsing with evil energy. It's radiating outward, making my heart beat off-rhythm.

Onyx is anxious too. At least, I think that's what's causing him to supersize. Like Jinx did when she first arrived, Onyx grows. He starts at the size of a gangly lab on an epically bad hair day and becomes the size of a Great Dane—still having a bad hair day.

His collar has a breakaway clasp and pops open, freeing him from the danger of choking.

I close the distance, taking up a position beside him in case he gets a dumb idea about running off.

"Show yourself," Gareth commands, straightening to his full height.

The being that shows itself is tall, its body composed of writhing tendrils of darkness that defy any solid form. Its eyes are a void, yet somehow they bore into my soul.

"What the fuck is that?" I whisper.

"A shadow wraith," Gareth and Azland reply.

"A Shadow *King*," the beast hisses.

I shudder, trying to shake off the feeling of being utterly exposed. Except it's not me it's looking at…

It's Charlie.

It licks its lips, eyeing my aunt with a hunger that makes my blood run cold.

I step in front of Charlie, my fiery gaze meeting the wraith's icy stare. "She's not for you. We saw what you do to people. You won't have her."

The wraith merely chuckles. "You cannot stop me, child," he hisses, his voice echoing in my mind. "I was trapped and starved for centuries and will not be denied sustenance."

A rush of dark energy pulses through the grove, and shadows crawl across the damp ground. The movement is unnatural and unnerving.

Gareth, Azland, and the hellhounds close in around Charlie. "Are you sure you want to do this?" Gareth asks. "Because we won't be put down like your other prey."

The wraith remains undaunted.

Gareth and I step forward, putting some distance between us and Charlie.

Then we call forward our fire elemental sides.

With a satisfying *whoosh*, my body is wreathed in fire, and I claim my woman aflame form. Flexing my right hand, I extend my element into a twelve-foot whip.

When my powers first awoke, I began training with a physical whip. Now, that's unnecessary. My flame whip is a part of me and coils and strikes at my will.

Gareth has embraced his demon side and has grown bigger. Thick, black horns come out the sides of his skull and curl forward as his forehead and hair crackle with orange flames. A massive stone and fire gauntlet sheathes his right arm and hand, and his tail swishes threateningly behind us.

Charlie gasps, but I don't turn because her shock, fear, or whatever is written all over her face right now is of no interest to me.

Gareth is who he was born, and I accept that without judgment. The man he chooses to be is caring, broody, and lives by a code—protect the innocent.

Behind us, Azland focuses his elemental magic on creating a shield between the shadow wraith and us.

The hellhounds bare their teeth and growl.

"Last chance," Gareth warns.

Our opponent is smart enough to assess us as an opposing force and look concerned. Still, it doesn't appear to be enough to stop him from attacking.

The Shadow King lunges forward, his dark tendrils reaching out for Charlie. I react instantly, staying between him and his target. A wave of dark energy hits Gareth and me in the face.

It knocks me backward and wraps me in its grip. I get my hands up and push my flames out. The searing heat melts through the attack, replacing the dark energy with a wall of fire to shield us.

Gareth straightens and stretches his neck. "Thanks, spitfire."

"You bet."

A *thud* on the other side of my wall tests the strength of my shield. It wavers behind the onslaught but holds without issue.

Gareth is ready to go on the offensive again.

Without effort, he steps forward and disappears through my wall of flame. *How did he do that?*

Sadly, there's no time to ask. The Shadow King sees Gareth coming and grabs a barren tree around the trunk. Ripping its roots from the soil, he angles the wood column and swings it.

Imagine being sideswiped by a telephone pole impacting you with the force of a semi-truck behind it.

That's all I can think of as I turn to catch the trunk as it approaches. Readying for the hit, I absorb the moment of connection and allow the Shadow King to take me on a ride.

I'm the ball cracked by the largest Louisville Slugger in the world.

The wraith doesn't keep his bat. *Oh, no.* He releases it during the follow-through, and I get caught behind the momentum of a massive wooden shaft.

That's not nearly as sexy as it sounds.

Gareth watches me soar by, and if his eyes weren't glowing red and on fire, he'd roll them.

What? How did I know this was going to happen?

I launch off the tree trunk, dive-rolling to cushion my landing. By the time I get back on my feet and rush back to help, Gareth is not only holding his own, he's advancing on his majesty, the Shadow King.

Swing after swing, Gareth dekes the incoming attacks and responds with brutal, ground-trembling return strikes. Both his defense and offense are preternaturally fast and lethal.

The Shadow King is furious, and when Jinx tears a chunk off several of his tendrils, I feel somewhat sorry for the thing.

With no one for me to fight and them having everything in hand, I observe.

The wraith is a formidable foe, but he's run out of steam. *'I was trapped and starved for centuries and will not be denied sustenance.'*

He's hungry.

A few months back, Rance and I were discussing my prejudices against The Six and he asked me if I judge a shark for hunting in its waters or a lioness for taking down a gazelle to feed its cubs.

I don't.

I hate how the Keeper threw people in this being's path, but if what the Shadow King says is true and he was trapped and starved, maybe it was a case of an apex predator trying to survive.

I eye the gaping hole at the heart of the tree. Could he truly have been trapped in there for centuries?

I study the beast in question and see the desperation in his eyes. Desperation and anger. As much as I want to protect Charlie and end this battle so we can get home to our family, my gut tells me there has to be a better way to end this.

"Enough!" I shout, my voice carrying over the sounds of the battle. I release a few flaring streams of flame and separate the wraith from Gareth and the dogs. "It doesn't have to be us versus you. I have a better idea."

With the fight interrupted, the Shadow King's dark, hollow eyes are fixated on Charlie, and his cracked lips twist into a sinister grin.

"No!" I snap. "I don't want to destroy you, but if you go after her, we will."

The wraith hisses at me. "Her energy…it's so vibrant, so full of life."

Eww. "I get that you're starving and somehow you got displaced and sealed into this tree, but maybe this doesn't have to be a 'you versus us' scenario."

The wraith hisses, his voice like a chilling wind. "I need to regain my strength to get free of this place."

I nod. "There's another way."

The Shadow King considers my words, his form still and silent. "Tell me of this other way."

Gareth looks at me and makes a face. "Yeah, we'd all love to hear what you've come up with."

It takes a bit of convincing, but after I finish, I'm pretty sure we can avoid more killing. Then I lead the group back the way we came, and over the next couple of hours, we get a better idea of what happened with the Shadow King.

Centuries ago, a group of wraiths came through this area of the fae realm and consumed the locals. The Keeper of the Grove—a governing partner to the Keeper of the Orchard—sacrificed himself to seal the Shadow King into the heart of the hollowed-out tree. The spell trapped both.

The Shadow King's people tried to free him, but the fae force holding him prisoner was too much.

"Many months ago, something shifted in the fae force," the Shadow King relates. "The spell encasing me in the tree weakened."

Gareth and Azland wear matching expressions of understanding.

I nod. "Yes, there was a global event called the Time of the Colliding Realms, and the veil between the fae and human realms fell. It has upset the balance of fae magic, for sure."

"Then I will take it as fortuitous indeed," the Shadow King replies.

At least it worked out for somebody.

Jinx and Onyx trot ahead on the path. When they sit and growl, we pay attention to our surroundings.

We must be almost back to the center of the orchard, because I feel the heat of watchful eyes clawing at the back of my neck.

I'm about to call for the Keeper of the Orchard when the wooden man drops from the canopy and launches at us. "You lied! You shall pay for your treachery!"

I brace myself for a fight, my fire powers sparking to life in my hands.

Gareth does the same, and it's obvious his demon form scares the bejeebers out of them because I'm pretty sure a few of them pee their mossy pants.

The Keeper of the Orchard raises his hands and dozens of branches around us come to life. They snake through the air, winding around us, trying to bind us in place.

I turn up my heat, and the crackle of wood sends sparks into the night sky. "Do you want us to burn this entire orchard to the ground? Because we will. Back the hell off, tree man."

The Keeper of the Orchard has the good sense to recognize when he's beaten.

Fire trumps wood. Every. Damn. Time.

Seething mad, the Keeper of the Orchard points back the way we came. "Get out of my orchard. You failed to kill the ancient evil, so you've condemned yourselves to spend the rest of your honorless, lying lives separated from your world."

"We didn't lie," I counter firmly, my voice steady despite the chaos. "We struck a bargain, remember? We agreed to remove the evil from your orchard in exchange for safe passage home. *Remove him.* We never said we would kill him."

The Keeper of the Orchard hesitates, his anger momentarily doused by my words. "Remove him?"

I nod, my fiery gaze locked with his. "We're upholding our end of the agreement. The Shadow King has agreed to leave your orchard. We'll find him a new home far away from here."

The surrounding fae glance nervously at one another.

Gareth steps beside me, his powers still in full, fiery force. "All you need to do is return us to our time and place as agreed. We'll take care of the rest."

The Keeper hesitates, his expression a mix of annoyance and uncertainty. He wanted the Shadow King dead, but our deal didn't specify how we would remove the evil.

After a tense moment, he finally nods. "Very well. We'll let you go, but don't return to our orchard."

"Then don't kidnap us and we won't."

Gareth bends forward to lean in. "If you *do* kidnap us again, you will be the Keeper of the Charred Lands."

There's a soft gasp from the locals, but I don't feel bad. "Send us back. We've had enough."

The Keeper of the Orchard steps back and presses a hand to the massive tree in the center of the orchard. He mentioned earlier that he was the intention and Aetherbough was the power.

Man, the tree is powerful.

The moment the Keeper touches the trunk's bark, a wave of magical energy hits us. I'm better prepared for it the second time around, and thankfully, Azland has hold of Charlie to keep her from assplanting.

When the power crackling in the air dissipates, the muted blue world is gone, and we're looking at the full-color sunset over the Montréal countryside.

"Is that it? Are we home?" Charlie's questions hang in the evening air.

I check with Gareth and Azland, then nod. "Yeah, Charlie. We're home."

"The bench is the portal link." Azland scowls at the innocuous piece of furniture. "Torch it, will you, Jules?"

"My pleasure." I grip the wooden boards of the seat and the backrest, and flames engulf the bench in an instant.

When we're standing over its ashes, I pull the flames back inside myself and release my fiery side.

Gareth hands me his keys and speaks to Jinx and Onyx before meeting my gaze. "Take my truck and go home with your family.

I'll call you when Jinx and I get back. Don't panic if it takes a few days. Time doesn't work the same way there as it does here."

"Okay. Be safe."

Gareth places a hand on the Shadow King's shoulder, and in a flash of dark energy, the ground opens and swallows them into the depths.

"Holy shit. Where did they go?" Micah's eyes are wide as he stares at the ground.

"Gareth is taking a shadow wraith to his father's domain."

Micah looks from the ground to us and the ashes of the bench. "Why do I feel like we missed something big?"

Charlie wraps her arms around his waist and waves Anna and Sammy in for a group hug. "Let's go home. I need a hot bath and a bottle of wine."

CHAPTER FIVE

A week without Gareth is lonely—and for a lifelong independent female like me, that's shocking. I'm not that girl. Although Onyx and I live with Briar, Kenzie, Zephyr, and by extension, Tad and now Hannah, I still feel my broody guy's absence like a weight of worry twisting in my guts.

He had to go to the hell realm because of me and my big idea to relocate the Shadow King. What will a trip there cost him? Will he have to see his father?

What will *that* cost him?

When his truck pulls up the driveway at the fire station, I rise from sitting on the retaining wall and brush off the ass of my dress.

Gareth is out of the truck and striding forward before I get off the front walk. His eyes flicker with flames, and his gaze roams everywhere the cut of this dress is supposed to highlight.

The dainty straps, the dipping cut toward my cleavage, the thigh hemline... "You look amazing. How about we cancel Rance and head back to my apartment? I've missed you."

I lean against the hood of his truck and fight the overwhelming urge to accept his offer. "I missed you too. And as tempting as that sounds, no."

He groans and adjusts the fall of his pants. "I was afraid you'd say that."

I brush my fingers over the dark scruff on his jaw. "I don't dress up often, so I don't want to waste it. Besides, Kenzie would kill me. She spent an hour on my hair, makeup, and nails."

He bends and presses his forehead to mine. "You're a wonderful sister, letting her have her makeover montages."

"Don't I know it. Tonight wasn't actually a sacrifice. I'm intrigued about the invitation to dinner with your brother and want to put past conflicts behind us."

He arches a brow, his gaze growing impossibly intense. "If you tell me this entire makeover was for Rance, blood will be spilled tonight."

There's a good dose of teasing in his words, but the graveled rasp in his voice tells me he's serious, too. I bite my lip and let his closeness seep deep into my bones. "It was definitely for you. I've never been one to get wrapped up in a guy, but I missed your face."

He grunts and kisses the tip of my nose. "Just my face? I must be slipping."

I laugh. "Oh, no. You're good. There are a good many other parts of you I've been missing too."

He waggles his brows. "Why not reschedule with Rance and we'll explore some of those other parts?"

I grip the seam of buttons at the front of his collared shirt. "Stop trying to seduce me. First dinner, then dessert."

Gareth chuckles. "As long as dessert is on the table."

I push off the bumper and make my way to the passenger door. "Oh, it is. I might have popped by your apartment a few days ago and let myself in to drop off a few personal items for your homecoming."

The growl that rumbles from the back of his throat hits me hard, and I worry I might combust. I close my eyes and try to rein in my libido.

"You realize you're killing me, right?" Gareth's lips brush my temple.

"Don't worry. It's mutual." I let my head drop back to rest against the door's window. "I hear delayed gratification makes things hotter in the end."

Gareth chuckles. "If things get any hotter, we're literally going to set my apartment ablaze."

He's not wrong.

Drawing a deep breath, I take his scent into my lungs and slide out from the frame of his arms against the truck. "Dinner, then dessert."

Gareth groans, grabs my door handle, and opens things for me. "Just know that I will be undressing you with my mind the entire night."

I climb into his truck and grab my seatbelt. "It's good to have you home, big guy."

As Gareth and I walk up to Rance's house, I forget all the warmth of sexual teasing. With every step closer to the stone mansion, anxiety and determination inundate me. Tonight's dinner is important for my relationship with Gareth, my family's future, and the elementals I'm protecting.

I draw a deep breath, feeling the warmth of the fire within me, and steel myself for the evening ahead.

It's going to be fine. Positive energy.

When the chiming of the doorbell ends, the door opens, and Rance stands in the entrance. In his dark charcoal suit and a black button-down, it's easy to see the royalty of his parents. "Jules, Gareth, welcome. I'm glad you could make it."

"Thank you for having us," I reply, my voice steady despite the nerves churning in my stomach.

We step inside, and Rance collects our jackets to hang them in the front closet. The last time I was here, his silver-haired assistant Miss Mabel played the part of the welcoming committee.

Tonight, it seems Rance intends to be more hands-on. When he finishes with the jackets and closes the closet doors, he pauses. "Jules, you are utterly resplendent in that dress."

I press a smoothing hand down the fabric and wish I was in jeans with my gun belt on my hip. That Jules is confident. This version of myself doesn't know what to do with a compliment like that.

Gareth collects my hand and laces his fingers with mine. "I told her the same thing. In fact, I tried to seduce her into blowing you off so I could show her how resplendent, but she refused. She insisted we come break bread."

Rance's smile widens. "I'm honored to hear it. Please, come inside." Rance leads us to a sitting area and gestures at the leather furniture and the well-stocked bar beyond. "May I offer you a drink while we wait for dinner?"

"Whiskey sour," I reply, taking in the space.

"Bourbon neat," Gareth requests.

I take in the room as Rance goes over to fix our drinks. Everything about him and his home is classy, masculine, and expensive.

He's a prince, and he lives like one.

"Here we are." He hands us our drinks a moment later. "What shall we toast to?"

"New beginnings?" I suggest.

He likes that and raises his tumbler. "To new beginnings, then."

"To new beginnings," Gareth repeats, and the two share a meaningful look. After not speaking for twenty-five years, I hope Gareth's family can accept and respect his lifestyle choices.

He wants to be more than the apex predator his genetics make him. He wants to be good.

As we sip our drinks, Rance makes small talk, asking about our day and what we've been up to recently.

I'm pleasantly surprised by how easily the conversation flows. Rance seems genuinely interested in what I have to say, and I'm warming up to him more than I expected.

We talk about the recent events in the corn maze and our encounter with the shadow wraith. Things get awkward when it comes to the part about Gareth taking him to the hell realm.

Family is tricky, and I don't want old wounds salted.

"How is production going for the synthetic essence?" I ask, not so subtly changing the subject.

Since testing the prototype of the synthetic fae essence Luc and Kenzie came up with, Rance has been revamping their other brother's drug factory for small-scale production.

"Very well, actually. I've selected and vetted a small group, and we've begun distributing it. We hope the medical testing in two weeks, two months, and six months all show what we expect."

"Which is?" Gareth asks.

"That the synthetic essence is truly feeding the cells and not simply acting as a placebo."

"I think you should be good," I reply. "The two people who worked on developing it vibrate at genius frequencies. They say it's our answer and I believe them."

Rance nods. "I sincerely hope so, Jules. I truly do."

If Rance will help protect the vulnerable fae races from the skoro and his siblings, maybe there is a chance for peace and understanding between our two families.

After we finish our drinks, Rance stands and gestures at the open door leading to the study off the living room. "Come. I have something I'd like to show you."

I glance at Gareth, who looks as curious as I feel.

Gareth guides us into the study with a hand on the small of my back. The room is stately, with shelves filled with ancient tomes and artifacts lining the walls.

In the center of the room on a small black display table lies a delicate keepsake that immediately catches my attention. It's small enough to sit in the palm of my hand and is woven with delicate silver strands spun into the most precious bird's nest I've ever seen. "This is so pretty."

Rance's gaze softens as he picks up the little nest. "This is what I wanted to show you. It belonged to our mother, the faery queen."

Gareth and I step closer, and as Rance tilts it in the light, it shimmers. Tiny leaves and vines twine around each other in an intricate pattern. Small, glimmering gems nestle among the silver threads, sparkling like stars in the night sky.

"Wow. It's so beautiful," I murmur.

Gareth nods, reaching out to take it. "Our mother didn't covet many things. She was humble and believed in people over objects. Still, this nest was one of her treasures. I didn't realize you had it. I thought it was lost, like everything else."

Rance sighs. "Our father was violently distraught when we lost our mother. He couldn't bear any reminder of her and removed everything of hers from our lives practically overnight."

How sad. "You weren't allowed to keep mementos of her?"

Gareth shakes his head. "The sorrow of missing our mother made our father even more volatile and dark. It wasn't such a bad thing to avoid that."

Rance nods. "I found him with a small box of her things not long ago, and he said I could pick something. I chose this, and I'd like to give it to you."

Gareth looks shaken by the offer and drops his gaze to the delicate keepsake.

Rance swirls the bourbon in the bottom of his glass and

smiles. "Our mother's grandmother was given it as a child, and it's been handed down from one generation to the next."

"Does it serve a purpose, or is it simply beautiful?" I ask.

Rance smiles. "It's a fae meditation talisman. Our mother used to sit out on her balcony in the palace of her realm and hold this gently in her cupped palms as she meditated."

Gareth hands the nest to me, and the enchantment's soothing energy pulses through my palms. The nest is cool yet radiates a comforting warmth that fills me with peace and calm.

When Gareth straightens, Rance smiles. "You are by far the most like her, little brother. I think she'd want you to have it, and therefore, *I* want you to have it."

Gareth hesitates momentarily, his gaze flicking between the nest and his brother. Then he steps forward and hugs him. "Thank you. This means a lot, Rance. More than you know."

When they break apart, Gareth examines the nest, and I slide it back into his palm. It's odd to see a man of Gareth's size and power tracing the delicate designs with such reverence.

I scan Rance's expression, searching for any sign that he's not being genuine or forthright.

There is none.

There is more to Rance Poreskoro than I thought.

Gareth hands me the nest and excuses himself to wash up for dinner. It's obvious he needs a moment to process, but nothing is said.

Rance takes the opportunity to speak to me privately. "I understand why you might be wary of me and my family." His voice is low and sincere. "I promise I'll do whatever I can to earn your trust."

I search his face for any hint of deception, but all I see is deep regret and a genuine desire to make things right. As the moment of understanding settles between us, a slow clap echoes through the room, shattering the fragile peace.

Rance's expression hardens. "Sasobek. Zissa. We weren't expecting you, sisters."

Gareth's and Rance's sisters step into the room, their attention locked on me.

I'm trapped in the lion's den, and the lionesses are home and on the hunt.

CHAPTER SIX

Zissa and Sasobek make a grand entrance by stalking into the study, scrutinizing me with predatory interest. Rance steps forward, and at first, I'm unsure whether he's moving to welcome his sisters or to protect me from impending attack.

Definitely the latter.

Zissa is strikingly beautiful in a fae princess type of way. The tall redhead with graceful antlers and plated body armor looks like an exotic deer-slash-armadillo hybrid.

Sasobek is almost wholly passable as a human except for her glowing yellow eyes. Those are freaky as shit and send a shiver down my spine.

Does she always look homicidal, or is that just me?

"What are you two doing here?" Gareth snaps, practically launching himself from the hall to land beside his brother. The two of them, tall and broad-shouldered, make a damn effective wall. "What the fuck, Rance? Did you invite them?"

Rance's frame goes rigid. "I didn't know they were coming. I swear."

I believe him. Rance is genuinely trying to rebuild a relationship with his only remaining brother.

Gareth's attention returns to his sisters. "Then you can go. You weren't invited, so you can leave."

"Nice to see you too, little brother." Zissa saunters forward, looking bored. "A quarter-century of pouting hasn't changed your disposition, I see. You're still spoiled enough to think we should do what you say."

Gareth stiffens in front of me, and I place a gentle hand on his shoulder blade. Normally, I wouldn't abide any man standing as my guard, but both of these men think it's necessary in the company of their sisters.

Who am I to counter their judgment?

"Fine. If you won't leave, we will." Gareth's grip is bruisingly tight on my elbow as he pulls me to his side. "Another night then."

"Nonsense." Zissa waves dismissively. "Sas will behave, and I, for one, want to meet your little elemental girlfriend. How about an introduction, little brother?"

Neither man moves, but it's silly.

I live in this city, and if they want to stalk me or try to consume my essence, they can find me when Gareth isn't at my side. Running away won't solve anything.

I turn and place my palm on his abs and wait until he looks at me. "It's fine. They're your family. I'm good."

Gareth wants to argue. It's obvious in every tense muscle and stress line. "I hate this."

I draw a deep breath and try to project more confidence than I feel. "S'all good, big guy."

He searches my gaze for a moment longer and scowls. "Fine. We'll stay. But if either of you makes one move toward Jules or her family, I will end you both."

Sasobek crows with laughter. "You can try, little brother."

"All right. Enough." Rance steps to the side, and I move to stand between them. "Jules, this is Zissa. You already met Sasobek when she raided your home and tried to have you killed."

I nod, my eyes locked on Sasobek. "I remember."

Sasobek's gaze flicks to the meditation nest I'm holding, and her eyes narrow. "Why is Raz's plaything holding Mother's nest?"

Rance answers without hesitation. "I gave Gareth the nest since he and Mother shared a special bond. I believe she would've wished him to have it. Jules was holding it while he freshened up."

Zissa doesn't care one way or another, but something about that is rubbing Sasobek raw.

Without further comment, Rance notifies the kitchen staff there will be two more for dinner. Once they add the table settings, we move into the dining room.

Dining with Rance Poreskoro is an elegant affair, and I'm glad I pulled out all the stops to rise to the occasion. Our family dinners were nothing like this, but *Maman* taught us manners and which forks to eat with what courses, so I hold my own.

Bacon-wrapped water chestnuts and cream of potato soup with seared eel to start. A lovely spinach salad with a lemon vinaigrette dressing. Iberian pork tenderloin with red berries and raspberry sauce next…

"Wow. Everything is delicious, Rance. Thank you." I dab my mouth with my linen napkin. "Please be sure to tell your chef how much I enjoyed everything."

Sasobek rolls her eyes. "You realize how stupid that sounds, don't you?"

I meet her attitude with mine and twist my napkin in my lap. "Why is that stupid?"

"Because the four of us are sitting here eating off our plates when we all know you're the tastiest thing at the table."

"Shut your mouth, Sas," Gareth snaps.

"Why? We're all thinking it. I'm just honest enough to say it out loud."

I meet Gareth's gaze, having a hard time swallowing.

He reads my expression as easily as always and reaches into my lap to grab my fist. "No. We're *not* all thinking that. I find her comment repulsive and have no desire to consume elemental essence. Sas is being a bitch and trying to get a rise out of us."

"Gareth's right." Rance glares at his younger sister. "Apologize to Jules."

"What? Do you seriously expect me—"

"I absolutely do." Rance cuts her off. "Jules is here as my guest and you are being rude."

"No, I'm hungry and think we should take advantage of having an elemental in the house. Now, if you're feeding her to fatten her like a Thanksgiving turkey, that's another matter."

The legs of Gareth's chair scrape the floor as he stands. He grips his knife and looks like he's about to use it.

Sasobek pushes out her bottom lip. "Aw, what's the matter, brother? Does the truth offend you?"

"Enough, Sas. You can either apologize or leave," Rance orders. "Those are your two choices."

She looks at him like he sprouted a second head. "You're serious."

"Deadly serious," Rance confirms.

The stunned incredulity in her expression hardens to a promise of revenge. "I'm sorry if the harsh realities of our world are offensive to you, Julie."

"*Jules*," Gareth growls.

She chuckles. "You are, and have always been, much too easy to wind up, little brother."

"Enough, Sas." Rance tosses his napkin over his plate and sits back from the table. "You're wrong about feeding on essence. That's over."

She arches a brow and shifts her creepy gaze to the oldest sibling, seated at the head of the table. "Oh? You think so?"

"I know so. Jules and her team have developed a synthetic fae essence, and I'm helping her with production. If things go as planned, there will be no need to harvest elementals going forward."

Both women grimace as if a wave of nausea suddenly hit them.

"Synthetic essence?" Zissa spits.

Rance spends the next few minutes informing them about the synthetic essence. They aren't impressed.

"Tofu isn't chicken no matter how you slice it." Zissa scowls at her brother.

Sasobek chuckles. "Prey should learn its place and be done with it. Have you ever seen a deer rise against a cougar? No."

My flames roar within, and I bristle. "My family and I are not deer."

"We shall see, elemental," Sasobek replies.

Flames arc from my fingers as my temper boils over. "If you think you can come at us and we'll simply bare our throats and give up, you'll end up as dead as Lamech and Draven."

The moment the words are out of my mouth, I realize my mistake. It isn't common knowledge that my parents and the Scaith Warriors took Draven down, and judging by the expression on Zissa's face, Sasobek hasn't told her that my siblings and I killed Lamech.

The sisters launch, sending the table flying.

Dishes shatter as Gareth and I ignite our powers. Flames explode from my hands and dance up my arms.

Rance steps in front of me, his body crackling with electrical energy. "Enough. Draven and Lamech made their choices. They attacked this elemental family, and it ended in their deaths. That is the way of battle."

"That seals their death," Zissa snaps.

"No. I won't allow further attempts on the Gagne family or their kind. Jules and her people have the right to fight for their survival, and they've gone so far as to help us with our feeding requirements. We will not return that effort with bloodshed."

Sasobek looks rabid. "You don't get to make those decisions, Rance."

"I sure as hell do. Now, both of you, go into the study for a moment while I show Jules and Gareth out. We have matters to discuss."

No one moves for a long moment, but when Rance doesn't give in, they stand down and storm off toward the study.

Rance escorts us out of the house and brings our jackets to the front porch. "I'm sorry about that, Jules." He steps behind me. "Our sisters are…passionate and can be difficult to control."

I shrug into my jacket and tie the belt across my waist. "I'm sorry I lost my temper and brought up your brothers."

He waves that away. "It was bound to come out. At least I'm here and will speak to them."

Gareth extends his hand. "Thank you for dinner and for trying to make peace."

Rance nods. "I meant what I said. If this is truly your path, I will do my best to ensure your happiness."

Gareth nods. "That means a lot. Thank you."

There's a loud *smash* in the house and Rance winces. "If I might make a suggestion. Perhaps you two should stay out of their way as much as possible in the future. I am not sure even *I* can control them when they get together and feed off each other's negative energy."

I slide in against Gareth's side. "Don't worry. I intend to give them a wide berth."

CHAPTER SEVEN

The next morning, I'm full throttle and pinning it through what little traffic is on the highway this early on a Sunday morning. My speed brings a biting October wind whipping around me, and if I weren't a fire elemental, it would likely be too cold to be out on Scarlett.

I *am* a fire elemental, so it's not.

Man, there's nothing like the rush of wheels against pavement and the throaty whine of one hundred and seventy horsepower vaulting you along the asphalt.

The faster I ride, the more my mind slows so I can think. Some people meditate. I break the sound barrier on my motorcycle.

This morning, my mind-spin is all about Gareth's sisters and what went down last night. It would be stupid to think Sasobek and Zissa will fold their hands in their laps and play nice because Rance tells them to.

I'm sure he's good—but no one is *that* good.

No. They'll come for us, and we have to be ready.

Gearing down, I take the off-ramp and come back to the

reality of life. A lot has changed since the veil fell ten months ago, but whether I'm a human cop for the Twenty-Third Precinct or an elemental enforcer for the Guild of the Laurentians, Montréal is still my city.

Yet, at the same time, it's not.

Somewhere in the land of fae I know nothing about, my birthplace waits for me to rediscover it—and not only mine. Kenzie, Zephyr, Briar, and I all hail from the elemental kingdoms of our biological families.

If you believe everything happens for a reason, growing up with my siblings is the universe's way to strengthen me for what comes next in our lives.

The guys at the Twenty-Third always teased me about being a lone wolf, but the truth is, I have a very small circle of people I trust enough to ask for help.

Very small.

Tiny.

It's not so much of a circle as a square. Four people. Me, Kenzie, Briar, and Zephyr.

Now, as enforcers for the Guild of the Laurentians, I get to work with them every day.

Doesn't get any better than that.

I wind through the streets, which were once familiar but are now a magical Wild West territory of chaos and crazy. Nature's response to an influx of fae magic has spun us all for a loop.

It's like living in the *Jurassic Park*-slash-*Harry Potter*-slash-*Game of Thrones* version of Montréal.

That might be an exaggeration, but it's not far off.

When I draw a deep breath, my stomach whirls, and my skin crawls. The crisp autumn air is tainted with a faint sourness, the prana growing more unstable by the day. Whatever is happening with the prana, it's getting worse.

Fiona says Merlin, Sloan, and a bunch of very smart and

magically gifted people are working on getting the veil back up, but it can't happen soon enough.

As I maneuver the busy streets, I think about Gareth. It's been a tough week for him. First, trying to assimilate with my crazy family, then returning to his father's realm, and the face-off with his sisters.

He was silent and broody last night. Yes, that's his normal factory setting, but it was more intense after we left Rance's home.

Not that it bothers me. I can be quiet and broody too so it doesn't faze me. Besides, it's hard for him, knowing his sisters want me dead.

It's worse knowing he can't be with me all the time.

I park Scarlett against the curb outside the city coroner's office. After locking things down, I adjust the fall of my leather trench and head for the entrance.

Gareth wants to protect me. He suffers from the regret and guilt of the violent damage caused by his family, and he's twisted himself up for decades to make things right.

He can't protect me and my family from his twenty-four-seven.

Such is the life we live.

Other than the family drama of death threats and past murders, on our own merits…things are great.

I have an exciting new job, an amazing home life, a hot and sexy boyfriend, and with the sun warming my skin and the freedom of the open road, life is good.

Then why is something still not quite right inside me? Am I looking for trouble, waiting for it all to fall apart? I don't think so.

No. It's more violent than that. It's within me. Am I growing too volatile? Is my fire side a darkness I can't control? I'm not sure. In the moments I've lost control and razed the world, I've felt so much better.

Is that a warning sign?

Inside the front doors, I stop and sign in at the registration desk. Once I have my visitor's pass, I clip it to the lapel of my jacket and take the stairs to the basement.

Luc's lab is at the end of the hall. I let myself in. My bestie is sitting at his desk, bobbing his head to the rhythm of the blaring rock music as he fills out a report on a particularly gruesome body recovery.

He doesn't know I'm coming, but I wanted to surprise him. He's been a rockstar lately, and I got him something special. If I touch him or call him, I'm going to scare the shit out of him. Instead, I pull out my phone and call up his contact info.

Visiting you. Standing right behind you.

His phone must vibrate in his pocket because he pulls it out and reads my text. He bursts into a wide smile as he swings his chair around. "Jules! You really *are* here. I thought maybe you were fucking with me."

He turns down the music and vaults out of his chair, only to be tugged back by the wires of his headphones.

I snort. "When are you going wireless and joining this century? You always do that."

He jerks back toward his desk, frees himself from his headphones, then hugs me. He's not normally a hugger, so it surprises me, but what the hell, it's been a minute. "I'm so glad you're here. I miss your face."

I squeeze him and step back. "I know. I suck. But I realize it, and I think that's half the battle."

"Self-awareness is a good thing." He steps back and flips his dark waves out of his face. "To what do I owe the pleasure of your company?"

"I come bearing gifts."

His eyes light up. "Gifts? It's not my birthday."

"No, but you've been such an amazing help, and I've used up your genius juju for fae stuff, the pheromone rings, and now for developing the essence aerosol. I wanted to get you something to say what I don't tell you often enough. You're one of my people, Luc. It's a select group, but you're a lock."

"Thanks, Jules. I feel the same." He holds out his hands, wiggling his fingers.

I hand him the package, and he's excited until he peels off the wrapping paper. Then his enthusiasm falls. "A book?"

"Don't worry. It's mostly filthy pictures." I make a face as I fan the pages open in front of him. "Disturbing cartoon porn pictures."

Luc snorts. "Manga isn't a cartoon. And don't judge art. To each their own."

I nod. "Exactly. So, here. You're welcome. Just save the perusing for when you get home. I don't want to cause any NSW events. HR already hates you."

He lets out an odd laugh, and I study him. He's about to say something but goes uncharacteristically quiet and shakes off the impulse.

I raise an eyebrow, curious. "All right. Spill it."

He hesitates, then grins. "Well, let's just say that not *everyone* in HR hates me."

"Oh, *really*?" I love the fact that his cheeks flush pink. Luc is good people, and if someone is taking notice, I'm happy for him. "I guess it pays to be on their radar, eh? All those visits and follow-up calls."

He snorts, waving away my teasing. "I don't want to jinx it. Let's just keep it between us for now."

I reach forward and squeeze his arm. "I'm happy for you. May the HR gods continue to smile upon you."

Luc chuckles and places the manga book in the drawer of his desk. "Thanks, Jules. I appreciate it, and I'll definitely enjoy it…in private."

My phone goes off, and I pull it out of the pocket in my backpack purse and smile. "Hey, Fiona. What's new in Toronto?"

"We've got trouble, and Sloan thinks the best way to defuse it is for your quint to pay us a visit. Can you get everyone together ASAP?"

I straighten. "Yeah, I'll call Tad to come get me, and we'll be there in a few."

"Thanks. I'll text Tad our location so he can start working out how close he can get."

"Perfect. On our way." I hang up and text the family chat.

A moment later, Tad *poofs* into the lab. "We'll need to grab Azland at Charlie's, but Briar is home."

My phone buzzes. "Kenzie and Zephyr are both on their way. Five minutes out."

"Aye, perfect."

I turn with a quick wave for Luc. "Later. Destiny calls."

He nods and smiles. "Later, Jules. Thanks for dropping in. Don't be a stranger."

I accept Tad's outstretched hand. "I couldn't be any stranger than you. Laters."

The moment we materialize in the kitchen of the fire station, I jog into my suite to change. Onyx loves it when I hurry. No matter the reason, he considers it playing a chasing game.

When I'm ready, I meet Tad and Kenzie at the kitchen table, pull out my phone, find Bakkali's info, and hit the call button.

"Miss Gagne, what can I do for you?"

"Just letting you know we've been called to Toronto for an elemental issue. Fiona says they need us and since they've saved our butts a half a dozen times, I didn't think to ask if that's something we do."

There's a deep chuckle at the other end of the line. "It's the whole point of the guild system. If we can help, we do. Let me know how things play out."

"Will do."

As I wait for everyone to get home, saws buzzing in the backyard grab my attention. I pat Onyx's side and jog downstairs and out the back door to find Briar and Gareth working on the hothouse.

My heart swells with pride at the progress they've made on our elemental sanctuaries. My lava pool is a fiery dream, and Kenzie's waterfall pool is straight out of a landscaping magazine.

Briar's and Zephyr's stations are well on their way, too. They might bicker and tease as any siblings do, but they insisted we get our restorative stations first when it came down to the order of the work to do.

They are true gentlemen.

I take a moment to appreciate the nearly finished hothouse, excited by the prospect of having Briar do his earth elemental thing and provide us with fresh greens, strawberries, and herbs all year.

As I jog to the guys, Onyx playfully races ahead of me, barking and wagging his tail.

Sadly, the shirtless days of summer are over, but Gareth is still a sight to see in jeans, a tool belt, and his muscles straining against his tight cotton top.

A man of all seasons.

When Onyx practically barrels into the back of his leg, he turns, and his gaze narrows. "Aren't you supposed to be at the Guild Tower this morning?"

"Change of plans. There's a problem in Toronto, and Fi called us for help. ASAP."

"We're helping *them*?" Briar straightens. "That's unexpected."

I understand his thinking. The Toronto team is formidable, and it's always been us calling for help in the past. "Fi said it's an elemental problem and thought we'd be the best to tackle it."

"Do you want me to come?" Gareth asks.

I shake my head and reach up to kiss him. "I always *want* you to come, but I think we can handle one elemental between Fi's team and us. You stay and do your thing, and we'll be back soon."

Briar sets down his saw and exchanges it for his sledgehammer. "All righty then. Let's go."

CHAPTER EIGHT

Tad's time in Toronto serves us well, and he portals us within a block of the chaos of their elemental event. I've never been to the city before, but I recognize the Toronto lakeshore from the pictures you always see in the media. Lake Ontario is to our left. The CN Tower and the dome are down on the right. And...

"Holy hell." Wide-eyed, Zephyr points at the stormy sky swirling beyond a building about a block away. "I'm pretty sure that's where we're heading."

Kenzie chuckles. "Yeah, I'm pretty sure."

The five of us race off, our gazes locked on the tumultuous skies overhead.

A wind elemental has lost control, and the devastation he's causing is everywhere. The air is full of flying debris. Screaming people are running for cover. Members of emergency services are struggling to keep up with the damage.

Sirens wail, lights flash...it's a cacophony of panic.

There's a teenage boy with his arms out and his body rigid, standing in the center of a grassy park area.

He's the epicenter of this event.

"Is it an Awakening?" I shout over the scream of the wind, squinting to keep my eyes from being whipped by my hair.

"If it is, this kid's going to be hella strong." Briar frowns. "Either that or he's like Z and the storm has been inside him too long, and he couldn't hold it."

"*Shit la marde*," I mutter, taking in the surrounding destruction. "Okay, Z, this is your wheelhouse. Do what you can, and we'll find Fi and help with containment and fallout."

Zephyr grips his storm staff and runs into the thick of things. As crazy as it is, the wind doesn't push at him. He jogs at the kid without having to crouch or brace himself against the gale force.

Briar curses. "Kenzie, you're up."

I follow his pointed finger to where enormous waves of water are cresting a low breaker wall on Lake Ontario and surging water is flooding the area.

Kenzie runs to help with the waterworks as Tad and Briar position themselves to evacuate the people stuck in the middle of all this. Azland and I continue to work our way forward, looking for Fiona or a member of the Toronto team.

"This isn't just a simple loss of control," Zephyr shouts, his voice barely audible over the howl of the wind. "There's something else going on here."

I stare at the boy at the epicenter of this vortex of volatility. There's so much debris circling that I can barely see what's happening. "Is it intentional?"

"That's not what I'm saying," Zephyr shouts. "But it's not an Awakening or a simple loss of control either."

"Hey, welcome to the party." Fiona materializes beside me with Sloan. "Thanks for the house call."

"Not a problem. We're happy to return the favor."

She frowns at Zephyr absorbing the chaos of the wind as he reaches for the boy. "Any idea what we're dealing with?"

"Not really. Zephyr says it's not intentional though, and he doesn't think it's an Awakening either."

Zephyr is facing off with the boy, assuming control and absorbing the hostile wind. He takes what he can and redirects the rest, shooting it straight up using his storm staff as he edges closer.

As the winds die down, our vision improves. One thing becomes clear. This kid isn't hostile, he's freaking out. Each time he tries to bring his arms down to shut things off, more elemental energy explodes from him.

He's not in a rage—he's in a panic.

The wind threatens to knock us off our feet as we force our way forward. Sloan and Fi have their palms up and shield us from flying debris while Zephyr does his best to counter the fierce gusts of air.

Azland looks from me to Sloan. "If I can get close enough, I can knock him out. I'm guessing if he's unconscious, this will all end."

The winds die down a little more, and I check on my brother. Zephyr looks nauseous, and his long black hair practically stands on end. "If you're going to do something. Sooner is better than later."

"I hear you, Z." I meet Sloan's gaze. "Can you *poof* Azland in behind the kid so he can whammy him and take him down?"

"Ye don't intend to harm the lad, do ye?" Sloan asks.

Azland fields the question. "No. It's more like a magic sleeping potion."

Sloan is okay with that and grips Azland's shoulder. "On three. One…two…"

On the count of three, Sloan and Azland disappear and reappear at the eye of the hurricane.

The moment Azland touches him, the kid drops like a rock, the wind dies, and the chaotic gusts transform into a gentle breeze.

The calm after the storm doesn't last long because as Sloan and Kenzie hunker down over the still form of the wind kid, Fiona looks at me and one of her older brothers, Calum.

"Canvass the witnesses and try to find out who this kid is and where he's from," she says. "Briar, if you can, help Tad and Diesel repair the destruction."

She gestures at a seven-foot-tall man rolling cars upright, setting them back on their wheels.

Damn, that guy is hella strong.

"On it." Calum tilts his head toward the onlookers creeping out from behind their cover.

I've worked with Calum before on other joint ventures. He and I fan out to assess the crowd. Since Calum used to be a Toronto cop—as all of her brothers were—he and I speak the same language.

The two of us check on people, chatting briefly about their experiences, and escort those who need medical attention toward the ambulances and cruisers.

The storm might have passed, but its aftermath remains. People are dazed, in shock, crying, trying to comprehend what transpired.

As we work through the witnesses, we ask the same questions I did for years on the Montréal PD.

Did anyone see how this started? Does anyone know the boy? Did anyone see him with anyone else prior to the incident?

Either they didn't see, or they don't want to get involved. That's nothing new.

My search leads me to a group of teenagers huddled together. While they wear the same masks of fear and concern, it's not for themselves.

Their focus is wholly on the downed kid and trying to see past Sloan and Kenzie.

I approach them. "Hey there. If you know that boy, it would

be a big help if you could tell us about him and what happened. What's his name? Where are his parents?"

The tallest of the group, a lanky kid with wild hair and a few scattered freckles, clears his throat. "His name is Ryan. He's a good guy. This wasn't his fault."

I shrug. "No one's here to lay blame. Is Ryan a friend of yours? Does he live in the area?"

The kid meets the gaze of the others, and it's a look I've seen a hundred times. They're about to bolt.

"Before you take off." I hold up my palms and release my essence. My hands burst into flame, and the kids momentarily forget their plan to beat feet.

"Holy fuck." The lanky kid takes a step back.

Now that I have his full attention, I try again. "My name is Jules. I'm an elemental, similar to Ryan, but my essence is fire."

"That's so freaking hot," another kid remarks while holding up his hand to test the heat of my flames.

"My brother Zephyr is the wind elemental that helped Ryan. I promise you, we're his best chance at coming out of this without a heap of trouble. If you care about him, you really need to help us help him."

The kids frown but seem more engaged. "What do you want to know?" my fire admirer asks.

"Does Ryan have family around here? Is there someone we should call?"

The kids shake their heads. "He's an orphan. He's been bouncing around on the streets since his powers showed up in the summer and his foster parents freaked and punted him to the streets."

My heart clenches. I'm not sure how I expected him to have a family and a home life. The lives and homes of elementals were destroyed twenty-five years ago.

Wait. If all the elemental adults were killed in the raids, where did this kid come from? He can't be any older than seventeen.

"You said Ryan has been bouncing around. Where has he been staying lately?"

A wild look of panic flips between the kids, and I back things up a bit before I lose them. "What about what happened here? Do any of you know how this started? What set Ryan off? Did something happen that caused him to lose control?"

They're wigging out, so I take another tack. "How about we go check on your friend? We'll see how he's doing, and if you think of anything, you can let me know, yeah?"

As the kids and I approach Ryan, his face is pale against the verdant grass, but he's breathing evenly. Kenzie sits by his side, her hand resting lightly on his forehead. Her brow is furrowed in concentration, her eyes sparkling with moisture.

"Kenz? What's wrong?" I ask.

"He's terrified," she whispers, her voice choked. "He's filled with so much fear, anger, pain...I can feel it. This isn't right. Zephyr's right. Something's going on."

I feel his struggle all too personally. A foster kid living on the streets, awakening as an elemental, and now at the center of a storm he never asked for.

It pushes more than a few of my buttons.

I look from her to Sloan. "Can you help him?"

"We're trying," Sloan replies. His voice is guarded. "But yer sister's right. There's somethin' else at play here."

Fiona joins the huddle and frowns. "Something else, like what?"

"I haven't figured that out, *a ghra*."

She considers that for a moment while biting her bottom lip. "Maybe leave the healing for a bit, hotness. See if you can dip into his memories. If you can tell us how this all started, it might lead us to answers."

"You can see his memories?" one teen—the lanky one—asks hesitantly.

"Aye, it's one of my disciplines." Sloan gently lays his palm over Ryan's forehead and closes his eyes. The tingling of Sloan's magical signature works across my skin and raises the hair on my arms.

After what seems like an eternity, Sloan frowns and removes his hand. When his eyes open, his attention swings to the three teens beside me. "It's not only Ryan who's afraid. Boys, ye need to let us help."

The look on their faces gets my adrenaline pumping. "Why? What do you mean? What's going on?"

"There's an entire network of street kids." Sloan scans the boys beside me. "They've been displaced, most of them after an Awakenin'. A man named Mr. Belvedere is roundin' them up with an offer of a haven."

Mr. Belvedere? Wasn't that a bad '80s sitcom?

"Belvedere is cagin' them and experimentin' on them. If they step out of line, there are others in place who drain their magical essence."

My blood boils in my veins and flames burst from my palms. "Draining them how?"

He frowns. "It's insensitive to say it like this, but it's like they're suspendin' them in a huge hookah bottle and smokin' them."

I freeze, knowing exactly what Sloan saw in Ryan's mind. "I'm sorry to tell you, guys, but you've got skoro and possibly a Poreskoro in your city."

"That's why his wind control is so out of whack," Zephyr adds behind me. "I knew it didn't feel right. This Belvedere asshole is fucking with their elements."

"Then we'll stop him," Kenzie snaps. "We'll fix this."

Yeah, we will. "Just lead the way and we'll—"

My words are lost in the breeze as we all turn to where, moments ago, the three boys stood.

"Where did they go?" Zephyr asks.

At some point during our revelation, the three boys bolted. I don't blame them. The world is a scary place, and they don't know us or have any reason to trust us.

"Even without the kids, Kenzie's right. We'll fix this. We are exactly the right people to help take down a nest of skoro siphoning off kids."

"Should we tell Gareth and get him to weigh in on this?" Zephyr asks.

I consider that and hate the idea. "He has enough trouble leaving the drama and destruction of his family behind. I'd rather not drag him into this mess. At least, not yet."

Fiona considers that. "Fine. We'll play it your way to start, but if it means finding him or not…"

I wave away her concerns. "Understood. We'll track down Belvedere and determine what we're dealing with. If it's better to involve Gareth, I will."

"All right." Fiona scans the group. "Let's find this Belvedere asshole."

CHAPTER NINE

Sloan gathers a good bit of detail from Ryan's mind as the boy lies unconscious. He learns how Belvedere lured Ryan into trusting him and made him feel like he'd be safe and free to live without the pain and judgment of being a fae freak.

He helps Kenzie direct her healing energy from the physical to Ryan's mental and emotional well-being. Even with both of them tending to the kid, they agree that we'll be in the same situation if he wakes up.

Whatever barrier nature sets for fae elementals to hold back their power has been disengaged in Ryan somehow.

"Then we keep him in a magically induced sleep for now," Fiona concludes. "Are you good with that, Azland?"

Azland nods. "Him being out isn't causing him any harm. He's merely suspended in a state of unconsciousness, which I can reverse at any time."

Fiona is satisfied with that explanation and turns to her crew. "Nikon, can you please snap Calum and Diesel to the Batcave?"

"Not a problem, Red."

"Good. Calum can go through the police database to search for any mention of Belvedere while Diesel checks the guild files."

The three of them nod and are gone in the next moment. Then Fiona's gaze swings to us. "Briar and Azland, would you mind staying here with Tad and Dillan to continue to repair the damage?"

Briar nods. "Of course."

"What do you need me to do?" Zephyr asks.

"I thought Dionysus could take you and Kenzie home to watch over Ryan. If people here are torturing him and causing him to self-destruct, keeping him within Tad's wardings against skoro is the best way to keep him comfortable and safe."

Dionysus steps up and waggles his brows. "I can add a little zhuzh to his wardings too, if you like?"

Kenzie nods and checks with me, and I'm good with that. "Hey, if a Greek god wants to lay some protection mojo on our house, have at it."

Dionysus nods, then he, Kenzie, Zephyr, and Ryan are gone, too.

That leaves me, Fiona, and Sloan.

"Where do we begin?" I ask.

Fiona grabs Sloan's hand and smiles. "In this part of the city, we've got an in with the homeless community. We'll start there and see what we can find out."

Knowing Sloan has a druid wayfarer affinity like Tad, I offer him my hand.

The moment he takes it, a warm, tingling sensation envelops me as we portal away from the devastated green space.

The world around us blurs, then sharpens again, and we're standing on the wide concrete front walkway in front of a soup kitchen.

This area of Toronto is busier than the lakefront, with cars rushing up and down the four lanes in an unending stream. People bustle by in both directions, taking up the sidewalk, their shared conversations swallowed by the honks and sirens of traffic.

I glance up at the bright signage. "The Queen's Table Community Kitchen."

Fiona grins. "Merlin owns the building and runs the soup kitchen and the club next door."

I step back to read the marquee and lights above the nightclub door. "Queens on Queen. Ah, I see the naming convention."

Fiona grins again. "Come on. We'll see if he's here."

She leads the way. I'm still digesting that Merlin—*the* Merlin of Arthur's court—runs a soup kitchen and what I'm guessing is a drag club.

I did not see that coming.

We step inside, and unlike many of the homeless drop-in businesses in Montréal, this soup kitchen exudes a sense of warmth and welcome.

The food line is busy but not crowded, and people sit in rows of tables eating, playing cards, and reading books.

I'm more accustomed to homeless people clutching old, tattered coats and fighting over threadbare blankets, their clothes worn thin and dirty.

This place is a cut above.

"Hey, Markie? Is he here?" Fiona calls to the woman dishing out food.

The silver-haired woman with the ladle fills a large bowl with soup and sets it on a tray. "Next door."

"Excellent, thanks. You need anything?" Fiona asks.

"Nope. We're good."

The three of us back out of the soup kitchen and change direction, heading to the club next door.

It has a retro, old-time feeling with the awning marquee hanging over the sidewalk and the show posters highlighted within glass cases lit with small, white globe lights all along the front wall.

Our entrance into the drag club is an assault on the senses in the best possible way. The colors, sounds, and energy are magnetic. The lights bounce off the sequined walls and floors, and the heady scents of spiced perfume and leather booths blend with the faint smell of stage smoke.

As we stand in the back, a majestic figure dominates the stage. She's a mountain of a woman, seven feet tall in her silver platform heels, her vibrant purple wig reaching for the heavens, and her body poured into a figure-hugging cheetah print dress. Her commanding presence steals every ounce of attention in the room.

She performs an energetic routine, her legs kicking up in time with the music as she belts out a heart-rending rendition of a sassy ballad.

It's a burlesque number, and her passion is palpable even in rehearsal. I can tell she's a force to be reckoned with, and her performance mesmerizes me.

The lighting guy, a wiry man in a black T-shirt, works with a singular focus to keep the spotlights on the diva strutting and spinning across the stage.

He's good because even with her energetic performance, he never loses track of her.

When the music finally reaches a crescendo, the woman kicks up her foot and waves her hands to salute the audience that isn't here.

Fiona claps and presses her fingers under her tongue to let out a loud, shrill whistle.

The performer shields her eyes with her hand and squints past the house lights. "Girlfriend? Is that you?"

"Yeah, baby. You rock socks, Pan Dora."

That earns Fi a glowing smile as she struts down the stage steps. As she nears, her vivid, painted eyes assess us.

There's a spark of curiosity in her gaze. She stops a few steps away, crossing her arms over her ample bosom, and strikes a pose. "What brings you three to my humble abode?"

Her voice is deep, sultry, and playful. That's when it hits me.

This isn't only Merlin's club—this is Merlin.

After filling Pan Dora in on what happened at the lakeshore, she jogs upstairs to change. Fiona takes one look at me and chuckles. "Okay, get it out of your system before he comes back. What's on your mind?"

I blink, my mind still spinning. "Merlin performs in drag and owns a drag club."

Fiona nods. "It's a long story, but the gist is that he's bonded to a dragon empress, and when her physical form was dying, he took her spirit into himself. That gave him a bit of a flair for glam, and even though it's all sorted now and Empress Cazzienth is fine, he still enjoys performing as Pan Dora."

All righty, then. "Consider me caught up. Thanks."

Fiona shrugs. "The important thing is Merlin's amazing and Dora's one of my favorite people on this planet, so live and let live."

"One hundred percent."

Merlin returns from the apartment above the club, and I'm shocked at the transformation. He is a fit, slender man with shoulder-length brown waves wearing black fatigues and army boots.

I know it's a drag club, but wow, the change between his on-stage persona and now is incredible.

"Jules Gagne, this is Merlin." Fiona goes the introduction route for a second time.

"It's such a mind-blowing honor to meet you," I remark. "Tad and Fiona have mentioned you a dozen times, but holy hell —Merlin. As in the legendary wizard and advisor to King Arthur?"

Merlin chuckles and nods. "That's me. Although I admit, the legends have grown exaggerated over time."

Fiona looks at me and laughs. "Close your mouth, Jules. Yes, he's Merlin, but he's also our mentor and friend."

I shake my head, still trying to comprehend that I've met one of the most famous figures in history. I've met powerful fae before, but this is on a whole new level.

"Tell me what you know about the people exploiting kids on my streets." He crosses his arms.

Sloan goes over everything he gleaned while working with Ryan, starting with the struggle to stabilize his wind essence and ending with the three boys booking it the moment we learned about the man siphoning their essence.

"My question is, why would they stay with him?" Fiona asks. "If those boys were allowed to leave the house, it begs the question, why go back?"

Merlin frowns. "The lines blur when you're desperate, girlfriend. At first, this Belvedere guy would treat them right. He'd give them food and a safe place to sleep and make them feel welcome and accepted."

"If they weren't experimenting with their elements, he'd likely get them hooked on drugs, too," I add.

"So, why stay?" Fiona repeats.

"It's a sad cycle, Fi. It could be the devil they know. It could be that he's blackmailing them with the safety of others. It could be the promise of their freedom. There's no way for us to know until we find them."

Fiona shakes her head. "Then we need to find them and find them someplace safe to live as kids."

Merlin grabs a long wool jacket and slides into it. "That's the plan."

As the four of us make our way through the city streets, I notice people are drawn to Merlin. They approach him with questions or to say hello, and he greets everyone with a warm smile and a kind word.

He's well-respected and beloved by those around him.

I feel a mixture of awe, gratitude, and curiosity. I want to know more about this enigmatic figure and how he survived and adapted through the centuries.

He makes me think of Bakkali. Montréal's Viking has the same sense of being there for the people as Merlin. I'm curious about him, too.

Although Merlin is much less intimidating.

As we continue our search for intel about Mr. Belvedere, we visit half a dozen homeless groups and cardboard communities down alleys or set up above the venting grates from the subway below.

It's only late October, but the bite in the air is sharp, and it gets colder after the sun goes down. This might not be Montréal, but it's the same story back in my city. Homeless people on the streets, battling the elements and wondering if they have what it takes to make it through another winter.

"Wonderful. Thanks very much." Merlin squeezes the arm of a woman tucked away in a blue tent. "Don't forget to come in and get something to eat. I mean it, Tracey. I'm going to ask my staff if you've been in."

The old girl flashes him a toothless grin. "Bossy, boy."

Merlin winks at her. "You know I wouldn't boss if I didn't care."

"Yeah, I know."

When he straightens, he meets us at the curb and gestures to the left. "There's a buzz to stay away from the old candy factory down by the lakeshore. The rumor is that the guy who bought it and renovated it is muling kids."

"What makes them think they're mules?" I ask.

"Just that there are kids coming and going at all hours and half the time, they look haggard."

"Which could also be because skoro are using them as essence drink boxes," Fiona counters.

Merlin nods. "That's another possibility, sure."

Fi texts Dillan, Calum, and the others to meet us at the location. Then Sloan *poofs* the four of us back to the lakeshore area.

The gentrification of the old candy factory into a modern condo building seems to have been an exercise in architectural alchemy. From the outside, the structure retains its majestic past. The original brick façade stands proud and tall, where time has added a charming patina to the deep red brickwork.

Grand arching windows punctuate the exterior, and I imagine they once flooded the manufacturing floors with natural light. Wrought iron gates at the entrance are original or beautiful replicas and provide a touch of vintage elegance.

Gone are the customary smoking chimneys and steam vents of a building like this. Now there is a lush green space offering panoramic views of the cityscape.

"I see why street kids prefer to live here," I comment.

"No doubt," Merlin agrees.

Fiona finishes a text and puts her phone away. "The others will be here momentarily."

As Fiona speaks, my gaze is drawn to a side door in the candy factory building. It swings open with an ominous *creak*, and a figure emerges.

Even at this distance, its black eyes are unmistakable, pools of bottomless darkness that seem to absorb the surrounding light. It's a sight that sends a chill crawling up my spine, not only because of what the creature is but because of what its presence here signifies.

This is one of the fuckers feeding on kids.

There's a moment of frozen silence when our gazes lock, and the world seems to hold its breath. Then, like a puppet jerked by invisible strings, the skoro twists and races back into the building. The door slams shut behind him.

"Shit!" I curse, the word slicing through the silence as I launch into a run. "We're blown."

CHAPTER TEN

When the skoro disappears into the building, I take off after him. Sloan and Fiona follow closely. The others call to them as they arrive and race after us. Our feet pound against the concrete, the echoes of our steps lost in the thrumming rush of adrenaline in my veins.

We can't let that asshole raise the alarm.

We don't know how many skoro are inside, so surprise is our best advantage. You don't know what you don't know and can't prepare for it.

Dillan catches up to me. He and I burst into the main lobby of the building, and the sight that greets us is a punch to the gut. Half a dozen skoro lounge in the elegantly renovated space, their demon gazes a stark contrast to the interior's sleek modern lines.

In the center of the room is a hookah pipe of unimaginable horror. Its massive glass chamber contains trapped fae. The skoro are drawing on several mouthpieces, sucking the essence from the kids too desperate and too trusting not to be caught in the snare of these monsters.

Flame bursts to my palms as the sight brings back the horrifying memory of being drained myself.

The skoro scramble and chaos of bodies and curses register our intrusion.

Dillan grins, bracing himself, his posture a perfect blend of readiness and resolution. "That's it, fucktards. How about you pick on someone your size?"

They come at us in a wave of malice and feral intention. The room fills with the *crackle* of druid powers, demon snarls, and the anticipation of making these Poreskro minions pay for Ryan and all the other kids they've been feasting on.

I launch myself at the first attacker.

My fire whip lashes out, wrapping around the skoro's wrist. When I solidify my intention, the whip tightens, burning through his limb until his hand falls to the floor, still clutching his dagger.

The beauty of the move is that my flame cauterized the amputation and the blood and gore are minimal.

With a rush of air and a flash of light, Calum, Briar, Azland, and Zephyr bust into the lobby and join us.

The first floor fills with an electrifying energy as everyone engages, transforming the elegant space into a fae battlefield.

"The gang's all here," Calum shouts.

Fiona throws a hand toward the entrance. "Seal the doors. No one gets out!"

I've already moved on to my next opponent, but when I swing around, I see Merlin pressing his hand against the doors and murmuring something.

A flare of pale green magic erupts from his hands and shimmers over the exterior walls. "Hotel California, Fi."

"You rock socks, my friend," Fiona shouts from the hallway.

Dionysus charges forward, sees the teens withering and suspended within the bottle, and presses his palms against the glass. The moment he touches the vessel, the glass is gone, and the two fae sink softly to the carpet on the floor.

His gaze is swirling silver when he looks around, and my stomach roils from the power he radiates.

Dillan races past with matching daggers in both his hands. "Take the fae to the Batcave, Greek. Get them somewhere safe."

The moment he says it, Dionysus and the two youths are gone.

Dillan continues to fight, his hands a blur as he deftly moves through the chaos, slicing and cutting through the enemy.

Azland finds a different path. He rushes to any skoro he can get close to, and with a touch, they drop to the floor. Their skin veins black as if toxic spider webs were infecting them.

"Jules, a little help." Zephyr is manipulating the air to create barriers and keep three off him. His eyes are the color of a stormy sky and bright with concentration.

"Gotcha, Z." I race over to engage, flick the length of my whip to wrap around my opponent's throat, and try my tightening technique again.

Skoro aren't the most susceptible to my flames, but fire or not, being beheaded ends the fight.

When the first head *clunks* to the floor and rolls, I'm happy to see the cauterization technique held.

One decapitated asshole and limited cleanup.

When the second head rolls, Dillan races past me. "Jules, you're with me."

I turn and follow without hesitation, on his heels as he races up the stairs one floor.

"With everyone locked down, we need to safeguard as many innocents as possible before they get used as hostage shields."

An excellent point.

We turn the corner and meet two skoro grappling a young fae girl. The girl's eyes are wide, and she's thrashing, trying to free herself from their grip.

I fling a barrage of firebolts over their heads. When they shift to assess the attack, Dillan throws his daggers and head-shots both of them square in the forehead.

They crumple to the floor, and my mouth falls open. "Holy

shit. Tell me that wasn't a fluke, and you knew you could make that shot."

Dillan grins at me and waggles his brows. "I'm just that fucking good, fire girl."

I laugh and jog forward to check on the girl. "Are you okay?"

The girl stares at us. "Uh-huh…I think so."

"Yeah, you are." Dillan presses his boot against the throat of his kills to give him the leverage to pull his twin daggers free. "You'll be even better once we find all your friends and get you out of here. Now, show us where your friends are."

Dillan and I follow, shifting focus from fighting to search and rescue because despite what's happening downstairs, we're here to safeguard the teens.

We gather as we go, and with them disoriented, weak, and scared shitless, we do our best to shield them and stash them on the third floor, away from the worst of the battle.

Room by room, we clear the four floors until we're sure we've secured the building.

Downstairs, the battle has grown quiet, the storm of chaos within the beautiful confines of the remodeled condominium dying off.

Dillan and I jog down the stairs and toward the group. Merlin and Dionysus have a couple of skoro prisoners bound to one of the couches and are trying to get information out of them.

Everyone else is filtering back from different directions, hauling any skoro that made it through this and still has a pulse.

"Who is Belvedere and what is he to all this?" Dionysus asks.

No one speaks.

"Is he a skoro demon like you or something else?" Merlin asks.

Still nothing.

I stride over, thinking that being interrogated by an elemental might knock them off their game a little. "Who is your maker? You can only be begotten from Sasobek, Zissa, or Rance."

The skoro guards exchange glances.

I laugh. "What? You don't think I know about the tie between you and the Poreskoros? Well, Lamech and Draven are dead and that means so are their spawn. Gareth never created minions, which means you three belong to Rance, Sasobek, or Zissa."

Fiona is looking at me with her eyebrows raised. "See, I knew bringing your team in on this was the right call."

It feels good to contribute to this partnership for a change. Usually it's the Toronto team with the skills and information, and we're the backup.

Going up against skoro and dealing with elemental issues means we're the in-house experts.

"The lady asked you a question." Dionysus wags his finger at them. "Don't make her ask you again. Who do you belong to, boys?"

The skoro remain stubbornly silent. I draw a deep breath and consider our next move.

As much as I don't like it, the play is obvious.

I pull out my phone and send a text. "Dionysus or Nikon, would one of you mind portaling to my fire station? I think we can clear this up rather quickly if we have the right person in the room."

Nikon nods. "Happy to. Merlin, are you going to let me out?"

Merlin drops the shimmering green shield locking the building down, and Nikon grins. "Back in two."

Fiona looks at me, her gaze curious.

I draw a deep breath and tell her the truth. "It's not widely known, but Gareth's full name is Razgarath Poreskoro. He's the youngest of The Six."

Nikon portals back with Gareth. The moment his gaze lands on the massive hookah bottle and the skoro bound and sitting on the couches, Gareth's eyes flip to scarlet flames. He storms forward, grabs one of the bound prisoners, and snaps his neck.

It's not like I'm squeamish, but the brutal ease of the kill is unnerving.

Something inside me argues to defend him. Gareth is half demon, and the world is better with one less skoro. Besides, we took out a dozen more since we've been here. I decide not to look too closely at it right now.

"They are Sasobek's," he growls, dropping the limp body of the skoro to the floor.

"You're sure?"

"Yeah, they reek of her power signature."

"Sasobek is who?" Merlin asks.

"My sister." Gareth sneers at him. "Before you ask. No, we're not close. No, I didn't know about this. And no, I don't condone torture or the draining of kids."

Merlin holds up his hands. "Hey, not all families can be like the Cumhaills, and I've lived too long to judge. We're good."

I know it's hard for Gareth to bear witness to the carnage his siblings cause, but I'm secretly relieved it upsets him so much.

I'd worry if it didn't.

Recognizing that Gareth needs some space, I lace my fingers with his and tug him down the main hall and away from the group's eyes.

He's amped up and gestures down the hallway. "You've been through these rooms? Searched for all the kids they had here?"

"Yeah. Dillan and I stashed them on the third floor."

Gareth thumbs the button on the elevator and steps inside. When we arrive on the third floor, he gestures for me to lead the way. Of course, his priority is to see to the well-being of the children.

That's who he is.

"From what Sloan learned from the wind elemental who brought us here, this was supposed to be a haven for them."

Gareth nods. "Kids with shitty lives and shitty homes get one look at a place like this and walk through the door, excited to live a new life. They don't realize that the door only swings inward until they're trapped."

When we get to the apartment where I left the kids, I'm pleased to see they've stayed put. "It's okay now, guys. The danger is over."

"What happened?" a scrawny girl with droopy antennae asks. "Are Casey and Shahir all right?"

"Who are they?" I ask.

"They were taken for this afternoon's feeding. Are they all right?"

Ah, the kids being drained when we got here. "As far as I know, yes. When we raided the place, one of our team transported them to the guild headquarters here in Toronto to get help."

The girl sighs and practically deflates. "That's good."

"What will happen to us now?" one of them asks.

Merlin comes in behind us. "We'll take you all to my soup kitchen. We'll get you fed, and after that, we'll sort through how and why you ended up here and figure out where you'll be safest and best cared for."

"We should take the elementals back with us." Gareth meets my gaze. "I can't stop my family from coming after them from another city, and these kids are younger than any elementals should be. We need to find out where they came from and where their parents are."

I think about the damage Ryan unwittingly caused. Sloan said Belvedere was experimenting on them and allowing the skoro to feed on them. Could he have wanted Ryan to lose control like that, or was that a side effect of being mistreated?

"Does that mean there are more of us?" I ask.

The question hangs in the air, heavy with the implication of more lost children and the mystery of how they could be here.

Maybe, like Azland, some elementals escaped the violent raids of the Poreskoro family.

Maybe they lived their lives and had families.

That thought blows my mind. For the past five months, we've been operating under the assumption that the handful of elementals placed in Montréal is all there are.

What if that's not true?

Gareth and I escort the kids down to the main floor and have Dionysus take the fae teens with Merlin to the food kitchen. The elemental teens go to the fire station with Nikon, Briar, and Zephyr.

I'm not sure what we'll do with six more kids to care for, but that's a problem for later.

For now, we need to figure out what Sasobek and Belvedere have going on here. Is it only a matter of feeding? Then why the experimentation?

Gareth and I explore the building, room by room, searching for answers. It's clear Mr. Belvedere has a taste for the unusual, but it's difficult to discern whether his interest in housing these fae kids is purely twisted or if he has an agenda.

"What the serious fuck?" I stand in the doorway of a room in the basement. The stench of melted metal singes my nostrils.

"The padlock on the door should've been a warning we were getting close," Gareth points out.

I shrug. "I was more focused on melting it off than preparing myself for what we were about to find inside."

I follow Gareth into the room, and my blood runs cold. There is a metal table in the middle of the room and a rack of strange and intrusive instruments—clearly designed for painful procedures.

I shudder. "This is no ordinary hobby."

Gareth's scarlet gaze scans the room. "No, it's darker than that. Knowing my sister, I wouldn't be surprised if she has places like this in a dozen cities."

That thought makes my stomach flip.

We finish our exploration, and it's clear something sinister has been happening here.

I take a few photos and a video of the surgical tools hanging on the rack. Maybe Luc or Rance can figure out what they were doing.

When I finish that, I turn to find Gareth sifting through the paper contents of a banker's box. "What did you find?"

"Procedure notes documenting the experiments Belvedere has been performing. He's detailed the race of the fae subject, the procedure and tools used, and the outcome."

"Which is what? What outcome was he working toward?"

He flips through a couple more pages and turns the last one for me to see. "He's perfecting his technique to extract and harness fae powers."

"For what purpose?" I wince and inspect the notes. "Does he think he can absorb or use the powers of other fae races?"

Gareth's jaw is clenched so hard I expect to hear his molars crack under the pressure. "I don't know, but whatever it is, it can't be good."

"Well, bring the box upstairs. It'll be up to Fiona and her team to find Belvedere and follow up on what he was doing here. We should get back to the fire station and check on Ryan and the other elementals."

"No. This is an elemental issue, and my fucked-up sister is at the center. We will handle things and keep Fiona and her team apprised of what we learn." Gareth tosses the papers back into the box and fits the lid on.

There's no room to argue the point, so why bother?

Heavy footfalls race over our heads and people are shouting. Gareth hands me the box, and we bolt for the stairs.

CHAPTER ELEVEN

Gareth takes the stairs three at a time, and I do my best to keep up. My pulse thrums in my ears as adrenaline fuels my cells. Did another wave of skoro arrive? Did one of her minions alert Sasobek that we're here?

We crest the top step and find Sloan pinning a man to the floor. "Are ye the one the kids call Belvedere? The monster who tortured and terrified an innocent lad until he nearly took down the city?"

"I don't think so," Gareth answers. "He's one of Sasobek's, no question, but from what the kids said upstairs, I think this is Rimmon, the skoro handler that oversees recruitment."

Sloan lifts the newcomer to his feet and hands him to Dionysus. "He's a little late to the party but better late than never. Take him to the holdin' cell with the others, sham. We'll let Garnet interrogate him. He holds a special hatred fer people who prey on children."

The man twists and curses, fighting to break Dionysus' hold. It wouldn't matter if he did. There are enough of us here that he wouldn't get two feet before another of us took him down.

Fiona picks up a large box of Timbits from the floor and pops the cardboard open. "He brought snacks. That's the party spirit, dickwad."

Dillan and Calum laugh as they dig into the box of donut holes. "Sweet, we take down this operation and get treats."

"What did you two find?" Nikon points at the box in my hands.

"Detailed experiment notes on Mr. Belvedere's techniques to extract elemental powers."

Calum pops a couple of chocolate spheres into his mouth and offers to take the box. "Awesome. I'll take it to the Batcave and start going through it. Looks like we've done all the damage we can do for today."

I hold the box and look at Gareth. "Uh, since this revolves around Gareth's sister and he knows best what she's capable of, we thought we'd like to dive in and tackle this one. The draining of elementals is something we're already too familiar with."

Fiona considers that. "All right. Let Calum take the box. We'll inventory everything and make copies for our files. Your team can take the lead, and we'll cover anything that happens here and keep you updated."

"We'll do the same," Gareth replies.

Dillan chuckles and offers me the box of treats. "And a good time was had by all."

I choose a chocolate glazed Timbit and a sourdough. As I chew on the first one, I scan the destruction of this operation and turn to Gareth. "I don't suppose this counts as us staying clear of your sisters."

Gareth arches a brow. The faintest hint of a grin plays at the corners of his mouth. "I don't suppose."

Nikon portals a bunch of us back to the fire station. The moment the power of his energy fades, the relief of being home washes over me. Until I take in the gravity of the surrounding situation.

"Thank the goddess you're back," Kenzie gushes. "Sloan, we could really use your help in here."

Sloan rushes out of the kitchen to join Kenzie and Zephyr in the living room.

"What's going on?" I ask one of the teens.

She's sitting at the kitchen table, rubbing Onyx's ears. "Ryan's not doing so good."

I scan the worried expressions of the other teens and sigh. We might have rescued them, but they look as scared and displaced as they did in that candy factory.

Pulling out my phone, I call the best person I know for a situation like this—Charlie.

"Hey, Jules. What's new, chickie-poo?"

I scan the scared faces and try to project all the calm and casual I can muster. "Lots. Are you busy? Could you and the kids come over?"

"What's wrong? Your voice is funny."

I stride across the kitchen and close the door to my suite. After explaining to Charlie what went down, I change and head back out.

"How's he doing?" I ask Briar.

Briar runs a hand through his sandy blond hair and exhales without answering.

Yeah, that can't be good.

The same look of hopelessness is mirrored on the face of every kid around the room. How are they here? Anyone who survived the raids was twenty-five years old or older.

By the look of these guys, they're all between fifteen and eighteen.

I lean back against the counter and look them over. "Where did you all come from?"

The kids exchange uncertain glances.

"From the streets," one of the water elementals replies. She's a petite little blonde with a wild mop of curly hair. "We've been hiding out, trying to stay under the radar. When some other kids invited us to crash with them in the condos, it seemed like we finally found somewhere to settle for a bit."

A loud *crash* in the living room has Sloan and Azland cursing and Kenzie squawking and readjusting her position. Whatever is going wrong with Ryan, it's going very wrong—and the kids know it.

"Hey guys, how about you take Onyx to the backyard with my brother Briar? He can show you our elemental stations. Which one of you is fire?"

A tall boy with brown curls raises his hand.

"What's your name, buddy?"

"Teddy."

"Well, Teddy, feel free to take a dip in my lava pool. There's a little change area and you can leave your clothes in there and get in behind the rocks so you have some privacy. I swear to you, there is nothing like it."

He nods. "Okay, maybe."

"The earth kids can enjoy my mud pit." Briar grins. "It sounds less appealing than it is."

"The rest of you can use Kenzie's pool," I add. "Tad spelled the water, so it's as warm as a bathtub even with it getting cold out. I heard we have two wind elementals, Ryan and…"

Another boy raises his hand. "Steffan."

I nod. "Hey, Steffan. Zephyr's iFLY wind tunnel isn't finished. Are you okay swimming?"

"Yeah, sure, that's fine."

"If you don't feel like relaxing, you can grab a beer or a cooler from the fridge in the garage bay downstairs and chill on the patio," Zephyr interjects.

I blink. "Hello? Can you say underage?"

Zephyr rolls his eyes. "Like we weren't drinking beer at sixteen. Please."

"Can we use the pole?" Steffan points at the shiny brass pole from our second-floor ceiling to the bay downstairs.

"Sure you can. We use it all the time. Just grab on tight with your hands, wrap your legs around it, and loosen your grip so you descend."

"For those who don't want to take the pole, I'm taking the stairs so Onyx can join us," Briar comments.

As they break off, I think of one more thing. "Teddy?"

"Yeah?"

"Don't be alarmed if Onyx jumps in with you. He's a hellhound, and he loves the lava."

"Seriously?"

"Yeah, so everyone else give the lava pool a wide berth. When the dog jumps in, lava flies everywhere."

Their excited chatter is better than their traumatized stares, so I take that as a win. Until I hear the garage fridge open and envision Briar handing out coolers and beer to those kids.

"Seriously. Aren't we supposed to set the example as guild enforcers?"

"Lighten up, Inspector Gagne," Zephyr urges. "They've had a shit day, and we're watching over them."

A groan in the living room has me hustling across the kitchen to where Sloan, Kenzie, and Azland are all working on Ryan.

Gareth moves in beside me and rests a hand on my shoulder. "What's happening to him?"

Sloan straightens and scratches the back of his neck. "His lack of control is growin'. We need to figure out how to contain his powers before we risk wakin' him, but everythin' we try unravels more of his control even faster."

"Do you have any ideas on how to fix that?" I ask.

"What if my station was finished?" Zephyr asks.

Azland sighs. "I don't think it would be what we need, but it's a moot point. It's not finished, and it's nowhere near close enough to being finished to try."

I look from Azland to Gareth to Sloan to Dionysus. "Any big ideas sparking in those minds of yours?"

Azland sighs. "I have one, but you won't like it."

"All right. Lay it on me. What are you thinking?"

"I say we take Ryan to Gailleann."

My mouth falls open. "You want us to take a kid in the throes of a total power meltdown into a devastated fae kingdom?"

"I mentioned you wouldn't like it."

He did…and he was right. "Okay, I'm listening. Tell me why we should take Ryan to Gailleann."

"Well, for one, wind is Ryan's element. He can't control it, but setting it free won't hurt him. It's who he is."

"And?"

"Behind the training academy, there's a station much like your regeneration stations. Except, instead of helping wind elementals control their element and keep things locked down, it allows them to release the storm that builds in so many of them."

I understand this completely because we saw what having his powers bound did to Zephyr.

"Can't he do that here somewhere?" I ask.

Azland blinks at me. "Did you miss the part where the kid took out a Toronto city block this morning? And that was with him still fighting to contain things."

Yeah, good point.

The idea of going to one of the elemental kingdoms excites and terrifies me. Would it help Ryan? Or would it put the rest of us in danger?

Azland told us the outer fringe of the elemental lands used to be treacherous, and after a quarter of a century, it is likely even more volatile. All five kingdoms took part in safeguarding the lands, and when the Poreskoro invaded with their armies, the elementals made getting in or out even more difficult.

"Let's say we decide to go." I try to stay objective. "How do we get to Gailleann?"

Fiona waggles a brow. "I can make that happen."

CHAPTER TWELVE

By morning, Charlie and the twins have agreed to take on the elemental slumber party at the fire station while we take Ryan to the fae realm, and hopefully to the vortex of Gailleann. "We've got this, Jules. Your job is to focus on helping Ryan and get back safely."

"Yeah, we've got this." Micah grins. "It's a hardship. Hanging out at your place, having a party—oh, wait! Did I say party? I meant holding down the fort."

I snort and point at him. "My bed might be slept in, but if I come back and find my room ransacked, I will burn all your clothes."

Micah's teasing smile falters. "Rude."

Anna laughs. "Just make sure you all come back in one piece, okay?"

I hug her with an extra-long squeeze. "Help Charlie and monitor your brother. He means well, but he can be a disaster of Zephyr proportions at times."

Anna laughs. "I feel you, Jules. Don't worry."

"What's your game plan?" Teddy asks, sending Ryan a worried look.

"I don't have all the details, but Sloan's been working with Azland, so we're in good hands."

"Yeah, you are," Nikon agrees, materializing behind us. "We're all set."

Anna and Sammy squeal in delight when they see Nikon. Honestly, I can't blame them. He's tall and blond with olive skin, Mediterranean good looks, and the charm of the ancients.

And he can portal.

Chuckling, I lean closer to the girls and whisper, "He's about a thousand years too old for you. Maybe you should get to know some of the new kids. They've been through a lot and could likely use a friend."

Anna rolls her eyes at me, snags Sammy's arm, and the two march off to hang out with kids their age.

Nikon claps Zephyr's shoulder. "If you guys have what you need, let's make this happen."

My stomach lurches at the thought. The elemental kingdoms. Until now, the idea of us coming from the fae realm has been abstract. Now we're going there.

Will I feel any different there?

Will my powers recognize being home?

Slipping back into my suite, I grab my backpack and scrub the top of Onyx's head. "Are you three ready?"

Gareth finishes his text and slides his phone into his back pocket. "Ready. I wanted to tell Rance what's happening and ask him to watch over the fire station in case my sisters get any big ideas about poaching your guests while we're away."

"Oh, man. With the preparations for the fae realm, I hadn't thought of that."

He winks. "Not a problem. I got you, boo."

I snort. "Did you really just say that to me?"

He shrugs. "You pick up a thing or two when you spend all your social time with teens."

I adjust my shoulder straps and snap the clip at my navel. "Do we have everything we need for the dogs?"

Gareth lifts a full-sized hiker's pack off the floor and swings it on. "All set."

After grabbing my water bottle from the counter and sliding it into place, I'm ready to go.

A scan of the kitchen tells me Kenzie and Briar are ready too. And Zephyr...he was packed, ready, and buzzing around before I had my first coffee this morning.

Not that I blame him.

Gailleann is his elemental kingdom. His father was the head trainer at the academy. This is his chance to see and feel where he came from.

That's beyond thrilling, I'm sure.

"All right, everyone." I stick my hand out between Nikon and me. "Hands in. Let's go."

Briar scoops Ryan off the couch and brings him to the kitchen. When everyone has their hands in, Nikon completes the circuit.

My skin tingles with the energy signature of his spatial magic. Then we're standing on a flat plane of green with a circle of standing stones to our left and four massive dragons to our right.

"Are you shitting me?" Zephyr's grin grows even bigger. "The wind kingdom *and* dragons? Could this day get any more fucking awesome?"

The dragons are breathtaking, their scales gleaming in the sunlight. The sight is awe-inspiring, and I shiver as nervous excitement runs through me.

We had the pleasure to meet two of Fiona's dragon brood last month when she brought two wyverns to the St. Lawrence Seaway to eat the fish that grew too dangerous because of the sudden influx of fae prana into the waters.

These are the same yet very different.

These are the dragons I picture when I hear the word. Four powerful limbs, enormous colorful wings, and a long row of spikes running from the collar around their scaly necks and down their backs to the spiked tips of their tails.

Incredible.

"How did you get them here?" Briar asks. "Are there going to be reports of UFO sightings or clips on the news that Toronto is under attack?"

Fiona chuckles. "No. Once they were a year old, they could glamor their presence to keep from being seen. No public riots will ensue."

"Excellent." Kenzie smiles at them wide-eyed. "Hello, beautiful beasts. Are you the siblings of Azure and Neak?"

Fiona gestures at a brilliant blue dragon. "Dart is the oldest of my dragon brood. Saxa is his mate. The vibrant green girl is Esym, and the deep red male is Torrim."

Zephyr whistles through his teeth. "Man, they seem so much bigger when you see them out of the water."

I chuckle. "Are you claiming the iceberg effect?"

Zephyr flashes me his middle finger. "Maybe."

Fiona continues. "To answer your question, Briar, these stone rings are connected by a dragon portal to an identical set of standing stones in Ireland. Merlin linked the two sites so Dart could visit his broodmates more easily. Now we use them to get from the island they live on in Ireland to here."

I glance around to gauge the others' reactions. Kenzie and Zephyr are brimming over with amazement. Briar is playing it cool. Azland looks completely unfazed. It's like he's seen dragons every day of his life.

I roll my eyes, not letting his stunted emotional range bother me.

"Yes, girl. They're incredible." I follow the rumbled timbre of Gareth's voice to where he's holding back an excited, wriggling Onyx and speaking to Jinx.

Wow, even the hellhound is in awe.

"How do we do this?" I ask.

Fiona raises her hand and approaches the blue male. "The first thing you need to do is introduce yourself. Dragons like to know who they're carrying on their backs and are quite particular about manners. They are not beasts of burden. They have free will, and we need to consider their wishes."

I frown. "And if we make a social *faux pas*?"

"Dart has been known to fry folks extra crispy and crunch them up."

I let out a squeaky laugh. "You're kidding, right?"

"Nope. That's true. Although he was younger and more impetuous at the time."

"Well then. Let's be thankful for mature dragons."

As we approach the deadly foursome, I can't help the pang of nervousness invading my cells. These creatures are massive, and their power tingles over my skin before I'm close enough to touch them.

I know we're here to work together, but will they accept us so easily simply because Fiona asks them to? A trained tiger will obey a ringmaster, but given the chance, it might still maul people.

Manners, she says.

I swallow my apprehension as we draw closer to the dragons. They tower over us, and their eyes are watchful as they regard our approach. The blue one, Dart, greets Kenzie with a stroke of his nostrils against her palm and a deep inhalation.

Taking a breath, I step forward and introduce myself to the vibrant green female named Esym. Her gaze bores into me as I speak, but when I finish, she nods.

Fiona grins mischievously. "The best way to get a dragon to like you is with roasted sheep or a barrel of mead. She's wondering what you've got there."

I hold up the large picnic lunch. "Thanks to Charlie, we've got enough food for a small army, but I'm fresh out of mutton and mead."

Fiona laughs and points at another large cooler. "Well, thanks to Charlie and Gran, there's certainly no risk of us starving."

Everyone gets a laugh out of that.

"What about the dragons?" Briar looks concerned.

Fiona smiles. "They hunt their own prey."

I breathe a sigh of relief. "Amazing. I don't want to start this adventure by letting them down on the food front. I can't imagine we want four hangry dragons."

Fiona waves away the concern. "No, we don't, but we fed them a huge stack of cattle and deer before we came, so they should be good."

That's reassuring.

"So, riding a dragon is all about trust." Fiona gets back on point. "You have to trust that the dragon has got you, and in return, the dragon has to trust you to hold on and take care of yourself while in flight. It's a relationship based on mutual respect."

I look up, up, up to where the dragon's back runs high above the ground. "Trust is good, but how do I get up there?"

Fiona takes a few running steps, vaults into the air, does some kind of acrobatic flip off Dart's elbow, and launches herself into an aerial. She lands, sure-footed and squarely on the flat of her dragon's back. "It's easy."

My mouth falls open. "You've got to be kidding."

Fi laughs again. "Of course I am. Tad, Nikon, or Sloan can portal you up. Come on. We're wasting daylight."

Sloan portals Gareth and me onto the back of the bright yellow dragon with burning amber wings. She's breathtaking, and from what he tells me, he's bonded to her as her dragon rider.

How freaking cool is that?

"These are yer saddle handles." Sloan points at three vertical rails mounted on a thick swatch of leather that wraps each of the first four spikes on Saxa's back. "If the skies are rough, hold onto the two outer grips and widen yer stance like this."

He takes hold of the handles and demonstrates. "If we fall under attack and ye need to defend, ye'll find usin' the center grip with one hand gives ye the balanced stance ye need to use the other hand to fight."

That this is part of the dragon-riding demonstration is alarming and intriguing. What kind of adventures have Fiona, Sloan, and her team had upon these creatures?

"As fer yer hounds, Nikon will create a spatial bubble around them. I suggest anchorin' them to Saxa's back with a harness, or I can cast a spell to keep them from fallin' off."

Ever the enthusiastic baby boy, Onyx can barely contain his excitement as his wagging tail thrashes his body around in happy butt wiggles. Gareth keeps a firm hold on Jinx and looks at me. "I can explain to the dogs what's happening, but you'll have to soothe him if Jinx doesn't take to this."

"I can do that." I tug Onyx to get him to sit his wiggly butt between my feet and the dragon spike I need to hold on to. "Go ahead, Sloan. Do what you need to do to cast your spell."

"Everyone ready?" Fiona shouts from the front spike of her blue dragon.

I scan our group spread out over the four dragons.

Gareth, Azland, Kenzie, Briar, Zephyr, and I make six from Montréal. Fiona, Sloan, Tad, and Nikon from Toronto add another four. Plus an unconscious Ryan and two anxious hellhounds.

Before we take off, I glance back to meet Gareth's gaze. He's right behind me, with Jinx lying at his feet. Without saying a word, I ask him if they're doing okay. The slight dip of his chin is all I need to release some of my worry.

"Yeah, we're good," I call, raising my thumb.

I feel a brief sensation of being pulled toward the ground. Then Saxa's powerful wings extend, and we take to the sky. The pressure of gravity dragging us down vanishes almost at once, replaced by a soaring weightlessness.

I grip the handles tightly, exhilarated and moderately terrified. The wind whips around us as we climb higher and higher. The ground quickly recedes beneath us.

It's unlike anything I imagined, and I'm caught in the moment's thrill. I see what Fiona means about trusting the dragons to carry us.

Man, when did my life get so crazy?

The city of Toronto sprawls beneath us, a glittering expanse of glass and steel. I gaze down at the CN Tower and the domed stadium beside it, marveling at the sight. It's not every day that one gets to view such landmarks from the back of a mythical creature.

Saxa zooms forward, leading the group over Lake Ontario. The vast expanse of water stretches out beneath us, sparkling in the sunlight. The power of the dragon beneath me is incredible. She's strong and graceful and carries us effortlessly through the air.

I'm only getting used to the sensation of flight when Nikon performs a complex series of movements in midair. I've seen him work his portal magic more than once, but it's no less impressive now.

Nikon's efforts open a rift between the fae and human realms. Crackling energy surges through the air as the dragons shift and shimmer, their scales and wings reflecting the flickering light of magical energy.

My grip on the saddle handle tightens as energy builds around us. The air ripples and distorts as if reality itself is twisting.

INTELLECTUS: ORIGINS DISCOVERED

A bright pulse shines through the swirling vortex of iridescence, covering all of us in its otherworldly glow. It's terrifying and also a coming home of sorts...

Holy freaking fireballs! We're going home!

CHAPTER THIRTEEN

Being in the elemental kingdom of the fae realm is surreal. It's an enchanting realm of wonder, its strangeness alien but beautiful. Vibrant colors and intricate patterns blend in a dreamlike landscape, stretching as far as I can see.

This is where I come from.

For twenty-seven years, I felt out of sync with my world. I searched for answers. I pored over the photos of the burned house where firefighters found me in a dead man's arms. I was searching for answers, but I was really searching for *myself*.

Cutting through the sky on the back of a sunshine yellow dragon, I feel truly connected to who I was born to be for the first time in my life.

It's as if magic infuses the air around me, and it's seeping into my bones and feeding my cells.

The reason is obvious. The elemental kingdoms are the foundational source of our elemental powers. I can almost feel the fire within me, a part of my soul, responding to the magic of this place.

Do Briar, Kenzie, and Zephyr feel it?

Does Gareth feel it? He's half fae.

"This place is incredible," Kenzie calls, her eyes wide.

We journey deeper into the magical realm, and I scan the landscape below. I spot a group of fairies dancing and playing among the branches of a cluster of trees. They don't glance up, unbothered by the dragons passing overhead.

We pass other fantastical creatures too. On a wide hilltop plateau, a pride of griffins lay sunning themselves, their wings tucked in, their lion tails flicking to keep the pixies off them as they relax.

"Are those unicorns?" I point at a herd of rainbow-hued horses below.

"Alicorns," Sloan corrects. "Unicorns don't have wings. Think of them like a pegasus with a horn."

Unbelievable.

At a waterfall off to the right, a group of creatures flutters into sight. They appear to consist of pure light, and they dance and weave through the air with a grace and elegance that seems too perfect to be real.

The sky is a brilliant tapestry of hues, ranging from deep blues and purples to bright pinks and oranges, as if a million galaxies have merged.

The air is thick with the scent of blooming flowers and ethereal music.

The dragons dip and soar, following Dart's path. Azland is up front with Fiona and Nikon, directing her and her dragon where to go.

Everything is like a fantasy dream.

"Incoming!" Sloan's voice snaps me out of my daydream. "Hold on."

I stranglehold both handles, looking around as a group of fae creatures swoops toward us. Their wings beat furiously to keep up with the speed of dragon flight, but they aren't getting left behind.

Small and nimble with razor-sharp teeth and claws, our attackers are intent on drawing blood.

"Kenzie, watch out!" I shout as another swarm heads for where Kenzie is standing on the green dragon, Esym. She's standing over Ryan, firing ice pellets with her free hand.

The fae creatures dive toward us, and the dragons unleash a burst of flames from their mouths. The little bastards are too quick, dodging and weaving through the flames.

I call flame to my palm and start hurling fire to defend myself and my siblings. The fae creatures come at us from all angles, their sharp claws glinting in the sunlight. I throw more fire, flailing to keep them at bay.

"What the fuck are these things?" Zephyr shouts, smacking one out of the air with his storm staff.

"They're pookas," Sloan explains, his voice tense. "They're mischievous creatures but usually harmless. I don't know why they're attacking."

Briar doesn't have much to work with this far from the surface other than solidifying his fists to solid rock and swinging at any pookas that come close.

Zephyr's having more luck. He's churning the air around the red dragon, Torrim, sending the little assholes spinning like cows caught in a twister.

Kenzie creates an igloo over her and Ryan. The pookas can't get through the icy dome.

Good.

The little shits call to each other, coordinating their movements in midair.

Fiona unleashes her battle bear, and he races across the dragons, snarling and snatching up attackers with his mighty paws before ghosting out and appearing on the next dragon.

In his spirit form, Bruin rides the wind and is an incredible force for our side. Even with our combined efforts, the fae creatures are relentless.

They dart in and out, refusing to give up.

I summon a protective fire barrier around the dragons and my friends, shielding us from the incoming attack. The pookas back off but continue to circle, their expressions a mix of curiosity and annoyance.

Azland's magic raises the hair on my arms, and I look over to see what he's up to. His eyes shimmer with a soft purple glow as he weaves a spell of illusion. Suddenly, the air is full of duplicate dragons and their riders, each as lifelike as the next.

The creatures hesitate, unsure of which targets are real and which are magical mirages.

The brief respite gives us a chance to catch our breath and strategize. "We need to end this." I frown in concentration as I summon another firebolt. "Before someone gets seriously hurt."

A terrible screech fills the air as if on cue, and all eyes turn skyward. A massive griffin, wings outstretched and talons bared, swoops down upon the battlefield. She snatches two of the fae creatures in her claws, crushing them with a sickening *crunch*.

"Enough!" she bellows, her voice echoing through the air. "Leave these travelers be, or face my wrath!"

There is no hesitation.

The pookas screech, scatter, and buzz off.

When the sky is clear, the griffin female circles to hover in front of our group. "I am Nesperia, and you are not welcome here."

I blink. "Rude much? We haven't done anything. We come in peace. If you saw what happened, those creatures attacked us totally unprovoked."

The throaty growl that rumbles in her lioness chest reverberated in my lungs. "You bring a demon and his dogs to our lands and claim innocence? No, little flame, you are judged by the company you keep, and you keep very poor company."

Flames spark from my palms unbidden, but Gareth straightens and shakes his head. I realize he can defend himself, but everything in me wants to tear this female down for being mean to him.

"I apologize if my presence offends." Gareth inclines his head. "In another lifetime, my father's demon side influenced my life and my choices. I turned to my mother's side more than three decades ago and have spent every day since making amends."

"You coming to these lands at all is in poor taste."

"No," I interrupt. "Gareth is here to help us restore a young elemental. He is a child of these lands and a fierce protector. Intentions matter, and his intentions are honorable."

The female looks down her beak at me, her eagle eyes pegging me with a haughty glare. "Honorable intentions do not excuse the past, little flame."

"I agree. His actions going forward are the only things that can do that. Escorting us to Gailleann is one of a hundred ways he works to make things right."

"Tell me of the child you bring to Gailleann."

"He is a wind elemental," Kenzie explains, absorbing the ice and snow of the igloo to motion at Ryan. "We hope that being here will help his powers sync. He's having a terrible time containing his element."

Nesperia considers that for a moment and lets out another piercing shriek. More griffins suddenly launch into flight below, their powerful wings stirring the air.

My heart races inside my chest. Battling one-handed against pookas was tough, and they are little shits. Battling midair against a pride of griffins would end badly for us.

Very badly.

Nesperia must read the same trepidation on the faces of our group because her demeanor softens. "If you are indeed here to escort a boy to Gailleann, we are here to escort you and your dragons."

"We welcome your company and will speak well of our encounter to all we meet," Sloan replies.

With a graceful turn, Nesperia arches into the sky, her fellow griffins following suit. Our dragons fall into formation, their wings beating in sync as we continue our journey to Gailleann under the watchful eyes of our new escorts.

CHAPTER FOURTEEN

The griffin lady and her friends guide us to a wide plateau overlooking the city of Gailleann. Saxa lands with a whisper of elegance that a beast of her size and power shouldn't be able to manage.

It blows my mind.

She's a dragon the size of a bus with spikes and talons, and somehow, she's still feminine and graceful.

Five stars for travel by dragon. Highly recommend.

Once Sloan releases Jinx and Onyx from the spell to keep them in place, he portals us all to the ground.

The griffins seem as infatuated with the dragons as I am, circling them and staring as if they aren't mystical, majestic creatures themselves.

"Dragons were once a vital part of our world," Nesperia remarks. "They were protectors, fierce and powerful. It's been many centuries since we've seen one. How is it possible to have you here with us?"

Fiona gives the griffins a quick recap about how the Queen of Wyrms protected twenty-three eggs in her lair for centuries until

Fiona facilitated the means to fertilize them for a new generation of dragons.

"That is incredible." Nesperia bows her head to Fiona. "The realms owe you a great debt indeed."

It's obvious that dragons are revered. I hope Fiona, being designated their human mother, will go a long way in ensuring the griffins remain our allies.

As they turn their attention to Jinx and Onyx, their admiration dissolves, replaced with disdain. "These beasts come as part of your association with the demon spawn?"

I bristle. "Careful, friend. Gareth isn't like others you might know. He is part of our group and deserves a chance to be judged on his own merits."

"Jules, it's fine," Gareth's words come out from between clenched teeth. "It's nothing I haven't heard a thousand times before."

"That doesn't make it right." I return my attention to Nesperia. "Gareth's father is a demon king, but his mother is a fae queen. He has a tie to this realm, as do we all. Yes, Jinx is his, but Onyx is mine."

I won't have anyone dissing my boyfriend or my dog.

She eyes the hellhounds warily, then dismisses the conversation entirely, moving on to bid us good luck in our quest to heal Ryan.

Whatever. Haters gotta hate.

"Tell us of the elemental kingdoms," Azland requests. "I haven't seen the lands of my people since the raids. What has life been like over the past decades?"

Nesperia flashes Gareth yet another withering glare. "While none of the five elemental cities are populated, now and then, a small party of elementals will venture back. Some stay for a time. Others see there is nothing left for them and leave."

Azland's surprise is obvious. "So there are others."

"Yes. A handful, maybe a few dozen."

It takes a moment to figure out the emotion of Azland's expression. I've never seen him look anything but dour. This is different. For the first time, Azland looks not only relieved but hopeful.

"That explains the younger generation." Kenzie brushes Ryan's hair away from his face. "Maybe they've come from one of those small groups, drawn together by the bonding magic of a quint or quartet."

I don't want to be the one to point out that something happened to them if their kids are orphans and living in the street but decide not to bring the party down unnecessarily.

Azland nods with a thoughtful smile. "I hope you're right, Kenzie. It would be more than I expected and would change everything."

I'm not sure what he means by that, but now isn't the time or the place. "Do you know how to get us to the Gailleann training academy from here?" I ask.

"I do."

"Then we shall leave you to your quest," Nesperia declares. "We wish you success in restoring the boy."

"Your support is well received," Sloan replies.

"Be well, friends," Fiona adds as she and Sloan bid the griffins goodbye. "Your intervention and guidance will be spoken of fondly."

Leaning close to Gareth, I whisper, "The way she and Sloan phrase things when speaking to people here is weird. Don't you think?"

His lips brush the shell of my ear as he responds. "Never thank the fae outright. Remember? It implies an indebtedness. There are many fae who might consider it a binding statement."

Right. He told me that before.

As Nesperia and her pride fly off, I'm in awe and a little relieved. I didn't like the way she talked about Gareth and the hounds. If it came down to it, I would throw down to ensure they didn't disrespect him.

Throwing down against a pride of griffins wouldn't be wise, so it's likely good that they're leaving.

"You can stand down, spitfire." He's smiling down at me, amusement heavy in his expression. "While I find it adorable that you'd raze the world in my defense, it's unnecessary. Nothing anyone says to me can be worse than what I have said to myself a thousand times."

That hurts my heart. "Then it's time to change the dialogue, broody boy, because I'll take down anyone who badmouths my guy—even you. Now, let's get Ryan to the vortex. Zephyr will combust into a cyclone if he doesn't get to explore Gailleann soon."

With a line of sight from the plateau above the city, Nikon can portal our entire group down to the ruins of the formerly thriving city and home to the academy of the Gailleann wind elementals.

A gentle wind blows through the empty streets, rustling the leaves and stirring the mist. Sunlight warms the air, casting a soft, ethereal glow over everything.

It's horribly sad to walk the abandoned streets and see how nature reclaimed them.

"It's like the vines and mosses have mummified the city." Briar brushes his fingers over the spongy sheet of growth covering everything.

Despite the destruction and decay, there's still beauty and power here that feeds something inside me. "Do the rest of you feel it? The magic of this place is still here. It's like Gailleann is waiting for someone to bring it back to life."

"We're dealing with the same thing in Ireland," Fiona

comments. "The island where two of my brothers live has a dormant city that has slowly been waking up over the past year. There's so much prana buzzing in the air that it makes our skin tingle, but all the buildings in the city are abandoned and asleep."

Walking the streets is eerie, but with birds chirping in the distance and small creatures darting in and out of the shadows, it's as if Gailleann refuses to be completely forgotten.

Tad points out the thriving plants and flowers growing in the cracks of the stone walls. "Nature always survives, even in the most unlikely places."

Kenzie nods. "It's a testament to the resilience of life. If the plants can thrive here, maybe Gailleann can be brought back to its former glory."

If the Poreskoro raids had never happened, would we have grown up here, surrounded by the magic and wonder of the elemental kingdoms?

There's no use dwelling on what might've been. We're here now in search of answers and a way to help Ryan sync up with his element.

We continue to explore. Zephyr walks ahead, eager to see everything about where he came from. "Guys! You need to see this!"

He's standing in front of a large, ornate fountain that has withstood the ravages of time and neglect. The water is still flowing, and I feel power emanating from it as we approach.

"Many of the fountains in Biotáille are like this." Azland reaches out to touch the water. The moment his fingers make contact, a ripple of magic shimmers across the surface. The water glows with a soft, ethereal light.

Kenzie's eyes widen. "That's so cool. What makes it do that?"

"Magic."

I chuckle. "Yeah, we got that. Thanks."

Sloan swirls his fingers across the water's surface and grins. "If the magic in Gailleann remains strong, perhaps the vortex we seek for Ryan might still exist and hold the power to help him."

Kenzie lifts both hands to show us her crossed fingers. "Azland? Do you know where we're going?"

"Of course. I was at the training academy frequently. It's that building up there on the hill."

We portal to the grounds of the training academy for the warriors of the wind kingdom, and standing there staring up at the place, its grandeur strikes me.

The sprawling complex of buildings, crafted from a mix of stone and crystal, shimmers in the sunlight. Spires reach toward the sky as if grasping for the element they harness.

Intricate carvings and murals adorn the walls, depicting wind elementals in fierce battles and moments of tranquility.

Zephyr takes it all in, and I see the wonder I feel mirrored in his expression. Of the four of us, Zephyr and I have always been the two obsessed with where we came from. We both sought answers.

Me because of being found in the fire in the arms of the dead man.

Zephyr because of the turmoil he grew up with brewing within.

Now we're finally getting those answers.

Although the academy has been abandoned for twenty-five years, the magic that once imbued the place is still strong. As we enter the main building, power emanates from the walls.

The academy's halls are vast, with high ceilings and wide, open spaces. The floors are smooth stone and shine like polished marble, and the banners and crests that once belonged to the warrior clans who trained here adorn the walls.

As we explore the academy, I notice the evidence of the raids that drove everyone away. Areas of disarray. Damaged walls. Scattered belongings. Broken furniture.

Despite its current state of ruin, the academy is still magnificent, a testament to the power and resilience of the wind kingdom.

I can almost hear the echoes of the warriors who once trained here, and I wonder about Zephyr's father.

Azland says he was the warrior in charge.

Zephyr's eyes are glassy as he explores the space. I rest a hand on his shoulder. "Are you okay?"

"Yeah. It's a lot, though, right?"

"Absolutely. It's also pretty amazing."

"I want to take it all in…every inch…every room."

"You will. Let's get Ryan to the vortex and do what we can to help him. Then you can have the time you need to absorb your heritage."

"Yeah? Do you think Fiona and her crew will mind sticking around so I can explore? I kinda figured they'd be eager to get back."

I shrug. "I'll talk to them and see what I can do. I promise, one way or another, you'll get your chance to learn about your father and your people."

Zephyr hugs me tight against his chest and kisses the top of my head. "Thanks, Jules. Love you."

"Love you too, Z. Now, let's take care of Ryan. Yeah?"

"Yeah."

The two of us find Gareth and the hounds wandering the halls. My guy looks haunted, and I can only imagine what being back here after decades of regret and self-recrimination is doing to him.

"You're not that man," I remind him, knowing he needs to hear it. "Your siblings swept you along with their armies, and it took you time to sort out your ideals enough to stand up for what you knew to be right. But you *did* stand up. You tried to stop this."

He looks at me, and his expression is cold and hard. "I hate everything about that period in my life. I should've done more to stop them."

I place my hands on both sides of his clenched jaw. "You were the youngest, the kindest, and the one least likely for them to listen to. I've seen your siblings in action. They are psychotic and scary. With armies behind them, they would never have listened to you."

He grunts. "I should have *made* them listen."

"Babe. That they locked you up and left you behind so you couldn't get in their way was probably the nicest thing they could've done. This is not on you."

It doesn't escape my attention that a very rigid and quiet Azland has joined Zephyr and the two of us in the corridor. I know it's hard on him to be around Gareth, but he's trying.

"The others have gone into the private grounds out back. If you're ready, they sent me to bring you out so we can get started."

I nod. "Of course. Let's go."

CHAPTER FIFTEEN

Azland leads Zephyr, Gareth, and me out a set of grand double doors at the back of the building and onto the grounds. As impressive as the architecture and fountains out front and the academy's haunted interior, the walking paths and gardens are like an HGTV episode on mind-blowing landscaping.

Sprawling lawns roll out before us, dotted with private arbors and gazebos. The carpet of lush green extends toward a thick copse of trees in the distance.

It's all wild and overgrown now, but that doesn't take away from what it was in its day.

Even distracted, I don't miss the change in the surrounding atmosphere. The closer we get to where our group is gathered, the more the hair on my arms prickles and stands on end.

"That's a good sign, right?" I hold up my arm to stare at the effect the electricity in the air has on me. "If it's this strong and we haven't started yet, that must mean there's still juice in the tank, don't you think?"

Azland nods. "It is encouraging, yes."

I hoped for more conviction and maybe a touch of excitement, but I'm not sure Azland has it in him. Was he always such a moody broody, or did that come with the annihilation of his home and family and having to take the form of our dog for a decade?

Swirling gusts of wind push at us, almost playfully, leading us forward along the garden path and into the cool shadows of the trees.

It's all very magical.

The fae forest has strange little creatures, glowing rocks, and a million different plants and flowers. I'd stop to inspect them if I weren't getting buffeted from behind to keep moving.

"Why do I get the sense the air is impatient?" I ask.

Zephyr chuckles. "It feels that way, doesn't it?"

As we round a bend, the trees open and we see the others in a clearing ahead. They're standing at the far edge of a wide conical dip into the ground. The walls of the funnel-shaped drop are polished stone. There are no stairs, and a person can't walk up or down with such steep walls.

The wind picks up, shoving us forward.

"Wow," Zephyr murmurs, raising his hands to greet the raw elemental power before us. "It's hard to believe there are places like this."

Azland grunts. "That's because you've lived your entire life thinking you're human."

True story. But hey, he was part of us living that lie.

"Good, you're here," Kenzie huffs, waving at us to hurry over. "Ryan's stuck in a state of turmoil, you two. Explore and reminisce after the boy is out of his coma."

I shrug. "Sloan and Azland said Ryan is resting in stasis. Zephyr needed a minute to acclimate."

"Jules is right." Azland surprises me by taking my side. "It's better Zephyr settled a little because he needs to focus for what comes next. Knowing his curiosity and mental chaos, getting his first barrage of questions answered is best for all concerned."

Zephyr's brows arch. "For what comes next? Am I part of what we're here to do for Ryan?"

Azland nods. "The most important part."

The wind howls as it whips around the clearing in a frenzied dance. In the center of the vortex, a swirling column of wind rises high into the sky, pulsing with energy. It is almost as if the wind is alive, twisting in a mesmerizing display of power.

The energy of the vortex courses through my veins, filling me with a sense of exhilaration and freedom.

Zephyr steps forward, his eyes wide as he raises his hands. The wind responds, swirling around him as if excited to be in the presence of one of its own. "It's like a living, breathing thing. I've never felt so connected to my element before."

Tad interjects, "It's beautiful, sure, but be cautious. This much raw power can be unpredictable. Fae magic has a mind of its own if yer not in full control."

I'm not sure if Zephyr *is* in full control. How could he be when he's never used his wind like this before?

I study Azland and the way he's watching my brother. He doesn't seem concerned.

"Are ye ready?" Sloan asks Zephyr, stepping up to the rim of the vortex where he stands.

Zephyr shrugs. "Not really, but I'm here for the kid. I know what it's like to have a storm inside you. No one helped me, and I suffered for years. I won't let that happen to him."

"Aye, then let's do what we can fer the lad."

Zephyr nods. "What are we doing?"

Fiona's husband gestures at the apex of the cone below. "Azland and I think it best if I portal us down. He'll remove the stasis spell, and I'll portal us back out straight away. If all goes well, ye'll stay with the boy and help him through his troubles."

Zephyr blinks. "And if all *doesn't* go well?"

Sloan waves away his concern. "Ye'll be fine. With the same

affinity, Ryan won't hurt ye with his storm even in a state of true chaos."

Sloan, Zephyr, and Azland chat more about positioning and logistics. As soon as they nail things down, Azland and Zephyr kneel over Ryan, and Sloan portals them down the stone slope.

From the moment they appear at the bottom, everything happens quickly. Azland removes the spell keeping Ryan sedated, then Sloan *poofs* him up to the rim of the funnel to wait with the rest of us on the lawn.

"What now?" Kenzie asks, watching.

"Now we wait," Azland replies.

Zephyr crouches over Ryan.

We wait.

"Okay...he's opening his eyes."

The moment the teen moves, the wind picks up. What had settled to swirling and breezy builds to gusts as Ryan's power flows through him and catches within the vortex.

"Don't be afraid." Zephyr stands to steady himself against the force of the air. "We brought you to a place where you can't hurt anyone or destroy anything. You're safe to let the storm out."

"I can't. I can't control it." Ryan rolls to his feet, panicked. By the look on his face, if he could run, he'd be high-tailing it up the side of the vortex and into the trees.

He can't—the slope is too steep.

Zephyr stands with his storm staff planted, and his arms outstretched. "Trust me, kid. We've got this. Let the storm free. I won't let your powers hurt anyone."

My heart squeezes. When Zephyr was struggling all those years, hurting someone was always his worst fear.

Ryan looks unsure, but Zephyr is confident and raises his hands. "Trust me, Ryan. I've got you."

The wind whistles before us, and I catch my hair as it's pulled forward. "Wow, this kid has juice."

Gareth looks down at me and nods. "Yeah. I feel for the kid.

Knowing how fire burned inside me, I can imagine what it's like to have the volatility of wind."

Yeah. After watching Zephyr struggle, so can I.

As the moments pass, Ryan stands straighter and seems more confident that his chaos will be contained. The relief on his face is exquisite.

He lets go bit by bit and adds more wind to the swirling column within the vortex. The raw power of it presses at my chest, and I wonder what it feels like to the two of them.

They don't seem bothered. The more Ryan releases his elemental power, the less solid he becomes as a young man.

"What's happening?" Kenzie asks, her voice uncharacteristically pitchy.

"It's fine," Azland assures her. "This needs to happen. It's exactly what I hoped for."

As we watch, Ryan's form becomes fluid and ephemeral. He flickers out of sight, his physicality diminishing until he sheds his human form completely.

Then he exists solely as swirling wind.

"Holy shit."

I blink at Azland. "What do we do?"

He looks at me like I've lost my mind. "We don't do anything. Like I've been telling you for months, you don't wield the power of your elements. You *are* the elements. This is Ryan's natural form. His trouble stemmed from his elemental existence being forced into human form."

"You mean we can all do this?" Kenzie asks.

"Fully become your element? Of course," Azland replies.

I think about that. I've come the closest to assuming a full-bodied form of my element, and it's amazing. While I've never given myself over to being a full fire elemental, my woman aflame form makes me feel powerful and free.

Is that because my human form *isn't* natural?

I watch Ryan for a few moments, awestruck by the sight of

him existing as a wind elemental. The power of his presence fills the vortex, racing through the air.

It's incredible.

So, this is what it could've been like to grow up and live within the magic of the fae realm.

"Uh, guys?" Kenzie breaks the silence, her voice tinged with concern. "Does anyone know how he changes back?"

We exchange worried glances and turn our attention to Azland.

Azland frowns. "This is his natural form. It should be a base instinct."

The pressure in my chest intensifies. "A base instinct if he was brought up understanding who and what he is, maybe. What if he's like us and knows squat about his powers or how to control them?"

"How do *you* reclaim your physical form?" Kenzie asks Azland. "Maybe you can describe it, and we can reverse engineer it for Ryan."

Azland shakes his head. "Magical elementals keep our humanoid form."

I search the expressions of Fiona and the Toronto crew. "What about you guys? Do you know?"

Fiona shakes her head. "We called you in because there's very little known about elementals in empowered circles."

Fan-fucking-tastic.

I glance at Nikon, hoping his millennia of knowledge might hold the answer. "What about you? Any ideas?"

The ancient Greek scratches his neck but ultimately shakes his head. "I've got nothing."

"So, he's trapped like this?" Kenzie snaps, pegging Azland with a glare. "First, he's trapped in a coma and now in a windstorm?"

Azland glares right back at her. "Relax. It's not like he's suffering. This is his natural state."

Zephyr rides the wind, rising straight from the massive stone cone, and lands on the grass beside us. "What's wrong?"

Kenzie and I fill Zephyr in quickly, and he shrugs. "Azland's right. He's fine for the moment. I feel his energy, and he's relieved and in a state of pure bliss."

Kenzie still looks like she might shred him to bits.

I intervene before the two come to blows. "As happy as I am that Ryan is enjoying himself, he can't remain in this form forever—can he?"

Gareth shakes his head. "No. We need to help him change back. If only to give him a choice."

"Maybe the academy library," Sloan suggests, pointing his thumb behind him. "If this is the academy for wind elementals, it stands to reason that the library would hold answers for its students. He can't be the first youth to get stuck in his elemental form."

"Zephyr's father was respected among the five kingdoms for his work here," Azland offers. "He was an accomplished scholar and might have something in his office that could help."

"Good enough." I turn toward the path that led us here from the academy building. "Fi, Nikon, Briar, and Kenzie, you stay here and watch over Ryan. Make sure he doesn't—I don't know—blow away or something.

"Tad, you portal Gareth, Zephyr, the hellhounds, and me to the administration area to look for Gale's office. Azland, you go with Sloan and head to the library. We'll regroup in an hour or sooner if we find something."

CHAPTER SIXTEEN

Tad portals our small group back to the Gailleann Academy building. We search through the rubble of the administration wing's abandoned halls until we find the office once used by Gale Halos.

It's a tough situation because as much as I want to take our time, easing open Zephyr's emotional doors, we need to find answers and get back to Ryan.

The four of us enter and split off in different directions. I veer to the left to check out the ornately carved wooden desk buried under an inch of dust and sediment.

Tad gets to work setting the filing cabinets upright to access their contents.

Gareth settles Jinx and Onyx out of our way and wanders over to a heap of textbooks haphazardly strewn on the floor below the window and in front of the credenza.

Zephyr faces off with the bookshelves to the right of the door. "Wow. This could be promising."

I round the desk, but as I straighten beside him, anxiety beats back my excitement. "Or it might be promising if we could read whatever language these are written in. How do we search the contents of a book if we can't speak the language?"

"Oh, sorry." Tad raises his hand. "I can help with that. I have a spell that will allow you to read the words of the elemental languages."

I blink. "There's a spell to Rosetta Stone the elemental languages?"

"Not only those languages. A more accurate description is to say it'll help you read the languages of your kind."

Magic still blows my mind, but yeah, that will make this quest a great deal more fruitful. "Sure. Go for it."

He stands before Zephyr and me and smiles. "Repeat after me…

In whispered tales, and ancient lore,
I seek to know the tongues of yore.
With heart attuned to nature's tale,
I delve into the mystic veil,
To grasp the words, the secrets held,
In languages of olden Eld."

Zephyr and I repeat each line after Tad, and when we finish, he directs us to have another look at the spines of the books.

"That's amazing." I grin at the words that have magically unjumbled themselves in front of our eyes. "Cool. I can read them now. It's like…"

Tad winks. "Like magic. Aye, I know."

Zephyr and I stand shoulder to shoulder in front of the floor-to-ceiling shelves, staring at all the books. There are hardcover texts, leather-bound tomes, parchments, and scrolls.

Among the spines are trinkets and personal belongings sprinkled over the shelves. Zephyr picks up a metal box with a shell inlay on the lid and brushes his fingers over the design.

"Whether these were mementos from travels or gifts or held some deeper meaning to him, we'll never know."

"You're probably right." I squeeze his shoulder. "But it's nice that we got the chance to be here and see what was important to him. Don't you think?"

Zephyr looks at me with emotions swirling in his eyes. "Yeah, I do."

"Guys, give me a hand with this, will you?" Tad gestures at a large cabinet lying over a pile of wreckage by the corner.

The four of us work together to clear a space on the floor and get the cabinet onto its base. As we sift through the wreckage, Zephyr is drawn to a large wooden chest tucked away in the room's corner.

It's buried beneath an old, dusty tapestry that fell when a section of wall collapsed. When he unearths it, Zephyr squats to examine its contents.

My hair flips and whips around as Zephyr's emotions manifest. "Hey, dude. Are you good?"

The wind dies down. "Sorry."

"There's no need to apologize. This is a big deal. What did you find? Can I see?"

He eases back, and I look. There is a collection of textbooks, a dagger with a sapphire hilt, a silver inkwell, and a photograph of a man and a woman standing together in front of the academy.

I study the photograph. It's obvious the couple is in love. The man is tall and muscular, with hair that seems to be made of the wind. He has a proud look on his face, almost severe.

The woman is beautiful, with long dark curls and sparkling eyes that hold a hint of mischief.

They are undoubtedly Zephyr's biological parents, and if I'm this moved by seeing them, I can only imagine what Zephyr's going through.

His father was a respected leader of this kingdom.

I brush my finger over the image. "You look a lot like your mom."

"You think?" His voice is thick and full of uncertainty.

"Yeah, the hair, the eyes, and that devilish smirk."

He lets out a shuddering breath, and I wrap an arm around his shoulders and pull him against my side. "You're good, Z. I've got you, little brother."

He turns and grabs hold of me. The wind picks up in the room around us again. "It's just a lot…you know?"

"Yeah, I know." When I look around, Gareth and Tad are nowhere to be found. Well, if they're giving us a moment of privacy, I won't waste it. "It's just you and me here. Let it wash over you however that feels. This room holds a lot of emotion to unpack, and I'm right here with you."

He considers that before he wipes a hand across his face and draws a deep breath. "No. My emotional baggage can get unpacked later. Right now, Ryan needs us to focus."

"Are you sure?"

When he looks at me, his eyes are glassy but determined. "Yeah. No sense having him suffer too. Now that I've found this, I can bring it home with us."

I hold his gaze for a moment and assure myself he's genuinely ready to move on before getting us back on track. "Okay, we're looking for anything that might tell us about elementals, transformation, or learning to control elemental forms."

The two of us focus. I'm impressed by the sheer amount of knowledge Zephyr's father collected here.

Time passes as we scour the shelves, occasionally finding something that might be useful and setting it aside for further examination. The sun dips below the horizon, casting an orange glow through the windows and creating lengthening shadows on the floor.

"Here. This one might be promising." Zephyr tugs on a leather spine to free the book from its neighbors. "*Elemental Transformations and Natural Forms of the Fae.*"

I step closer to look, and Zephyr opens the book on a small table Tad set upright by the window.

Zephyr points at a passage on the page, and I skim through the text.

Tad comes in from the corridor. "What did ye find?"

I shift to let him see. "This says there are several ways to help elementals struggling to maintain their human form. Grounding techniques, physical touch, focus, or magic."

I read the highlights to the group. "Under grounding techniques, it says wind elementals can struggle to hold their human form because they get too caught up in the wind's energy. We should try deep breathing, meditation, or physical exercise to help anchor them in the physical world."

Zephyr snorts. "How do you get a cyclone to focus on his breathing? The kid is literally a swirling mass."

I shrug. "If that's a no-go, there is also physical touch. According to this, physical touch can be a powerful tool in moments when the elemental can become corporeal. We're supposed to hold their hand or place a hand on their shoulder to help them feel connected to the physical world and grounded in their human form."

Zephyr shakes his head. "Next."

"Encourage them to focus on a specific task. Wind elementals deal with mental chaos, and distraction can lead to them losing their human form. It says giving Ryan a specific task to focus on, such as reading a book or practicing a spell, could help him remain focused and anchored to his human form."

Zephyr tilts his head from side to side. "I suppose that might work. If I can communicate with him, I might get him to focus on something, although not reading a book. That's dumb."

"I think that's in other instances. Not when he's full wind and stuck in the vortex."

Zephyr nods. "Okay, what does the last one say?"

I return my attention to the last paragraph in this section and read the advice for using magic to stabilize corporeal form. "If all else fails, we can try casting a spell that enhances the connection between their human and elemental forms or a spell that helps anchor them in the physical world. But there's a warning here. It says to use caution because the overuse of magic can be draining and potentially harmful if used too frequently."

"For Ryan or us?" Zephyr asks.

I frown, rereading the paragraph. "Not sure. It isn't really clear."

Zephyr scowls. "Is it just me, or were those proven techniques less than helpful?"

I sigh and pass Tad the book. "It's not just you, but it's all we've got. Did you guys find anything else?"

Gareth is standing to one side, holding a dusty book. "I found this in another room, but it's not about helping Ryan regain his form."

"What is it?" I ask.

He looks sad as he glances at me and hands it to Zephyr. "It's a journal, and it looks like it might've belonged to your father."

Zephyr accepts the book and flips through a few pages. It's written in ink with flowing script and attention to detail. Not at all like Zephyr's scratch and scrawl. "Thank you, Gareth," he murmurs. "I appreciate this."

Gareth squeezes Zephyr's shoulder in reassurance before stepping back to join me. The look on his face tells me everything I need to know. Being here is hard for Zephyr, but it's hard for him, too.

Knowing his siblings destroyed the lives of so many is tough to bear. Seeing the destruction and the ripple effect of the loss in our lives is much worse.

"Not your fault," I whisper.

He graces me with a sad smile but says nothing.

"Ah, here ye are." Sloan strides in with a stack of books in his arms and Azland at his side. "Did ye find anythin' that might help?"

I snap out of the moment and shuffle over to show them the

grounding techniques in the book we were reading. "What about you? Are all these books about stabilizing a corporeal form?"

Sloan chuckles. "Och, no. Just some light readin' I thought I would scan through. I left a note of the titles in the library and will return them, I swear."

Tad blinks at Sloan. "It's not like the library is up and running. I'm sure no one will notice."

Sloan shrugs. "The spirit of a lending library is that yer on yer honor. I'll bring them back all the same."

I give the massive stack another once-over and try to wrap my mind around that being some "light reading."

Any who... "We should head back to the vortex and let the others know what we've found."

The scene when we return to the vortex is much the same as when we left. Ryan is a swirling wall of wind. Kenzie is worried. Briar and Nikon are on guard and keeping watch. Fiona is laughing with her Kodiak companion and shooting the shit.

Seriously, she's relaxed and looks like this is another day in her life.

I can't imagine things like venturing into the fae realm to rescue a wind elemental becoming ordinary, but then again, I'm only months into this life, and she's got years on me.

"Thank goodness you're back," Kenzie calls when she sees us. "That took forever."

I check my watch and frown. No, it didn't. "Did something happen?"

Briar grunts. "No. Nothing."

He grumbles about that like he's bored, but for once, I'm glad he is. "Okay, so we found a few things to try. Tad has the book we found, and I think Azland and Sloan have a few ideas."

"Cooleroo." Fi grins and smacks her hands together. "So, the healers can heal, Zephyr can do the wind elemental backup, and Azland can add the magic touch. We're in good shape."

Is it really that simple?

She seems to think so.

I step back and watch as the players involved do what Fiona said. Sloan talks Kenzie through a healing technique. Zephyr returns to the bottom of the vortex funnel to work with elemental Ryan. Azland raises his hands and gives off a faint purple glow.

As the air around us crackles with energy, the velocity of Ryan's spinning slows.

"Yeah, baby." Tad high-fives Fiona. "That's what we're talking about."

Agreed. It's encouraging.

Ryan's body solidifies as the magical glow of Azland's efforts grows brighter. The previously unstable wind form becomes more and more human-like, the teenage boy emerging from the chaos.

After a few more moments, Azland releases his hands, and Zephyr steps forward at the bottom of the stone cone. "Hey, kid. Glad to have you back, buddy."

Ryan is standing, looking around like he's still a little lost. "Did this really happen?"

Zephyr chuckles. "Yeah. Your wind got the better of you there for a bit, but we've got you back now."

"Yeah, we do." Briar grins. "Well done, folks. That was some good empowered teamwork."

Hells yeah, it was.

"Bring them up, Greek," Fiona calls.

Nikon appears beside the boys a moment later and portals them to the grass where we stand at the vortex's upper rim.

Kenzie is the first to break ranks and hug the kid. "Are you okay? How do you feel now?"

Ryan stills and looks around as if considering her question. "It's weird. I feel amazing, but it's almost too quiet inside me."

Zephyr nods. "I know exactly what you're saying. When my element first unlocked, and I started training to control it, the calm serenity almost drove me crazy."

Ryan chuckles. "Right?"

"You'll get used to it. You'll sleep better. You'll feel less on edge. If all goes well, you won't take out half the city the next time you get worked up about something."

Ryan winces. "I'm sorry about that."

Fiona waves away his concern. "Not your fault, buddy. We've got your back. We fixed the damage, took down the assholes tormenting you and your friends, and smoothed things over with the humans."

Ryan's eyes widen. "Seriously? I'm not in trouble?"

Fiona shakes her head. "Nope. You're off the hook, and as soon as Azland and Zephyr run you through a few drills and train you to control yourself, we'll head home."

Ryan looks around and frowns. "What if I don't want to go back?"

CHAPTER SEVENTEEN

After successfully returning Ryan to his corporeal self, we gather around the boy, introduce ourselves, and explain the situation. "You won't be going back to that candy factory to be tormented," Zephyr tells him. "You can stay with us until we figure things out."

While I understand Zephyr's instinct to take the kid under his wing, one of the first lessons I learned as a beat cop in Montréal was that I can't take home every stray I find on the street.

Okay, so I ignored that with Anna and Micah.

And Sammy.

And now Ryan.

I chuckle. I'm terrible at this rule.

"What do you remember about what happened?" Kenzie asks.

Ryan steps over to sit on the circular bench that runs around the circumference of the vortex. "You know about the witch doctor, right?"

"Mr. Belvedere?" Kenzie asks.

"Yeah, that's him."

Zephyr sits beside him. "Yeah, we know about him, and as

soon as we get back to the human realm, we'll track him down and make him pay for what he did to you kids."

"What did he do?" Gareth asks.

"You don't have to give us details if you're not ready," Kenzie adds. "But the more you tell us, the faster we'll be able to catch him and stop him from hurting other kids."

Ryan looks from her to Zephyr. "You said you cleared out my friends, though, right?"

"Yeah. Steffan, Teddy, the two girls, and the lanky kid with all the freckles."

"Seamus," Ryan fills in. "The girls are Macy and Zara. What about the kids who weren't elementals?"

"A couple of them needed medical attention, but the last we heard, the rest of them were with a friend of ours, getting spoiled until we figure out where they can go and still be safe."

Ryan nods, biting his bottom lip. "That's good, I guess. But there isn't anywhere they'll be safe. Not with the way things are right now."

"Don't worry, buddy," Zephyr reassures him. "We won't let anything happen to them. We'll figure it out. But first, we need to know how you ended up losing your shit. What is Belvedere doing?"

Ryan shrugs. "I honestly don't know. Once or twice a week he'd come to our condo and drug one of the six of us with elemental affinities. When we passed out, he'd have one of those black-eyed freaks take us out of the room. Then we'd wake up later back in our apartment and feel like shit."

"You weren't awake during the procedures?" Kenzie asks.

"No."

That's bad for our investigation but a relief for those kids. Maybe they can move forward easier if they don't have to relive being experimented on.

"What do you remember about yesterday?" Zephyr asks. "Did Belvedere pick you?"

Ryan nods. "Yeah. He drugged me like normal, then instead of waking up in the apartment with the others, I woke up by the lake."

"You must've been disoriented," Zephyr offers.

Ryan nods. "Seamus was there. He, Adrian, and Markus saw Rimmon take me away, and they were afraid Belvedere killed me. It turned out he fucked up my wind and couldn't shut it down."

Luckily, Belvedere threw him away and didn't kill him. He likely thought he'd end up killing himself.

"I was terrified," he continues. "I tried to hold it together, but the more I panicked, the more things fell apart."

Zephyr nods sympathetically. "Stress doesn't help calm that particular storm. Been there, done that."

Fiery anger boils in my blood for all the years Zephyr struggled. I'll never forgive our adoptive parents and Charlie for keeping the truth about our lives hidden.

If we knew earlier, Zephyr wouldn't have suffered.

Maybe helping Ryan will heal some of those wounds.

I hope so.

"I won't let that happen to you, kid." Zephyr's gaze is on mine, and I know what he's asking without him saying it. "Will we, Jules?"

Dammit. He knows I can't say no to him.

Reaching out, I pat Ryan's shoulder and offer him a warm smile. "Zephyr's right. We've got you, buddy. You can stay with us as long as you need to."

Ryan looks up at me, his eyes shining. "Thank you."

I meet the questioning glares of Briar and Kenzie and shrug. "You're welcome. Now, let's figure out how to strengthen your control so we can avoid taking out Montréal the way you did in Toronto."

Over the next couple of hours, Azland and Zephyr run Ryan through various exercises and techniques to help him maintain control over his element and his human and wind forms.

As they train, Ryan makes progress and gains confidence. His wind manipulation becomes more focused and controlled.

"I think I'm getting the hang of it." Ryan's face is alight with a genuine smile.

"It's all about balance," Azland reminds him. "Don't let your emotions overwhelm you."

Ryan nods, clearly taking the words to heart.

When they decide he's learned enough of the basics to keep everyone safe, we break out lunch.

"Between Charlie and Gran Cumhaill, we have a feast." Briar grins at the spread.

Nikon grins. "We certainly won't go hungry."

Ryan pauses with his plate half full and scans the crowd. "Thanks, everyone. No one's ever had my back before. I don't know how I would've survived this without your help."

"No problem, kid." Zephyr claps his back. "We're family now, and that's what family does."

"Don't feel bad." Azland grabs some cutlery before retreating to the bench. "It's not uncommon for elementals to struggle with the balance of holding one form or the other. The only real problem was that it happened in the human realm instead of here, where our people can manage it."

Fiona frowns. "So, should we expect more of the same happening?"

Azland shrugs. "We don't know how many elementals there are in either realm or what shape they're in. If you asked me three months ago, I would've said there were maybe a dozen elementals left in existence. Now, after the Awakenings, finding the kids in Toronto, and hearing what Nesperia told us about the elemental travelers, I couldn't even guess."

The thought of there being groups of us dispersed and trying to survive makes me excited and sad.

"I hate to think about others out there suffering," I comment.

"Forget about the destruction. Elementals shouldn't have to suffer through things like this on their own."

"I wasn't suffering once you got me here, and I could let loose," Ryan chimes in. "That was incredible."

Azland pauses with his fork at his mouth. "As it should be. Embracing your elemental self is healthy and freeing. It allows us to better understand and control our elements."

Zephyr sets his plate on the bench and launches to his feet. "You know what? I want to try it. If it's a natural part of us being elementals, I want to go full windstorm and see what it's like."

The group goes silent as everyone exchanges worried glances. I admit I'm one of them, but curiosity mixes with my concern. "What do you think, Azland? Would it be dangerous?"

"Of course it would be dangerous," Kenzie snaps. "We barely brought Ryan back to his corporeal form, and he's young. We know how strong Zephyr is. How will we possibly help him if he gets stuck?"

Zephyr frowns. "I hear what you're saying about the risks, Kenz, but I can do this. Ryan had trouble because he was scared and overwhelmed. He didn't understand what was happening. None of those things apply to me."

Briar grunts. "It's ballsy, but if you think you can manage it, I say go for it. We're here, right? Better to try here when we have the vortex to help mitigate the danger than in the backyard of our fire station."

True story.

Kenzie steps forward, placing a gentle hand on Zephyr's arm. "I'm not doubting your abilities. It's just… What if something goes wrong? We can't lose you. Who will get us seats at all the music nights? We'll have to line up and go early like the common folk."

Zephyr snorts. "Heaven forbid."

His expression softens as he looks at us. "I appreciate your concern, guys, but I want to do this. I need to know what it feels like and if I can handle it. Besides, you'll be here to pull me back from the brink if things go south, right?"

Briar crosses his arms, his brow furrowed. "You know we've got your back, Z, but you have to promise to be careful. If anything feels off, you pull yourself out immediately."

Zephyr nods, his gaze flicking between us. "I swear. Now let's do this."

With that, Zephyr steps away, plants his staff firmly against the ground at his feet, and calls to the air around us. Wind swirls, picking up speed until it lifts him off the grassy lawn and gracefully lowers him into the vortex's funnel.

The wind howls around Zephyr, and for a moment, I think I see a flash of fear in his eyes before the brave determination he always seems to wear replaces it.

I banish any lingering doubts. If he's got this, I'm not going to jinx him.

Looking up at us, he winks. "Here goes everything."

The air around Zephyr distorts and ripples as he shifts and changes shape. The gale force bends to his will, and his body becomes less defined. It's fast. Too soon, his physical features blur and fade away until all that remains is a swirling mass of wind and air.

The cyclone howls and whistles as though it is singing. He moves in gusts and eddies, twisting and turning in a wild dance of energy.

"Wow. He shed his human form much easier than Ryan did," Briar observes.

My focus stays locked on our brother in the vortex below. "Maybe that has something to do with his level of calmness and understanding of the situation."

"Or maybe it's a control thing," Kenzie suggests. "He's trained so hard to master his element."

True story. Of the four of us, Zephyr is the one who has worked the hardest to excel. I think the past twenty-five years of being our troubled fuck-up—his words, not mine—has driven him to prove himself.

Not that he ever needed to prove himself to the three of us.

Despite the apparent chaos of his wind form, Zephyr's movements have a sense of order and purpose. He swoops and dives, rising toward the sky in a tight column before plummeting back into the vortex, all while maintaining a sense of grace and fluidity in his movements.

Laughter echoes through the air as he dances before us, a tangible manifestation of his elemental power.

After a while, we break out of our stunned silence, and the magnitude of his accomplishment sinks in. I press my pinkies under my tongue and let out a shrill whistle. "Go, Zephyr! You rock, brother."

Kenzie and Briar call accolades, and Fiona and Nikon clap for him.

Ryan watches with wide-eyed wonder. "He's really good for his first time. He makes it look so natural."

"Because it is natural," Azland replies. "If our people hadn't been hunted and forced from our lives, you would've grown up knowing that."

I throw Azland a pointed look. "Enough with the recrimination, Judgy McJudgerton. We all understand what happened, but this is where we are. We were all molded by our lives and the way things played out.

"Yes, it could've been different, but it wasn't. This is us. Like it or lump it. I, for one, think we're pretty fucking awesome. I grew up in a city I love, with siblings I would die for, and now we find out we're basically freaking superheroes. It's time to stop pointing fingers and griping and embrace life as it is."

"Damn straight." Briar nods. "Eyes front."

The flexing muscle in Azland's jaw tells me he doesn't appreciate my take on things, but tough titties. I wouldn't give up Briar, Kenzie, and Zephyr for anything. Not even living a life in the fae realm. We can't go back anyway, so why groan about it?

Returning my attention to Zephyr's big win, I realize I missed him winding down. The wind has eased down to a breeze, and he's reclaiming his corporeal form. When he's finished his transformation, he levitates to join us, grinning ear to ear. "That was abso-fucking-amazing."

I hug him, laughing. "You made it look easy, Z. It might have scared the hell out of me, but I'm so proud of you."

Zephyr wraps his arms around me, his smile never fading. "Thanks, Jules."

As we pull apart, Briar and Kenzie take their turns, offering their congratulations and relief that he's safe.

"That was amazing." Zephyr takes a moment to catch his breath before continuing. "Being a powerful force of nature, a being in tune with the natural world and the elements that make it up...there's nothing like it. You guys need to try it."

I exchange glances with Briar and Kenzie, considering the possibility of fully embracing our elemental selves.

"I don't know, Zephyr," Kenzie hesitantly replies. "I mean, I love my water abilities, but I'm not sure I'm ready to take it that far yet."

Briar nods in agreement. "It's definitely something to think about, but I think we should take it slow. We're still learning about our kingdoms and our place in all of this."

I nod as well, although the idea of fully unleashing my fire powers is tantalizing. "Let's focus on learning more about our kingdoms and the range of our power first. We don't want to go off half-cocked and put people in danger."

Z shakes his head. "First, I'm always fully cocked. Second, if not for the experience, I think you should do it for your well-being. You know that angsty feeling we've talked about since the magic started to sour? Yeah, well, that's gone. I feel better now than I have in my entire life."

Well, that's something. Maybe Zephyr has a point. "All right. Once we've got a better handle on things, we can try embracing our elemental forms."

"When we have a safe place like you being in the vortex," Kenzie adds.

Zephyr's enthusiasm blooms. "Then we should go to the other kingdoms. I have my dad's trunk and his journal to go through. Maybe we can find out stuff about your families, too."

Briar nods. "Yeah, I'd like the chance to visit Litaui and learn about my parents. I think I should be able to find them mentioned in books or their likeness painted in portraits."

Kenzie chuckles. "As the king and queen of the kingdom, I suspect you're right."

"I love the idea," I agree.

Gareth holds up a finger. "Going as a group could prove difficult. The fire and water kingdoms aren't welcoming to other elementals. Between the lava geysers and the underwater palace, those two are intended for the members of their communities only."

"Then we'll go to Litaui with Briar," I say. "Our fair prince deserves the chance to explore his heritage."

As my siblings chime in with their agreement, Fiona shakes her head. "I wish we could stay, but Sloan and I are due back. With the way time passes in the fae realm, a day can be weeks, and a week could be months. We have family and guild responsibilities that need our attention, sorry."

"Does that mean we all have to go?" Zephyr asks.

"Not at all. Sloan and I can take Ryan back to the human realm, and Nikon can bring you back when you're ready."

Ryan raises a hand. "I want to stay here, too. I want to learn more about myself and what I can do."

Zephyr frowns. "You'd probably be safer back home."

He shakes his head. "There's no one back there who has ever cared about me or the shit I've been going through. You get it. I want to stay with you."

The look of desperation he flashes at us is more than any of us can bear. Zephyr grasps the back of his neck and pulls him against his side. "Then you stay with us, and we'll figure it out together. But I gotta warn you. My siblings might seem cool, but they're really annoying and giant pains in the ass."

Ryan laughs. "Consider me warned. I'm good with that."

CHAPTER EIGHTEEN

Fiona and Sloan bid their farewells before mounting Saxa and ascending into the sky with Nikon. As the sunshine yellow dragon rises, a colorful burst of magic opens a portal in front of them and she pumps her stunning orange wings. As Saxa disappears, Nikon materializes with our group on the ground and closes the portal above.

"That was dope, dude." Ryan holds out his knuckles for a bump.

Nikon grins. "Thanks. I aim to please."

With the departure of Sloan and Fi, our group moves to the remaining dragons left for our transport.

Dart, Esym, and Torrim are ready to fly, their scales shimmering brilliantly under the sun's rays.

"All right, let's make the most of the daylight we've got left," Zephyr suggests, his enthusiasm infectious. "To Litaui!"

I laugh, and Kenzie and I share a look. This energetic, cheery Zephyr is new to us. It's fun to see him so unburdened by life.

I'm no better prepared to climb onto the back of a dragon now than I was earlier this morning, so I accept a quick portal from Tad. He helps calm the hounds and secure them to Dart's back.

When I'm sure Onyx and Jinx will be safe, I move to the saddle on Dart's second spike and widen my stance to brace for takeoff.

How crazy is it that I know the pre-flight procedures for a dragon voyage?

Man, I love my life.

Glancing over my shoulder, I catch Gareth eyeing me and chuckle. "Are you checking out my ass, broody?"

"Every chance I get," he confirms without an ounce of apology. "Why do you think I took the spike right behind yours, spitfire?"

I grin and wiggle my butt. "Enjoy the show."

Dart's powerful muscles shift beneath us, and he brings his wings out to his sides. "Everybody ready?" Tad shouts, glancing around. "Hold on, and if ye fall off, scream like a maniac so Nikon hears ye and can save ye from certain death."

Kenzie snorts. "Babe, if one of us falls off our dragon, you can bet your bippy we'll scream like a maniac."

We take to the sky in a rush of unbelievable power, and the wind whips through my hair and makes my eyes stream with tears. I squint until we level off, then glance to the side and watch the earth grow smaller below us.

The kingdom of Gailleann treated us well. Let's hope Litaui does the same.

I'm unsure what kind of mileage dragons in flight can achieve, but it doesn't take long before the terrain below changes. The rolling hills and lush forests of Gailleann give way to a breathtaking city built in harmony with the rocks and mountains of the earth.

The dragons circle lower, and I study how the city doesn't only sit at the base of the rocky terrain. It is *part* of the terrain. The palace of the earth elementals is built into the mountain's stone face, its walls and towers made of the same granite and marble as the surrounding cliffs and waterfalls.

Stone caves and caverns dot the mountainside, and I assume those would've served as homes and gathering places for the city's citizens.

Dart takes us so close we can see inside the homes long abandoned. Some are small and cozy with simple furnishings, while others are grand and cavernous with vaulted ceilings and intricate carvings over the stone doorways.

As we draw closer to the palace, I suck in a deep breath and study the towering structure with massive stone columns and archways leading into a grand courtyard. The façade boasts ornately carved intricate symbols and mosaics.

They depict scenes from the history and mythology of the earth elementals.

I'm so excited for Briar. "If my heart is hammering this hard in my chest, I can only imagine what kind of shape your ticker is in, B."

Briar meets my comment with a smile. "It's pretty spectacular, isn't it?"

"It absolutely is."

We hover over the city courtyard, and I swear the surrounding stone pulses with a deep, steady energy. The air is thick with the scent of earth and minerals, and when the dragons touch down, I can almost feel the solid strength of the mountain beneath my feet.

Litaui is a place of strength and stability, a testament to the power and resilience of the earth elementals.

The dragons come to a graceful stop in the courtyard. Their talons *click* against the stone as we settle down.

When everyone has dismounted our dragons and Jinx and Onyx are free to sniff around, I wrap my arm around Briar's broad back. "All right, My Prince, where would you like to start?"

"Technically, he's the king," Azland corrects.

Briar chuckles, his gaze locked on the lands of his birthright. "I don't know about that. I can't believe we're really here. Thanks for not making us rush back."

I pat his hip and rest my head against his arm. "There's nothing in Montréal or the human realm more important than this. For this moment, we're exactly where we need to be."

"It's so beautiful," Kenzie whispers, her voice soft and reverent. "You should be very proud, B."

His adoring gaze continues to drink in the scene. "I am. It's like stepping into a dream."

Briar walks ahead of us, scanning the city with wonder and sadness. "This is where I come from. This is my heritage."

"And it's incredible," Kenzie murmurs, her eyes wide with wonder as she runs her fingers over the smooth surface of a nearby column. "It's like the entire mountain was hand-carved."

"It was," Azland confirms. "Think of the earth kingdom as the birthplace of master stonemasons. They could shape rock and stone as easily as a potter molds clay."

Kenzie gestures at the numerous fountains and pools scattered throughout the area, her blue skin shimmering in the sunlight. "Why are there so many water elements in an earth city?"

"All five elements are bound and need each other to survive and thrive," Azland explains. "It's only natural that the elements are all intertwined. Think of how green and lush Gailleann was."

"That's how it should be," Tad agrees, his hand resting lightly on Kenzie's shoulder. "The elements are all connected in a delicate balance."

We continue our journey through the abandoned city, and the sense of wonder and excitement fades, replaced by a growing feeling of unease.

The haunting emptiness surrounding us mars the city's beauty, and the air grows heavier with each passing moment.

"Something's not right," I murmur, scanning the abandoned city. "Can you feel it?"

Gareth squeezes my hand in his but makes no outward sign that he's uneasy. Something lurks in the shadows. We're not alone in this forgotten kingdom.

We move through the abandoned city, and the unease and danger follow us.

Briar is guarded, frowning at the stone structures and statues as we walk the silent streets. "The sooner we reach the palace, the better."

We quicken our pace, and I'd swear I feel the weight of unseen eyes on us. The rumblings of the earth grow more frequent, the tremors quaking beneath our boots.

As we turn a corner, Kenzie gasps, pointing at a statue. "I swear that thing is staring right at us."

I glance at the statue, and yeah, its stony gaze seems to be locked on us. My sister and I exchange uneasy glances before continuing, only to come across more statues, each focused on our group.

"What the actual fuck?" Zephyr asks. "The first thing you do as king is take your sledgehammer and smash these statues, brother. They are creepy AF."

Azland and Gareth seem the most bothered by the stone sentinels. The two of them have taken up defensive stances, each calling their elemental powers to their palms.

"What is it?" I call fire to my palms as well.

"These aren't statues," Gareth advises.

Aren't statues? My mind stumbles on that. I'm about to tell him the pressure is getting to him when the statues suddenly come to life. Shifting from their stone forms, they grow in height and breadth until they are towering earth elementals.

"I don't suppose they're a welcoming committee," Kenzie remarks. Her gaze tracks the growing number of hostiles closing ranks.

Zephyr pulls Ryan to his side and raises his hands, calling a gust of wind to encircle us. "They don't seem welcoming, no."

They move toward us, their intentions clear—we're under attack!

"Incoming!"

Feral earth elementals rush us from all sides, their bodies made of solid stone. Whatever offense we've caused, they have no interest in giving us a chance to explain. They are out for blood.

I focus my element, stoking the heat coursing through my veins, and call my fire whip. A twelve-foot fiery lash extends from my hand as I wreath myself in an aura of flames.

Gareth has already shed his human form and grown into his terrifying demon form. Black horns protrude from his temples, and a massive gauntlet resembling molten lava encases his clawed right arm. He slams his fist to the ground with a roar and a wall of fire ignites, creating a barrier between my family and our attackers.

The intense heat tingles over my skin, feeding the power surging through me.

Despite the onslaught, we're not overwhelmed. We're a formidable force between the powers of our quint, plus Tad, Ryan, and the hounds. If we needed more firepower, I'm sure the dragons would also come to our aid.

I scan the scene of chaos and ensure everyone is holding their own.

A layer of stone armor covers Briar's massive arms. His fists meet the hand-to-hand attacks of the earth elementals with equal and opposite force. His face is contorted with frustration as he tries but cannot communicate with them to de-escalate the fight.

Zephyr and Ryan are working together, their wind powers sending cyclones to knock the attackers off balance. Zephyr's storm staff crackles with electricity, the threat of a lightning storm brewing overhead.

Azland sends waves of magical pulses toward our attackers, knocking them back, freezing them in place, and confusing them, depending on what they get hit with.

Kenzie is taking full advantage of the nearby fountains, manipulating the water, summoning waves, and freezing her opponents in place with ice.

"Kenzie, give us a fog screen," I call, gesturing at a group of five stone elementals pushing through a break in the wall of flames.

My sister swings her attention my way and a thick wall of mist rolls in, blocking visibility to our attackers.

"Enough," Briar shouts, his voice laced with a frustrated growl. "Stop this!"

They won't stop. Wherever they're coming from, there seems to be an endless supply.

Briar drops to one knee and slams his fist into the ground, causing the earth to quake and split open. The chasm swallows several of our attackers whole. I'm not sure what that would mean to an earth elemental.

After that, he summons boulders and rocks to hurl at the remaining foes and erects barriers of stone to protect us.

Zephyr and Ryan have taken to the sky, using targeted gusts to push back the horde. When Zephyr lifts his storm staff, the sky above darkens, churning with the promise of a whirlwind of chaos. Lightning flashes and thunder rolls, threatening the next stage of our defense.

Jinx and Onyx have super-sized into their offensive forms and are picking off raiders and taking them to the ground. It amazes me how in tune Gareth is with Jinx, the two of them fighting with such coordination that I wonder how long it took to develop that skill.

With the full fury of his demon side, Gareth is melting the

ground beneath our attackers, and Jinx is tackling them and causing them to sink into the molten earth.

Despite our best efforts, the battle against the feral earth elementals rages on with no clear victor emerging.

With the arrival of more and more of them, we're outnumbered, and it's becoming increasingly obvious they will eventually tire us out.

I search for Tad and Nikon in the mix and make my way through the crowd to them. "I say we evac and regroup."

The pair are portaling in quick succession from one side of their attackers to the other, to their back. They shift position again and again, keeping their foes disoriented.

Nikon nods at me. "When and where?"

I scan the surroundings. Briar isn't ready to give up on finding out about his parents, and I won't be the one to take that away from him. "Take us to the palace."

Nikon's power signature surges with a wave and our entire group is whisked from the battlefield to land on the palace's front steps.

The surrounding area is still, and as we catch our breath, I survey the damage we've sustained. Gashes and bruises, but nothing Kenzie can't take care of.

Considering the fight…

I'll take that as a win.

CHAPTER NINETEEN

With the adrenaline from the fight still coursing through my veins, I scan the elaborate stone courtyard at the front of the palace. Thankfully, no statues and no earth elementals are closing in on us.

It'll take them a bit to figure out where we've gone and travel from the vast courtyard of the city proper to here. "I suggest we get inside and do our exploring on the quick."

"Fine by me," Briar grumbles. "My people are assholes. They wouldn't even let me introduce myself or explain why we're here."

Azland chuckles, wincing as Kenzie knits a deep gash across his shoulder. "Earth elementals are known to be difficult. Where do you think the term 'stubborn as rocks' comes from?"

"We made it out in one piece, thanks to Nikon," Zephyr comments. "Thanks, Greek."

Nikon inclines his head. "You're all welcome, but I agree with Jules. The sooner we get inside, the safer we'll be."

I exchange a worried glance with Gareth and Azland. He's right. It's only a matter of time before they find us and force us to confront them again. "Yeah, let's get inside."

We move in a bustle of groans, our tired and weary setting in fast. As we flop to the floor in the center of a grand foyer, Zephyr and Briar drop the door bar, and Tad spells the entrance closed.

When he's finished that, he looks at us and frowns. "I'm going to make a quick scouting run to ensure these halls aren't full of elementals and we're not about to get ambushed again."

"Do you want one of us to go with you?" I ask.

He shakes his head. "No. If I run into anything, I'll pop back here and Nikon can evac us back to the dragons."

"We're not going anywhere until I have my chance at answers," Briar grouses.

"In a perfect situation, yes." I pat his shoulder. "If it comes down to our survival versus your curiosity, there's really no call to make."

Briar exhales heavily. "I hear you. I don't like it, but I hear you."

Zephyr reaches down and helps Ryan to his feet. "In the meantime, let's explore your life, B."

Ryan grins. "This place is tight, man, but it's a bit of a fixer-upper."

Briar looks around at the crumbled wall, and the section of the banister tangled and twisted on the foyer floor and chuckles. "Yeah, I'm not sure the maid showed up this morning."

Ryan laughs. "Or this decade."

The seven of us dust ourselves off and decide to stick together for the exploration until we hear from Tad. The palace is a maze of corridors and chambers, with crumbling walls and faded murals that speak of a once-great kingdom.

Briar's rough edges from the battle smooth out as we venture deeper. His curiosity about his family and the kingdom they ruled win him over in the end.

"Can you imagine growing up here?" I ask Briar as we wander the halls. "These bedrooms are as big as our entire floor at the firehouse."

Briar shakes his head. "It would've been great, sure, but if it took away the years the four of us spent figuring out who we are... Nah, everything happened as it was meant to."

"Agreed." Because while my chest is tight with sadness for my brother, knowing he was robbed of the chance to live in this place as a prince and learn about his heritage, he's right. We are the people we are because of the life we lived and how we grew up.

We continue to explore, each room revealing more of Litaui's lost history.

In one chamber, we find an ancient map of the kingdom detailing the various regions and landmarks that made up the once-vibrant land. Briar traces a finger along the map, committing the names and locations to memory.

In another room, we discover a collection of dusty, worn books filled with stories and poems written by Litaui's citizens. Briar picks up a book, carefully flipping through its pages, his eyes lighting up as he reads the words of his ancestors.

"Yo, Briar, check this out," Zephyr calls, pointing at a mural on the wall of a long hallway. The painting depicts a great gathering of elementals high on a mountain plateau. It showcases the people of Litaui gathering around the royal couple, celebrating on a glorious sunny day.

"It looks like they knew how to throw a party," I comment.

Zephyr chuckles. "Definitely a gene they passed on to you."

Briar grins. "I'm not sure there's a party gene."

Zephyr waves away the skepticism. "Of course there is, and you got it. Look at all those people celebrating with them."

We stand there, taking in the scene depicted and I draw a deep breath. "They look happy, don't they?"

Briar nods. "I wonder what kind of rulers they were. Did their people love them? Did they make a difference in the kingdom?"

I place a hand on his shoulder. "They had to be amazing to have a kid like you."

Briar hugs me to his side and kisses the top of my head. "Thanks, Jules. That means a lot."

I run my fingers over the muted colors. "I think they'd be proud to know you're here, trying to learn about them and their kingdom."

"They would," Azland says. "I never met them personally, but where the fire and wind elementals often had civil friction and discord in the leadership of their kingdoms, the people of Litaui always loved their king and queen. Your parents cared about their citizens, and I think Jules is right. They'd find comfort in you being here."

Briar nods, his eyes locked on the mural. "I wish the people out in the city felt that way. I want to talk to them, not fight. I want to find out what's happened in this kingdom since the death of my parents. Who knows, maybe I can be part of the solution and honor them in some way."

Kenzie hugs Briar's arm and rests her cheek against his shoulder. "That's a lovely thought, big guy. Maybe a memorial or something for the lives lost. However that looks, we'll help you make that happen."

He stands there for a moment longer, taking in the mural and the story it tells about his biological parents. "All right. Let's continue our exploration."

Tad says, jogging up the hall. "Hey, guys, I'm glad I found you. This place is massive. I was worried I'd never catch up to you."

Kenzie greets him with a hug and eases back to kiss his cheek. "Did you find anyone?"

"No. We're alone in here, but I found something really cool." He holds out his hand to get us to stack our palms to portal. "Wanna see?"

It takes a moment to get everyone connected. Where Nikon

has the power to transport a large group without physical contact, Tad's wayfarer gift doesn't.

Once we've completed the circuit and I have a hand on Onyx, and Gareth has Jinx, Tad portals us all to another part of the palace. "Ladies, gentlemen, and hounds, I give you the royal throne room of Litaui."

We step into the throne room, and I take in the sheer beauty of it all. The shimmering crystals lining the walls light the cavernous space. They catch the natural sunlight outside and transform it, casting a soft, ethereal glow throughout the room. Stone stalactites hang from the ceiling like chiseled icicles, their pointed ends threatening yet beautiful in their way.

"Wow," Kenzie whispers. "Just, wow."

"Look at this." Briar glides across the vast stone floor, drawn to the massive geode that houses his parents' throne against the back wall.

Built for two people, a leather-cushioned bench seat with intricate designs nestles within the hollow of an enormous split amethyst. Purple crystals, polished to a fine finish, jut out in natural chaos within the stone shell, hovering over the bench.

The geode is incredible, but with the addition of the light from the crystals, deep purples and pinks shimmer across the walls when the light catches them.

The effect is dazzling, casting rainbows across the walls and floor.

"That's one hell of a throne, brother," Zephyr comments.

Agreed. "Take a load off and see how it feels."

He meets my gaze and hesitates. "Do you think I should?"

"Absolutely. You have more right than anyone to sit there. This is your birthright."

Briar glances at Azland. "Is that true? Was the ruling order of Litaui based on bloodline or election by the people? Maybe the survivors have already elected a new king."

Azland shakes his head. "It wouldn't matter even if they did. You were born Taranis Stoneheart, heir to the Stoneheart reign."

Briar blinks. "Why is this the first I've heard of my birth name?"

Azland shrugs. "You never asked until now. I figured you would when you were ready."

"Do you know all our birth names?" I ask, eager to learn something about myself.

He nods. "Your surnames, yes. Laurette knew the circumstances behind each of your placements."

My mind is spinning out. "So, what's my name?"

"You're the daughter of Emberald Blazeweaver."

"Juliette Blazeweaver." I make a face as it hangs in the air. "Jules Blazeweaver-Gagne?"

Kenzie shakes her head. "Jules Gagne Blazeweaver?"

"That's a mouthful."

Briar rolls his eyes. "Seriously? How did this become about you, Jules?"

I laugh. "It's not. Look away. Nothing to see here."

He pins me with a look, but there's no heat behind it. Briar goes back to staring at the throne. "This is my family's legacy. Am I supposed to carry it on? Do I have what it takes to lead?"

"Lead who?" Zephyr asks. "The assholes who jumped us in the city square?"

He shrugs. "Maybe they wouldn't be assholes if I could talk to them. I could explain about our Awakenings, and Hannah, Payton, and the kids in Toronto, and how there are survivors other than them. We could work on rebuilding a community."

"I really want to be on Team Briar for this, but after going all-out in a battle of stones and boulders outside, I'm with Zephyr. They're assholes. They wouldn't even let you speak."

Briar frowns at me. "But they're my people. My parents died while ensuring I would live and Litaui would have someone to watch over them. I have to help them."

Kenzie scoffs. "You mean the homicidal gargoyles that tried to kill us? I don't think they need your help."

He crosses his arms and digs in. "They do. I could feel their energy, and it was all wrong. Azland said elementals need to balance their human and elemental forms. We know what it feels like to be out of balance on one end of that spectrum. I think the elementals in the courtyard are examples of what happens when we're too long in our elemental form."

Zephyr frowns. "You think they've gone full Kerell?"

Kenzie shakes her head. "More words. What is full Kerell?"

Tad chuckles. "It's a race of stone people in D&D."

"The game with the weird dice?"

Tad nods. "From yer perspective, aye, that's it."

Briar waves that off. "We're getting off point here. I'm saying I think they have stayed stone too long and have lost their humanity. Maybe if I can access my full earth form, I can show them I'm one of them and reach them somehow."

Kenzie sighs. "Briar, it's great that you want to help them. But just because your parents were royals doesn't mean you have to endanger yourself for a group of people who want us dead or gone."

Briar shakes his head, his expression resolute. "I disagree... and if I see a way I can get through to them and help them, I'm going to take it."

I raise a hand to stop Kenzie's rebuttal. When he gets like this, there's no changing his mind. What was that Azland said about the people of Litaui?

Stubborn as rocks.

"For now, let's take things one problem at a time. We're all in this together, and we all support you in whatever you decide to do." I meet the raised eyebrows of Kenzie and Zephyr. "Don't we, guys?"

No matter how reluctant they are, they nod and get on board. "Of course we're with you," Kenzie agrees.

Zephyr exhales. "Well, if you're king, I'm going to be your sergeant at arms. No way am I letting those assholes come at you again. You're royalty, for fuck's sake."

Briar chuckles, and a grateful smile forms. "Thanks, guys."

CHAPTER TWENTY

Gareth, Jinx, Onyx, and I leave Briar with the others in the throne room. He's determined to access his full earth elemental state, and I'm not sold on it being a good idea. "If he felt he was ready and wanted to extend his understanding of his abilities, that would be one thing, but he's rushing himself to reach strangers who might not be open to him or to reclaiming their humanity."

Gareth squeezes my hand. "Your brother has a strong sense of duty and being here has probably amplified that. Wanting to access his true form could be about them, but it could also be something he wants for himself. I haven't known your brother long, but he doesn't seem like a reckless guy."

No. He's not. "I'll give you that. Zephyr is our impulsive one. Briar is deliberate, but he's also very protective, and that can lead to rash decisions."

Gareth pulls me to a stop and turns me to look up at him. "He's also smart and knows his limits. Trust that he'll be cautious and won't put himself in unnecessary danger."

I sigh, trying to let go of my worry. "I just hate it when my siblings are facing tough situations."

He chuckles. "Sorry, that's a totally alien emotion for me. I've spent most of my life hoping my siblings would spontaneously explode and have their body chunks eaten by hounds."

I arch a brow. "That is both gross and disturbing. You're a sick man."

He grins. "Thank you."

"You don't feel that way about Rance, do you?"

"Not anymore. I'm not sure if it was the decades of distance, your family taking out Lamech and Draven, or him evolving beyond the violent superiority of our parentage, but he's changed. He's becoming the brother I always wanted."

I step closer and wrap my arms around his waist, pressing my cheek against his chest. "I'm glad. You deserve that."

His arms around me are comforting, and I take a moment to soak in his strength before easing back. "All right. I'll stop being an overprotective big sister and trust that Briar knows what he's doing and what's best for him."

Gareth kisses the tip of my nose. "As wise as she is beautiful."

"You've gotta work on your pickup lines, broody."

He chuckles and steps back, feigning offense. "I don't know. I've had no complaints."

I wave away any conversation of past lovers and hook my arm through his. "Next subject. Unless you want to play the 'All my exes' game and compare."

He glances down at me and makes a face. "Hard pass. I can't see how that would ever work in our favor."

"Agreed. So, unless we run into one of our past mistakes on the street and need to give the other person context, there have been no others."

He nods. "I can get behind that."

"Good, because I can be possessive, and with my new abilities, I might leave a trail of charred breast implants and stilettos if I have to deal with women who have seen you naked."

He studies me, amusement dancing in his eyes. "First, your assumptions about my tastes are insulting."

"But likely accurate."

He rolls his eyes. "Second, would you really torch someone for me?"

I push up on my tiptoes and brush his lips with a quick kiss. "Nothing but smoking stilettos, baby."

"Violent *and* possessive. I'm touched."

"What would you do if one of my past lovers came sniffing around?"

Scarlet flames ignite in his gaze as his demon side rises to the surface. "In the interest of saving lives, the 'Don't know, don't tell' approach is in effect."

"Agreed. We are the only two people we have ever fallen for."

He grins. "Agreed."

With that settled, we continue our walk, exiting through a door and discovering a greenhouse garden near the back of the palace. Onyx and Jinx don't follow us in. With sections of the glass ceilings broken, rain has kept things watered, but still…the wild overgrowth of this place is incredible.

The living walls are mind-boggling. It's like a jungle has taken root inside the palace.

I blink at the sunlight filtering through the skylights. The sun's heat on my face feeds my cells and makes the entire space feel alive and vibrant.

"These plants have taken over." I touch a few waxy leaves climbing the stone wall. "I suppose it's nice that not everything died out here after the raids."

Gareth makes a gruff sound at the back of his throat as his gaze traces the tendrils of vines. "It's a testament to the power of nature. Even in the face of destruction and decay, life finds a way to thrive."

I study the lush growth, my attention sharpening. There is

something about how they move—not swaying with the breeze so much as twitching, skittering, or maybe moving with purpose.

Suddenly, like snakes striking from the underbrush, the vines lash out.

One thick tendril wraps around Gareth's wrist, yanking him forward as another entwines around my ankles, pulling back fast and taking me down.

I hit the stone floor hard, my hip screaming in protest as my full weight lands. Then my shoulder connects. I manage not to crack my head against the floor, but it's close.

The oasis of wild beauty from a moment ago is now a murderous trap.

Gareth is quick to react, summoning a burst of flame from his free hand and scorching the vine holding him. The blackened plant sizzles and retreats.

The hellhounds growl from the doorway.

"Jinx! Onyx! Stay!" Gareth calls.

More vines come, thicker and faster than before.

A cluster races toward my head and I scramble with flaming palms to keep it from wrapping around my throat.

"Jules!" he shouts, throwing a massive ball of fire at me. The explosion of heat is intense, the flames licking over me like being dunked in a pool of fire. My skin pulses with energy while the vines recoil, some turning to ash upon contact.

Drawing my elemental power, I direct a concentrated jet of fire at the base of the wall, where the vines seemed thickest. The flames erupt, causing a cascade of fire to climb the vines, severing the attacking tendrils.

The attack continues for what feels like ages but is likely only minutes. The vines writhe and snap, but each meets with our fierce and fiery retaliation.

The scent of burning vegetation fills the air, and the black and gray of char and ash replaces the vibrant green of the plants.

As suddenly as it began, the assault ceases. The remains of the once lush green vines lay smoldering around us.

Gareth grabs my wrist, hauls me onto my feet, and yanks me stumbling through the doorway. We escape the greenhouse and slam the door behind us.

Leaning against the wall in the hall outside, we double over to catch our breath. Onyx nudges me.

"Fucking plants," Gareth gasps, his voice ragged.

I chuckle, wipe sweat and soot from my brow, and scrub my pup's ears. "So, no houseplants in our forever home, then?"

He pegs me with a look and rolls his eyes.

"Too soon?"

He sags forward and laughs. "You're ridiculous. Come on. We better get back. Who knows what other murderous landmines have been set in this place? Let's go find your family."

Gareth and I have nearly recovered from our *Little Shop of Horrors* escapade when we run into Kenzie and Tad wandering the halls.

Kenzie takes one look at us and giggles. "You know, subtlety is an art form. Look at us. We are completely presentable."

I scoff. "I was attacked and dragged to the ground."

Her attention shifts to Gareth. "There's something to be said about the sex appeal of alpha males. I suppose letting the demon loose can get rough."

He blinks. "We were attacked by killer plant life. Us being ruffled and singed isn't the result of getting swept away in a moment of demon kink."

She sighs. "That's disappointing. It was much more interesting my way."

Tad reins my sister in and looks us over. "Yer well though, aye?"

"Yeah." I'm thankful at least one person seems concerned

about our well-being. "But I advise you not to go in the greenhouse unless you can druid through strangling vines and attack plants."

He nods. "Thanks for the warning. I'm sorry I wasn't there to help."

"We did okay." Gareth's scowl tells me he's tired of this conversation.

"Did you guys find anything interesting?" I ask.

Kenzie turns back the way they came. "Come see."

We follow them through an arched doorway and into a series of corridors leading—if I'm not totally turned around—back toward the grand foyer where we left the others.

"Check out these troughs." Kenzie points at what I took to be bulkheads running the length of most walls. "They're filled with water, and we think they cycle through the palace, creating an aqueduct system."

"For drinking?" I scrunch my face at the stone bulkhead, not loving the idea of drinking water that's been moseying around the palace's lazy river for who knows how long, gathering who knows what kind of contaminants.

"I don't think it's potable," Tad corrects. "In the kitchen, we found taps that lead up to an impressive cistern system on the roof."

"Rain catchment," Gareth supplies.

"Yeah. From what we could see, it's an intricate system that's still in working order."

"These troughs don't seem to connect to that system," Kenzie adds. "From what we could see, these feed the living walls, the water features, and the fountains within the palace. It's a brilliant way to keep the palace alive and thriving even when there's no one here to maintain things."

The four of us chat more about that as we return to the grand foyer where we first entered the palace. The hellhounds' nails *click* on the floor as they walk with us.

The tension in the room is palpable, and I look from Briar to Azland to Zephyr, then at Nikon and Ryan. "What's going on? What did we miss?"

Zephyr huffs. "He wants to remove Tad's warding and open the doors, even though he feels the energy of the feral gargoyles from hell and they're still out to get us."

"Then why would we invite them in?" I ask.

Briar scowls. "Because I can't very well talk them down when I've barricaded myself in here. If I'm to convince them to trust me, I have to trust that they'll listen to reason."

"And if you're wrong?" Kenzie asks.

"I don't think I am."

I shake my head. "I get what you're trying to do, and I admire it, but we don't know what state those elementals are in. Sure, they might be too long as stone and be confused, or they might be fully rabid and unreachable. In which case—"

"They're not!" he snaps, the ground beneath our feet shaking. He closes his eyes and draws a deep breath. "Sorry, but they're *not*. I feel it. Maybe I'm taking a risk, but I feel it in my gut. There is a chance to reach them and restore some measure of humanity to their elemental forms. I have to try."

I don't like this, but what Gareth said earlier still bounces around in my head. Briar isn't reckless or rash. He knows his limitations, and he's not one to endanger others.

Swallowing, I draw a deep breath. "Okay, if you're sure and you've thought it through, I'm behind you."

Kenzie and Zephyr look at me, and despite their misgivings—which I share—they nod their agreement.

Zephyr scoffs. "Fine, but if they try to kill us again, I'm going full lightning strike on them and reducing them to pebbles."

Briar offers us a quick nod. "Fair enough. Thanks, guys." Then he turns to Tad. "If you'll do the honors, I'd like to invite my people inside to chat."

Tad glances at Nikon and Azland, and when they nod, he moves to the barred door and removes his protective spell.

Briar waits until Tad jogs back to stand with Kenzie. Then he strides to the entrance, lifts the bar, and opens the double doors.

Stone people crowd the other side of the threshold. Briar raises his hands in a gesture of peace. "Please, listen." His voice is firm but calm. "I am not your enemy. My birth name is Taranis Stoneheart, son of your king and queen. As heir to the Stoneheart reign of Litaui, I come to you as a fellow earth elemental, one who seeks to understand and help."

As he speaks, the elemental energy around us shifts and intensifies.

I admire his conviction and courage, but I'm still not convinced it will be enough to reach the feral elementals and bring them back from the brink of madness.

When scanning the ready stances of our party, it's easy to see I'm not the only one with reservations. At the heart of things, we are Briar's family, and beyond that, we are warriors.

We're ready for a fight if that's how they play this. So are Jinx and Onyx.

"My parents sent me away to survive the raids. They hoped I could one day return and serve the kingdom of earth like they did."

As Briar speaks, I watch the seething group of elementals. I'm not sure if it's their intention or simply the result of people pushing to get a better look, but the ground beneath us is alive and pulsing as they inch toward my brother.

A massive surge in the elemental energy around us has my adrenaline thundering.

Briar's body changes, his limbs thickening as his skin becomes rough and rocky. He's shifting into his earth form, assuming his true elemental state.

Only it doesn't look joyous or freeing like when Zephyr did it.

"What's happening?" I shout, staggering to the side as the ground shakes beneath our feet. "Is he doing this, or are they?"

The feral earth elementals aren't that close to him yet, and still the transformation continues.

"I don't like this," Zephyr mutters, his hands flying to the sides to steady himself. "He wasn't able to assume his earth form while he was practicing. I'm not sure this is his doing."

That's good enough for me. I drop my hands to my sides and call my flames, wreathing my skin in fire.

Before I can reach him, the ground cracks and Briar drops out of sight. The feral elementals jump forward and vanish into the earth in the same place.

Everyone launches forward, reaching the hole as it seals shut, swallowing them whole.

I reach the spot where Briar stood only a moment before, my mind reeling. "What the hell just happened? Where have they taken Briar!"

CHAPTER TWENTY-ONE

Briar's sudden disappearance leaves me in a state of shock. My heart pounds as I realize my brother is in danger and I have no way of helping him. We have to find him. But how?

"Did that just happen?" Kenzie stammers, her eyes wide. "Did they just take Briar?"

Zephyr curses. "They sure as fuck did. What do they want with him?"

I clench my fists, fire arcing off me like sun flares. "I don't know, but we have to get him back. He was trying to help them, not hurt them. They know that, right?"

Tad steps forward with his brow furrowed in thought. "I'm not sure they care, Jules. They're feral. Their connection to reason seems to be compromised."

I hate the sound of that. "Well, we'll make them understand. They don't get to take our brother into the depths and walk away from it."

I'll do whatever it takes to get Briar back. I don't care if I have to gut this entire kingdom. "Tad? Can you open the ground back up? You're a druid. You have control over earth and stone. Can you get us down there? There must be a tunnel or something."

Tad is frowning at the spot on the ground. "I don't have dominion over the earth like elementals do, but I can try. The bigger problem is that we don't know what we'll be walking into."

"Does that matter?" I search the others' faces. "Whatever is happening down there, it's happening to Briar. We go in, no matter what."

"I'm not suggesting we don't," Tad replies. "I want to take a beat and consider what we might come up against down there. If there are tunnels, earth elementals could close them and bury us alive. Up here, in the courtyard, we have a foothold. Below ground, we'd be totally in their domain."

Azland nods. "Tad's right, Jules. If we go down there, we're sealing ourselves into a lair with hostile elementals that can close the stone around us."

"Tad won't let that happen." I check with him to be sure. "You can keep that from happening, right?"

The look he flashes me doesn't give me much confidence. "I won't *let* it happen, Jules, but that doesn't mean I'm all-powerful and can stop it from happening."

"What about portaling us out if things go south?" Zephyr asks.

Tad checks in with Nikon, and they both nod. "We've got a good chance of that working. Still, we don't know what kind of offensive they have."

"But we know they have *Briar*," I insist.

Everyone considers that. Then Azland steps forward. "There's no good alternative. We'll go down, but if things go sideways, Nikon will do a mass evacuation and pull us out."

"Ryan should stay here." Zephyr frowns at the kid. "It's too dangerous."

Ryan makes a face. "Are you seriously suggesting I stay up here alone with creepy, homicidal stone men lurking around?"

"The kid's got a point, Z." I meet Zephyr's gaze. "We can't leave him here, and we can't afford to split our party."

Zephyr considers that for a moment and curses again. "Fine, but you stick close to Nikon at all times, and if we have to bug out, you make it easy on him to evacuate."

"Deal."

Tad kneels on the ground with his hands pressed firmly against the broken stone tiles. He draws a deep breath, then recites a druid spell to open the earth. He speaks in old Irish tongues, and honestly, if my brother weren't missing, I'd sigh in girly contentment.

As it is, I'm too worked up to fall under his sexy spell. His voice takes on a musical quality, the Irish words flowing together in a rhythmic chant that echoes through the earth.

I don't understand what he's saying, but his magical signature tingles across my skin.

His words take hold, and the ground beneath his hands trembles and shifts. After another few moments, the floor splits open, forming a narrow passage leading down into darkness. I step forward and peer into the opening. The others close in, but I decide that I should be the first to take the plunge since I pushed the hardest.

I lower myself to sit on the edge and dangle my legs into the hole. "Once I'm inside, it'll be fine."

"That's what he said," Zephyr mumbles, only half paying attention.

Kenzie smacks his arm and tilts her head toward the kid. Zephyr has the good sense to look abashed.

Despite the shared trepidation, once I drop into the hole and light my fist like a torch, the group follows my lead.

Gareth is the last to jump down. Onyx squirms in his arms.

When he hands him to me, he wriggles and wiggles and licks my face.

"That's disgusting." Kenzie scowls at the PDA—Puppy Dog Affection.

"What? He was anxious about me going into the scary dark hole." I set him onto the dirt floor of the tunnel and wipe my face with the sleeve of my shirt.

Gareth raises his hand, and a moment later Jinx jumps down to join us. "Which way, girl? Take us to Briar."

Without hesitation, Jinx sniffs the air, then drops her nose to the ground and strikes off.

"Hellhounds. Not just for killing demons anymore," Zephyr intones like a commercial announcer.

I grunt. "Jinx and Onyx have proven to be a vital part of this team. They are more than demon defense."

Kenzie pats my arm. "Of course they are, Jules. He was lightening the mood a little."

I get that. "I guess I'm touchy about the hounds after the griffins spouted off. We're good."

We make our way through the tunnel. The air grows chilly and damp. The packed earth absorbs the sound of our footsteps, so other than the occasional drip of water from above, we're pretty much silent.

Descending deeper, we walk in single file, the tunnel narrow, the tension thick. Adrenaline has my fire simmering below the surface, ready to ignite at the smallest provocation.

I think we're making good time until we turn a corner and the tunnel ends.

Jinx sits in front of the wall ahead, undaunted by the seven-foot wall of dirt, roots, and rock in front of us.

"What is this place?" Kenzie whispers, her breath condensing in a cloud as she speaks.

"I'm going with underground death trap." Zephyr frowns at it.

"Seriously, Z." I peg him with a look. "There are thoughts you can think and other thoughts you say out loud."

"Tell me you weren't thinking it."

Kenzie shivers. "Briar better appreciate this. I'm more of a tropical waters girl."

I hold my hand in the space between me and my sister and release a ball of flames.

Kenzie reaches forward, warming her hands over my flames. "Thanks, Jules."

"Not a problem."

Tad scans the intricate network of roots and rocks that form the wall blocking us from our destination and presses his hands against the dirt. He whispers another incantation and the passage before us shimmers. "Any chance someone can give me a boost?"

Azland and Nikon move to either side of him and add to the magical output.

At first, only a faint, ghostly light struggles to break through the wall of earth. Then the dirt and debris give way, and the hole is big enough for us to crouch and climb through to the passage beyond.

"You rock, Irish." I pat Tad's shoulder as I straighten on the other side. "Okay, Jinx. Lead the way, girl. Where's Briar?"

When our hellhound guide trots off along the tunnel, we fall in behind her and are off again.

I'm not sure if it's light deprivation, the uncertainty of what's happening to Briar, or the myriad twists and switchbacks in the tunnel system, but it feels like we've been lost for hours.

"You're sure Jinx still has the scent, right?" Zephyr asks, mirroring my concerns.

Gareth tilts his head for a moment, focusing on his hound. "Yes, she's sure."

His words say he's sure, but his tone makes me wonder. "What is it?"

"She also said we're not alone. She senses something ahead."

"Some*thing* or some*one*?" Nikon asks.

Before he answers, the shadows ahead stretch, distorting our vision. If I can believe what I see, a gargantuan figure is rising from the earth.

It looks as if it's been hiding here for centuries. The beast's eyes—gleaming gold gems against its rocky surroundings—snap open.

"Is everyone seeing this?" I widen my stance.

"I'll never *unsee* it," Kenzie replies.

The beast before us rises, dirt and debris falling from its frame. Its emergence reveals a sinuous physique that melds seamlessly into the shadows. Its limbs are long and slender, ending in sharp, talon-like fingers. Two luminous eyes pierce the black, their color constantly shifting from gold to silver to an eerie shade of violet. Devoid of pupils, they ratchet up the creepy factor and send a shiver up my spine.

"Intruders! Why have you come?"

His bellowing words shake the tunnel, and I worry he might cause a cave-in. "We seek the ones who took my brother. We have no interest in disturbing or offending you. If you step aside, we'll be on our way."

"The earth elementals allow me to live here and in return, I protect their domain. You shall not pass!"

I stiffen. "Listen, Gandalf. My brother has been earth-napped, and we will get him back. We aren't looking for a fight, but we're certainly not afraid to start one."

Its shadowy form advances. A tattered cloak made of pure darkness clings to its form. It flutters as if caught in a perpetual wind, even in the stillness of the tunnels. When it looks at me, its eyes flare brighter. "You shall not pass."

The narrow space explodes into a barrage of chaos. Tad *poofs* Zephyr and Ryan behind the thing as Gareth, Kenzie, and I move in from the front.

Jinx and Onyx grow to their massive battle forms, and it's game on.

Wind gusts from behind make the cloak flutter wildly, but its feet remain planted.

Kenzie conjures streams of water through its filmy silhouette and hits Tad and Zephyr instead.

Gareth and I summon our fire, and twin torrents of flame engulf his form. I expect him to crumple or retreat, but he stands taller, grinning as his eyes glow scarlet. "It's been a long time since I've felt warmth in my bones."

"That's not good," I mutter.

Gareth grunts. "No, it's not."

"What the fuck are you?" Zephyr asks. "I ask with curiosity and knowing your answer will help us decide how to attack you next."

The beast's grin does nothing to bolster my confidence. "Nothing you've ever come across before, boy."

Another round of frenzied fighting lights off, and we all bombard the thing at once.

Azland is casting, and the ground around its feet glows. "That should lock it in place," Azland shouts. "Knock it off balance and—"

Before he finishes that sentence, the creature smashes its fist into the ground, shattering the glow of the spell and sending forth a shockwave that throws us off our feet.

Tad steps forward, raising his arms and shouting something in Irish. The cavern quivers, and suddenly, roots and vines emerge from the walls and floor, wrapping around the shadow's legs, trying to restrain it.

Our attacker roars, and I take that as the first good sign since this started.

The cavern is alive with chaos as we all attack at once. Except, every move we make, every elemental force we summon, seems to have no effect other than pissing it off.

Each strike, whether a gust of wind, a splash of water, or a flare of fire, meets with a thunderous counter. It's as though we are children trying to bring down an ancient power.

We're all giving it as hard as we can when Gareth steps forward with his hands raised. "Stop, demon! Razgarath Poreskoro, prince of hell, commands you to stop!"

Demon?

Our attacker freezes mid-swing, its eyes locking onto Gareth. There's a heavy pause, the air thick with tension. Then he drops his gaze to the dirt.

"You interfere with our mission, demon. Whether or not you have an agreement with the elementals, your fealty to the Kings of Hell supersedes it."

The rest of us exchange baffled looks.

"I did not recognize you in this form, young prince."

Gareth growls, acting much gruffer than his usual broody self. "The size of this tunnel doesn't allow for my true form. I assure you, I speak the truth. And you see my hounds."

The demon's gaze slides to Jinx and Onyx. "You carry the blood of the demon king. I am at your service."

"Then respect our request and let us through."

With a bow of his wispy frame, he steps back and dissolves into the shadows. "Be of care, young prince."

Gareth shifts uncomfortably under the scrutinizing gazes of our group. "I didn't realize what he was at first, and I detest pulling rank."

"But you did it to keep us safe and get us moving," I add, stretching to kiss his cheek. "Thanks, broody."

There's a round of head nods when a muffled scream echoes through the underground passages. The sound is faint, barely discernible over the distant rumble of the earth, but it is enough to send a jolt of adrenaline coursing through my veins.

"That's Briar!"

CHAPTER TWENTY-TWO

Briar's muffled scream reverberates through the underground labyrinth as we sprint through the twisting passageways. My breath escapes in heavy pants of condensation as I push to close the distance. Hot on Jinx's heels, I lead the way, my fiery palms illuminating the darkness before us as we run.

The others stay close, our footfalls beating a threatening rhythm.

The scream sounds again, louder and more desperate this time.

It's undoubtedly Briar. That he's afraid or in pain only fuels my determination to reach him.

Thankfully, Jinx's keen senses help us navigate the winding paths. Even when we come to intersecting ways, we follow her without hesitation.

At last, we enter an expansive chamber. The flickering light from my fire casts eerie shadows on the walls. The room is seething with earth elementals in full stone form. I search for my brother, but...

I suck in a gasp when I spot him.

He's a massive male, broad-shouldered and encased in stone.

He's standing in the center of a mass of elementals and by the looks of things, he's not being tortured, bound, or held prisoner.

He's one of them.

"Briar!" Kenzie shouts.

The mob of earth elementals turn and don't seem to appreciate the interruption.

"He did it," Zephyr marvels. "He's a fucking beast."

The ground vibrates with the movement of the stone behemoths, sending tremors up through my feet and into my bones. My flames flicker and dance, illuminating the harsh, unyielding expressions of the stone-faced earth elementals.

Jinx tenses beside me, growing into her fighting form. The rest of the group forms a protective circle.

We're outnumbered, surrounded, and from the low rumbling sounds emanating from our brother at the center of the chamber, not welcome.

"Briar?" I call, searching the face of the massive figure I think is my brother. His once gentle eyes are cold and unyielding. His chiseled stone features show no recognition.

It hits me like a sledgehammer—he's one of them—lost in his elemental transformation.

The room feels suffocatingly still for a heartbeat. Then, like a landslide, the earth elementals surge forward.

Zephyr curses, whips up a vortex, and pushes back several of the stone warriors. They recover quickly.

I lash out, swiping fire through the air at anyone who comes too close.

To my horror, Briar lunges forward, his heavy fists aimed at me. Shock must take over because I don't move. I'm stuck in place staring at those stone fists barreling toward me.

A feral roar echoes inside my head a moment before Gareth steps in front of me and takes the hit. Gareth in his demon form is huge...but so is Briar.

The punch connects with a *crunch* of bone, and it throws

Gareth back and off his feet. He's so close that he takes me to the ground too. We fall in a breath-stealing crash, crumpling to the chamber floor.

Strangely enough, I watch the whole thing from outside myself. Instead of fear, a pang of grief courses through me.

A hit like that from Briar could've killed me. "It's me, Briar! It's Jules!"

He's not seeing me. He grabs my arm, yanks me out from under an unconscious Gareth, and throws me against the hewn stone wall.

I cry out before my breath is forced out of my lungs in a rush as I hit the stone and drop.

"Jules!" Zephyr's shout draws my attention to where he and Ryan are fighting foes.

He's too far to help me.

I scramble to my feet, my legs wobbly and my left arm hanging limp at my side. Briar comes at me again, and tears sting my eyes. I flame up, but fire isn't wholly effective against stone, and it won't stop him, especially with me barely able to stand.

His glazed gaze falters, revealing a glimmer of confusion...or maybe of recognition.

"Briar, it's me!" I gasp, tears sizzling on my cheeks and evaporating as quickly as they fall. "You don't want to kill me. You love me."

He presses forward. The noise from the battle around us fades into the background. All I hear is my heartbeat echoing loudly in my ears.

His hard-as-stone stare shimmers with inner turmoil.

"That's right, big guy." I sag against the wall to stay upright. "You love me, B. Come back. Focus."

The muscles of his chiseled jaw twitch as he struggles with himself. The overpowering weight of his elemental form bears down on him, causing his shoulders to slump and his massive form to waver. He drops to his knees with a heavy thud, and his head hangs low.

He extends a shaky hand, stopping short of touching me as if he's afraid he'll hurt me again. "I...fuck, Jules. I'm so sorry," he murmurs, his voice breaking. "I couldn't...I didn't mean to..."

My legs give out, and I drop to my knees, throwing my good arm around him. The surface of his skin is still mostly stone, but beneath that, there's the warmth of my brother again.

"I'm so sorry," he sobs next to me.

"It'll be okay," I whisper, wincing as he seeks solace. "I'm a little busted up, but—"

"But nothing!" Kenzie moves in and shoves Briar back. "We told you not to rush your transformation. We told you not to take such a risk for a bunch of feral lunatics, and did you listen? No. You're stubborn, and you almost killed Jules."

Zephyr kneels beside us, his expression fraught with worry. "Shit, Jules. Your left shoulder is way fucked up."

"Yeah, Briar yanked it out of the socket and crushed it when he slammed me into the stone wall."

Briar looks anguished. "I'm so sorry."

"You should be!" Kenzie shouts. "We told you to stop and think about things. You nearly got us killed, and you could've gotten killed yourself."

Briar takes the hit. We all know this is Kenzie's way of saying he was stupid and he could've died.

"Uh, guys?" Tad waves at us from across the chamber. "Any chance we can save the family drama fer later and address the more immediate issue here?"

The four of us look up to find the entire room of elementals focused on us.

"Well, at least they're not attacking us," Zephyr comments.

"They shouldn't have attacked us in the first place," Kenzie snaps, turning a withering glare on them. "He's the heir to your kingdom, and we're his family. Instead of attacking us, you should've welcomed us. We wanted to meet you, to help you, and to learn from you. What the hell were you thinking?"

Tad grins. "Are ye really rippin' a strip off a room of homicidal earth elementals?"

Kenzie props her hands on her hips. "Damn skippy, I am. If they need to focus to get their heads on straight, they can focus on this. I don't care what you've been through over the past twenty-five years. At some point, you descended from this kingdom, and our brother is your sovereign. Pull your shit together and step the hell back. If you can't play nice, take your ball and go home."

Briar grunts as he stands, raising his palms as he did at the palace's entrance. "What my sister is so passionately trying to say is I'm Taranis Stoneheart, son of your king and queen. I came to Litaui to find my people and help them. So, let me help you."

Between checking on Gareth and Kenzie healing my shoulder, clavicle, and ribs on my left side, I miss the planning session of how we're going to help the feral elementals. Honestly, I don't care what happens next. Briar is back to being Briar, so they can take our help or leave it. I don't give two shits.

The only way I'm invested in this is on Briar's behalf. He truly wants to do his parents proud and for his sake, I hope we can leave this place better than we found it.

From what I can see from my spot on the ground, the elementals are still wary of us and hanging back.

With the combined magical efforts of Azland and Nikon, Tad's druid efforts, and Kenzie's healing efforts, they work out a spell that might help stabilize the feral elementals and bring them back to their humanoid forms.

Gareth has one hell of a headache from taking Briar's punch, so we watch from a safe distance with the hounds protectively sitting guard.

"I'm sorry Briar hit you." I lean against his chest.

He runs a finger along my forearm and bends his head to kiss my shoulder. "Better me than you. The way his fist was swinging, he might've taken your head off."

I shiver, not wanting to think about it. "He'll feel bad about it forever. It might even smooth things over with him about you."

Gareth chuckles behind me. "He's wanted to hit me for a while now."

"I didn't mean that. I was saying you taking the hit and protecting me while keeping him from killing me will move the needle with him."

He sets his chin on my head and wraps his arm around me. "If it's better for you that he likes me, that's great. Honestly, I'm here for you and you alone."

I know that, but damn, it must be lonely.

"For now, that might be true, but if this lasts the way I hope it will, I want you to be part of the family."

"Family is overrated."

"It can be," I agree, thinking about all the domestic calls I responded to when I was a cop. "It can also be magical."

He grunts. "I'll have to take your word for it."

I turn my head to look up at him. "You're a good man, Gareth. I know you don't think so, but I do. If you stick around long enough, others will see it too."

He brushes his lips over mine. "I'm not planning to go anywhere."

The two of us settle in and watch the progress of restoring the elementals.

Since Azland and the others began working, several wild elementals have dropped to their knees, their bodies trembling. One regained a noticeably human form while another remained in his stone form but seems to be lucid and in full control.

It makes sense because if our elements are our true forms, we should be able to exist in that state and thrive. Just because we're not accustomed to our fully elemental state doesn't mean it's not perfectly natural and healthy.

Each time an elemental reclaims a humanoid form or their lucidity, Kenzie rushes over, helps them up, and gives them some extra healing. It's incredibly slow work, but given how long they've likely been in that form, coming out of it will take some effort.

Energy crackles in the air, and magic builds in the cavern, rising to a crescendo.

The feral elementals sense it too. Their pacing grows more erratic and their eyes widen with fear and confusion.

A sudden burst of energy ripples through the cavern, and I raise my arm to shield my face from the blinding light. There's a collective gasp, followed by heavy, labored breathing.

When I lower my arm, almost all the transformed elementals are lying on the ground, disoriented.

"It's all right." Briar kneels before them, sitting on his heels. "You're safe, and while you might not remember it, I'm here to help."

A swell of pride rises in my chest. Despite the odds and the risks, Briar accomplished something truly remarkable here today. "He's going to be an outstanding leader."

I glance at Briar, who is deep in conversation with one of the transformed elementals. His face is serious, but there's a light in his eyes that suits him. It's clear this victory means more to him than any of us could truly understand.

I always knew he was a prince among men.

CHAPTER TWENTY-THREE

Nikon and Tad portal all who care to join us back to the city above. Not everyone is ready to socialize and not all the elementals are happy to be brought out of their natural state.

Once we emerge into the sunlight, the group gathers around the grand fountain in front of the palace.

"What happened to you?" Briar scans the faces of his people.

The elementals exchange glances, their expressions a mix of relief and uncertainty.

An older elemental, his skin still flecked with bits of stone, steps forward. "We were away during the demon raids. Trading, traveling, or living away from our homeland."

A younger woman joins in. "We heard what happened and were afraid to return. We stayed in hiding for years and didn't dare return."

"Where did you hide?" Kenzie asks.

"There are a few encampments here in the realm, and a few groups went to the human realm."

The older man nods. "When we were certain it was safe, we came back. The palace, our homes, everything above ground was in ruins."

"But the elemental power..." The woman's voice trails off, her gaze distant. "It was pure and had been undisturbed and untapped for years. Everywhere we went, we felt it. It was intoxicating, overwhelming..."

"It was too much to resist," another adds, her voice barely a whisper. "We spent longer and longer periods basking in the power of our elementals until we couldn't change back. We were trapped in our element, lost and disconnected from our humanity."

As they speak, our group listens, our expressions a mix of sympathy and understanding. We know all too well the allure of power and the danger it poses if left unchecked.

"But now you're back," Kenzie points out.

The young woman glances around the sun-washed courtyard and smiles. "It's a strange feeling to be human again after so long. I think we'll need time to adjust, to rediscover ourselves and feel comfortable in our skin."

Yeah, I'm sure that journey won't be an easy one.

The older elemental nods solemnly. "Without the balance of a robust community, we became more stone than man. We won't let that happen again."

The young woman looks up, tears glistening in her eyes. "We had no anchors. The allure was too strong, and we were adrift and lost."

Kenzie places a hand on the woman's shoulder. "You're not lost now. You're back, and we can help you restore energy balance to your kingdom."

"Consume it, you mean," the old man counters. "That's why he's here, isn't it? The Poreskoro prince is here to finish what he started?" He points at Gareth, his contempt clear for everyone to see.

I shake my head. "Gareth never took part in the raids. He spoke out against them and suffered the wrath of his family for it. He's here because he is part of our family."

Nikon steps forward. "Time tends to change not only situations but people as well. Almost three decades have passed since the raids on your people. Restoring your freedom is a new beginning, a chance to ensure the past doesn't repeat itself."

"If you didn't want a repeat of our destruction, you shouldn't have brought a Poreskoro and his demon dogs here," a man retorts from the back.

The mood in the group is shifting fast as tension fills the air. Confusion and mistrust morph into them radiating anger.

I step forward. "Gareth might have been born into that family, but that doesn't mean you know him. He's a good guy and lives his life dedicated to helping the fae."

An elemental man with sharp green eyes points at Gareth. "A change of heart doesn't erase the horrors his family caused."

Gareth meets his gaze squarely, his voice steady. "I understand your caution. I know the weight of my family's sins, and I am determined to make amends."

The green-eyed elemental sneers. "Words are easy. How do we know we can trust you or your kind?"

A murmur of agreement rises among the earth elementals, their collective mistrust growing palpable.

I raise my hands. "We're not here for any nefarious purposes. We only want to understand, to help, and to heal. Briar only recently learned his parentage, and he wants to be here for his people."

The old man scoffs. "By bringing our enemy here? He might have learned about his heritage, but him trusting a Poreskoro proves he's no Stoneheart. Our royal couple were amazing leaders. They died fighting to keep our people safe."

Briar draws a heavy breath, his disappointment and desperation obvious. "But I *do* want to keep you safe. I came here to learn about my people, and we brought you back from the madness you were trapped in. I have no ulterior motives. I genuinely want to reconnect, to learn about our heritage and my family."

The burly elemental with the stony skin glares. "You don't know what it is to be a Stoneheart. You aren't one of us."

"No, he's not," I snap, moving to stand beside my brother. "Because he's better than you."

They don't like my opinion much, but I don't care. "This man might have been born Taranis Stoneheart, but he was raised Briar Gagne. He's gracious, forgiving, loyal, and brave. He risked his life to save you—strangers he's never met—because he cares deeply about people and has a sense of responsibility that goes well beyond being your king."

"He's not our king," the old man snaps.

"You're wrong about that, and you're stupid to deny him. Having Briar as your sovereign would be the best thing to happen to your kingdom in two decades. If you're too blinded by the past to see the future he offers, that's your loss."

The old man narrows his gaze. "That's twice you've called us stupid, girl."

I shrug, not caring one bit about the disdain in the way he calls me *girl*. "Just calling it as I see it, old man. Fire elementals run hotter than most, and I don't give two shits if you're offended or not."

He shakes his head and looks at the surrounding elementals. "We've heard enough. Leave. And don't return."

"Are you fucking kidding me?" Zephyr scans the crowd. "We risk our lives rescuing you from a madness made of your greed and poor judgment, and you take issue with us and order us away? We fucking saved you."

"And we're grateful," the young female says. "Of course we are."

"But?" Briar asks.

"But we don't know you. Maybe you're the son of the Stonehearts, or maybe you're not. Maybe the Poreskoro among you is the outlier for his family, or maybe he's not. Maybe we're being stupid, as your sister says, or maybe we're not."

"You definitely are," I interject.

She glares at me and continues. "The point is, we've spent two decades locked in our survival instincts, and our reasoning is shaky. Maybe leaving isn't such a bad idea…at least for now. Give us time to clear our heads, and maybe we'll see things differently."

"That's an awful lot of maybes," Kenzie points out.

Briar lifts his hand to stop us from weighing in. "All right. I'll give you time and space to clear your minds—but I'll be back. My entire life, I've wondered about my ancestry and my parents. If they meant for me to return and restore their kingdom, nothing you can say or do will stop me from trying."

She nods. "That's fair. Thank you."

"You're not serious." I turn and meet the heartbreak in Briar's gaze. "What about learning about your parents and your kingdom? We're here. They can't make you leave. Your answers are in that palace and this city."

Briar straightens, and I know he's locked in and will be stubborn about this. "It's my first test at being their leader, Jules. What they need from me is time to sort out the fog of emotions. I was only lost to the elemental power for a few hours, and I feel the weight of it. They were lost for decades."

"And you rescued them."

"They know that. Let's step back. We'll round up the elementals at home and return once they've reconnected with reality."

"There are more of you?" the man with the stone skin asks. "More of us?"

I nod. "Dozens. The magic binding our identities failed recently, and the elementals sent to the human realm are surfacing. We came because Ryan needed to stabilize his powers and we could only do it in the vortex of Gailleann."

Their attention moves to the blond teenager glued to Zephyr's side. "This kingdom isn't yours just because you're here and you say so. If my friends or other emerging elementals need it, it's their kingdom, too."

Zephyr rests a hand on Ryan's back. "Yeah, it is. Well said, buddy."

Ryan's words seem to impact, and more than a few of the earth group bob their heads.

Briar straightens. "There are others and more every day. We have a chance to rebuild not only as a race of fae but also as a community. I need you to think about that and let it sink in. Hopefully, the next time we come back, you'll see what we see and will be ready to move beyond the tragedy of the past."

"Says the boy who neither lived with the horror of that tragedy nor the fallout," the old man chides.

Briar's eyes are filled with an aching sadness as he's slammed with rejection again. "Maybe that's true, but it also means I'm not consumed with hate and negativity."

"Which is also why you think it's okay to befriend the Poreskoro."

I laugh harshly. "Not all of them. Our adoptive parents died killing Draven, and we killed Lamech. The Six are now four because our family stood up against your enemy. When we tell you Gareth isn't like them, that isn't naivety. That's a fact. Like I said, you don't know us."

My revelation stirs the crowd as they chew on that.

The young woman steps forward and nods. "You've given us a lot to think about, and when our heads clear and we *can* think, we'll talk things through. Safe travels back to the human realm. Whatever happens, we thank you for what you've done for us today."

Briar accepts our dismissal and stands straight with his head held high. "I see a bright and flourishing future for elementals, and I want to share my vision with the kingdom my parents and grandparents established. I sincerely hope you give me that chance because I would much rather we be united. We've spent much too much time divided."

With that, he nods at Nikon, and the Greek transports us back to the dragons.

"I'm sorry, B." I hug my massive little brother. "They don't know how amazing you are and that's their loss. But it sucks that you didn't get to learn more about your family and get your answers."

He shrugs. "There's still time. That door might be closed to me right now, but I'm a patient man and will wait for my chance to open it."

Kenzie chuckles and comes over to join our hug. "You're not patient, Briar, you're stubborn."

"Same result."

Zephyr moves in and makes it a four-way hug. "If you need help to freeze that door open, blow it, or burn it down, we're right there with you, brother."

Briar's smile grows stronger as he looks at us. "Yeah, and I thank the powers for that every day."

With a collective sigh, we break up the love fest and return our attention to the rest of the group. They're talking to the dragons and preparing to leave.

"Shotgun," I call, jogging over to them.

Tad laughs. "What exactly does that look like with dragon flight, girlfriend?"

I don't know, but everyone laughed, so it doesn't matter.

CHAPTER TWENTY-FOUR

We materialize inside the fire station, and the familiar scent of home washes over me. The place might look more like a cabin at summer camp than our usual home, but it doesn't matter.

We're back, we're intact, and that's all that counts.

"Well, look who's back! You look like you've been through the wringer." Charlie greets us with a wide grin, her eyes twinkling with humor at the sight of our disheveled appearances.

"What, you don't think I'm rocking this look? I was thinking of auditioning for Snow Queen at *Fêtes des Neiges*," I retort with a weary smile.

Glancing around at my siblings, they all seem to share the same mix of exhaustion and relief as me.

Ryan heads toward the sound of teenagers, and the moment he's visible to the kids in the living room, they surround him.

"What happened?"

"Are you okay?"

"What is the fae realm like?"

"Did you get in trouble for taking out half of downtown?"

Ryan gets tugged into the wake of his peers, and we disperse.

"Man, I'm starving." Zephyr rushes the Tupperware containers lined up on the counter.

"We're off to shower and sleep for a week." Kenzie grips Tad's wrist and pulls him toward her suite.

"Hey, B. There are brownies." Zephyr holds up the container.

Briar reaches out and accepts the chocolaty bliss, then pulls up a place at the breakfast bar. With his elbows on the counter, he pops the sealed lid and digs in. "I hope no one else expects any of these because I'm claiming them all."

I pat his shoulder. "I'll get you a glass of almond milk."

Charlie frowns and leans on her elbows across from him. "Are you okay?"

Briar manages a tired smile. "I'm fine. We had a rough time and a few setbacks in the earth kingdom."

Her brows pinch. "I thought you were going to the wind city."

"We did." Zephyr joins the conversation, setting himself up with butter tarts a couple of stools over from Briar. "We started in Gailleann, and that went pretty great. Then we wondered about the other elemental cities."

"The fire city wasn't a good group trip for obvious reasons." I slide a tall glass of milk in front of Briar. "Azland said the water kingdom was limited to outsiders too."

"So we went with earth," Zephyr adds.

As my brothers begin their baked goods binge and decompress, my gaze falls on Gareth standing off to the side with Jinx. He looks lost in thought, his brow furrowed as he stares at the floor.

I know he blames himself for Briar's trouble with the earth elementals, but it's not his fault. We have no choice about what family we're born into. All we can do is try to rise above it and pave our own path.

He's done that. If others can't see past his mixed race or his last name, that's their problem.

I walk to him and lay a gentle hand on his arm. "Hey, there. Are you okay?"

It's a testament to how far we've come that he doesn't reply. A few months ago, he would have either gotten angry because I was prying or lied and told me what he thought I wanted to hear so I'd stop asking.

I've also learned a few other things in the past month. Gareth is a loner who doesn't open up or relax when other people are around.

Lacing my fingers with his, I tug him down the stairs, across the garage bay, and after making a quick stop at the downstairs bevvy fridge, outside to the back patio.

The dogs follow at our heels and rush out to play in the moonlight of the backyard.

"Do you want to get nakey and soak in my lava pool?"

He smiles, but it doesn't touch his eyes. "Not tonight. I think I should probably go."

I point at the patio chairs and hand him his beer. "It wasn't your fault."

"It was, but I'm grateful you don't blame me."

I twist the top of my beer and toss the cap into the bowl on the table. "Of course I don't because it's not your fault."

Gareth sits heavily, and it's like the weight of his past is dragging him down once again. He opens his beer and takes a couple of long gulps, but I'm not sure he tastes it.

"You might never get out from under your family's shadow, but that doesn't mean we give up."

His gaze shifts to mine. "We? Are you sure you want to die on that hill?"

"Without hesitation." I shift closer and sit on his lap, wriggling to make room between his chest and the table. "I see you, broody. I believe in you, and I know who you were, who you are, and who you want to be. I am Team Gareth until the end."

He draws a deep breath and studies my resolve. "Where did you come from, Jules Gagne?"

"Funny enough, I've spent my entire life asking myself that same question. Do you know what I learned?"

"Always. I want to know everything about you."

I kiss his cheek. "Aw, sexy and sweet. Two points for that one, broody."

He chuckles, and his amusement jiggles me in his lap. "What did you learn?"

I set my beer bottle on the table and shift to straddle him in the chair. Facing him, I cup his square jawline with both hands and lean close. "I learned that everything we live through, good or bad, consciously or unconsciously, makes us who we are. It doesn't matter who I was or where I came from. What matters is who and where I am now."

His dark gaze studies mine, and I know he's searching for any sign that I'm placating him.

I'm not.

"All the stuff that came before—your mixed parentage, your siblings, the demon stuff, the raids, your imprisonment by your siblings—was all part of you becoming this version of who you are. And I, for one, love who you are."

His brow arches at the use of the L-word.

We haven't said it to one another yet. I'm not one hundred percent sure it wouldn't send him running to save me from the fate of loving him. But it's becoming more and more apparent.

I'm falling for him. I just need him to understand that's not a bad thing.

"The next time we have time to go to the fae realm, will you come to Lasair with me? I want to check out the fire kingdom and see what it's like to embrace my true form completely."

After the past two days, the thought is thrilling and terrifying. Still, I've never been one to cave to fear.

"If you want me there, I would be honored to escort you. No

doubt you'll be exquisite." The catch in his breath when he says that does all kinds of wonderful things to my insides.

"Your element is fire, but when you go full-on, your form is still humanoid. Is that an in-between stage or is that your full form?"

"That's my full form. My demon genes combine with my element, and that is what I become."

I search his face to see what he thinks about that, but as usual, his emotions are well-guarded. "Does that make you sad? Would you like to be fully fire?"

He purses his lips as if considering that. "Is it wrong if I say no?"

"*No.* Don't ever think I'll judge you for telling me what you really think or feel. You said you want to know everything about me, but that goes both ways."

He nods and exhales. "This is going to sound weird. As much as I hate the whole Poreskoro stigma and what's been done in the name of my father's influence, I don't hate my father or that side of me. My demon side is powerful, cunning, and fearless."

"And your elemental side?"

"My mother gave me compassion, conviction, and the confidence to stand on my own."

More than one person has said Gareth is much more like his mother—a fae queen—than his father. I'm not sure. If his strength, cunning, and fearlessness come from his demon side, I think he's also very much like his father. "The best of two worlds."

"Hmm." A soft smile curls his mouth. "My parents loved one another. They weren't supposed to be together, and the fae powers tried to step in and forbid it, but they wouldn't be parted. They defied social opinion and believed in their love."

A little like us. Not that I can say that to him.

Not yet anyway.

"How about we check in with the chaos inside, then say good-night and go to your place? Naked time in the fireplace might do us both some good."

He's out of his chair and slinging me from his lap to over his shoulder before I can catch the squeal that escapes my throat.

Yeah no, there's nothing wrong with demon strength.

Inside, the elemental kids still listen to Ryan with rapt attention, asking about griffins, dragons, our battles with the shadow demon, and the feral earth elementals.

Then come the pleading gazes and them asking when they can go to the fae realm. Not all of them, but most.

"Before any of that happens, we need to find out about your parents, your lives, and what Mr. Belvedere was doing in that house," I tell them.

"Why does that matter to us?" a fire boy asks. "We're here now. The witch doctor won't get us."

"No, but when there are people out there experimenting on our kind and draining and harnessing our elemental energy, we need to know who and what is behind it to ensure it doesn't happen again."

Charlie rolls her eyes and moves toward the living room. "What Jules means is we're going to take every precaution to ensure you and all those like you are safe."

I lift my hands and shrug. "That's what I said."

"Only you said it badly." Anna giggles. "Not everyone is used to your blunt cop talk. Some people need a bit more hand-holding."

"Yeah, well, that's not my strong suit."

"No shit," Micah agrees.

"Language!" Charlie shouts from the living room.

Micah ducks his head. "Geez, she's got good hearing."

Briar and Zephyr laugh. "Kid, wait until you try sneaking in at two in the morning. She can wake from a deep sleep and be tapping her foot on your bedroom floor in minutes."

Anna laughs and shoves Micah's shoulder. "You're a little late on that warning, boys. He lost his gaming keyboard and mouse for a month."

Of course he did.

"Hey, everyone." Hannah comes over to kiss Briar and welcome us back. "I knocked but didn't think you heard me, so I let myself in."

I wave away her concern. "It's like an underage social club around here. Not a problem. How have things been?"

Hannah is an empowered cop who works on Rene's outreach team under Mayor Tremblay. She's good people. The fact that she's an earth elemental and is enamored with Briar is even better.

If they make it work, they might start the next generation of pureblood earth elementals.

"How was your trip?"

Briar starts telling her all about it, so I tug Gareth into my room to keep me company while I pack an overnight bag. He doesn't need to relive the hostilities, and even though Briar knows it's not his fault, he's disappointed and kinda blames Gareth for that.

When I'm all packed, the two of us return to the kitchen and find Hannah rubbing Briar's back and consoling him.

That's our cue to keep moving.

"Good night, all. If you need us, we'll be at Gareth's."

Kenzie arches a brow. "You realize we have a house full of teenagers, right?"

I grin. "Absolutely. Now that we're back, Charlie will go home with Sammie and the twins, and two or maybe three of the girls can use my bed. Thoughtful of me, isn't it?"

Tad chuckles. "Ye really sold it, Jules. Full points."

"Thanks, Irish. Portal over to get us if anything happens."

"But text first," Gareth adds with a look. "It might be best, for all our sakes."

Tad nods. "Aye, I'll be sure to text first."

The two of us take our leave, grab the dog harnesses, and call the hounds to get into the truck cab ahead of us. When we've buckled in and the engine is rumbling, I reach across the console to squeeze his thigh. "I wish there was something I could do to make you feel better."

Gareth winks at me. "Knowing that you care enough to listen and try to understand means more than you know."

I'm glad because Gareth deserves someone in his corner. With my purse in my lap, it strikes me I'm not the only one in his corner.

I unzip my bag and ease his mother's meditation nest out to cup it in the palms of my hands. "In all the chaos, I forgot this was in my purse. Maybe a little motherly Zen might help you."

He chuckles. "I'll save this for when I'm alone at home. I don't think I can zone out when you're so close. Having you near has the opposite effect on me."

"Are you saying I'm chaos in your life?"

"You are, but no. I was saying you rile me up."

I waggle my brows. "Oh, yeah? Tell me more or better yet, show me."

He flips the truck into reverse and gets us cruising down my driveway toward the road. "Hold that thought. I'll be happy to show you what you do to me the moment we get home."

We drive to Gareth's apartment and make it upstairs in record time. It seems like the elevator is set to climb at a snail's pace, but we make good use of the time.

Look away. Nothing to see here.

It's hard to walk while making out, so Gareth solves our stumbling problem by picking me up. I wrap my legs around his hips like a horny koala, taking full advantage of my position against his chest.

Then he stiffens.

Not in the good way.

He ends the kiss, and my instincts kick in. I drop my boots to the floor and study his expression. He's focused on Jinx, and Jinx is focused on his front door.

"What is she telling you?" I whisper.

"We've got company."

"How many?"

"Six."

The hounds morph into full battle mode, snarling and snapping that intruders dared to invade their home. Jinx's eyes burn with the intensity of hellfire, and while Onyx isn't as big or fierce as his mother, he's doing his best to prove himself as a fierce protector.

"Stay behind me," Gareth orders.

I nod, knowing better than to argue with him in a situation like this.

"Onyx." My puppy turns his head as Gareth calls his name and gives him a command in a language I don't understand.

I'm about to ask what he said when my boy falls back and presses against my thigh.

I stroke my fingers through his wiry coat and take comfort in his protective nature—Gareth's too.

Gareth reaches for the door handle and glances back at me. "Be safe," he mouths.

"You too," I reply the same way.

After sharing a meaningful look, I nod, and we rush through the door.

CHAPTER TWENTY-FIVE

The sight that greets us is nothing short of devastation. Gareth's pristine apartment has been ransacked, with overturned furniture and broken belongings scattered everywhere. Skoro skulk around in his hall, the kitchen, and by the couch in the living room.

At the center of them all stands Sasobek, her yellow eyes cold and menacing as she surveys the destruction she's caused.

"Where is it?" she demands, her voice filled with anger and desperation. "Where's Mother's nest?"

Gareth's frame stiffens as he steps forward. His fiery fury roars to the surface. "What have you done?" he growls. "And why?"

Sasobek sneers. "You will give it to me, little brother."

"Like fuck I will. The moment Rance entrusted it to me, I locked it away for safekeeping."

If I didn't know it was in my purse and hanging at my hip, I'd believe him.

Sasobek's expression darkens, and she stalks forward. "Tell me where it is."

Gareth laughs. "Did you know three of Jules' close friends

have the power of global teleportation? It's nowhere you'll ever find it, so fuck off and get out of my home."

"Tell me where you hid it, or we'll kill your little play toy." Her gaze locks on me, and the moment she moves, the hounds leap into action.

Teeth bared and eyes blazing, Jinx throws herself at Sasobek while Onyx hangs back to protect me from her goons.

I waste no time releasing my element and creating a whip of flames. Fire might not be the most effective weapon against demon spawn but wrapping it around their throats and tightening the noose until they drop makes them just as dead.

I lash out at the nearest skoro and do that, squeezing until he crumples to the floor. That draws the attention of three others.

Fighting alongside Onyx, I'm amazed by my young hound's ferocity and skill.

Behind you. Down!

The command in my mind is so emphatic that I obey without question, and Onyx leaps over me, taking down another skoro with his powerful jaws.

"Did you talk?" I exclaim, astonished. "Gareth! Onyx can talk in my head!"

Gareth is grappling with his sister. He grunts in response. "Yes, spitfire. Maybe we can discuss that later?"

"Right." I refocus on the battle at hand and resume my assault.

I take out another of Sasobek's henchmen while Onyx rips two to ribbons. Together, we make one hell of a bloody mess, but in a fight to the death, us versus them, they are going down.

My flaming whip.

His powerful jaws.

Bodies falling. Bones snapping. Flesh tearing.

It's a brutal but beautiful thing.

Although formidable in their own right, the skoro are no match for the combined might of Onyx and me. I wonder if Gareth had this type of bond in mind all along.

He gave me Onyx as a pup when we barely knew each other. Did he want me protected even then?

A loud *crash* behind me has me spinning to check on Gareth's battle against his sister. The two of them have crashed through the kitchen table, and he has her pinned with both hands clamped around her throat.

He's let his demon out and is crushing his sister's windpipe with his massive, clawed grip. Sasobek is frantic, smacking his arms and flailing with her legs to buck him off.

It's not going to happen.

Breathing heavily, I step back, allowing Gareth to confront his sister alone. Jinx stands guard, ready to come to his aid but trusting in her master's skills.

As the battle between the two reaches its end, Rance bursts through the door and rushes across the wasteland that once was Gareth's home. "Raz, stop," he calls as he moves toward his brother. "Gareth, no."

Gareth's expression when he turns to look at his brother is haunted and homicidal. "She won't stop coming for me, Rance. She came at Jules—*again!* She dies, and this ends."

Sasobek's flailing is growing slow and sloppy.

My legs are shaky, and I plop down on one of the leather cushions in the middle of the living room floor. Onyx lays across my lap, and I pat him, watching the Poreskoro drama unfold.

Rance is on his knees with his arm over Gareth's shoulder, whispering in hushed tones close to his ear.

I've seen Rance fight. If he wanted to pull Gareth off their sister, he could do it. His lightning attacks are brutal and would knock Gareth on his ass.

He doesn't want to go the brute force route.

Likely because Gareth is just beginning to trust him again. He hadn't spoken to his oldest brother—or any of them—in almost thirty years after they dismissed his feelings, overpowered him, and locked him away so they could raze the world and not have someone with a conscience try to stop them.

Now the tables have turned.

Rance is the one pleading for compassion and staying the death sentence.

The difference is...Sasobek isn't innocent.

She brought this on herself, and if the situation were reversed, she wouldn't hesitate to kill him, me, or any of my family members.

I won't feel bad if this brotherly chat takes too long and Sasobek gasps her last breath.

Yet, Rance still tries.

Why? Sasobek is a blight on humanity—a greedy, selfish waste of air.

"Get off her!" Zissa shouts, racing in to join the family feud. "What are you doing? Raz! Let her up."

The moment Zissa rushes toward Gareth, Jinx snarls, and Onyx launches to join his mother in creating a barrier between them.

"It's fine." Rance stands and pulls Gareth to his feet. "Stand down, Zissa. Sas lives."

Zissa's green eyes are wild as she looks from Sasobek lying statue still on the wooden splinters of Gareth's kitchen table, to Rance, then at Gareth heaving for breath and trembling with rage.

"You'd really end one of us for her?" Her tone is more confused than accusatory. "Your entire life, you've lectured us about what family means and condemned us for the destructiveness of killing, but you'd kill a member of our family for your girlfriend?"

Rance curses as Gareth turns on his sister but doesn't move to get between them.

"Jules is *MINE!*" he roars, his seven-foot frame becoming even bigger with the emotion of his statement. "*She* is my family, my home, my heart, my confessor, and my love. I will not only kill anyone who comes after her, I will *destroy* them."

Zissa blinks. The shock on her face is genuine. "But we're your family…"

Gareth shakes his head. "Not even close. Family isn't a given because of the blood you share. It's forged by the care you take of the people in your life. Jules and her family and friends have shown me more kindness, forgiveness, and interest than any of you—save Rance—and that is new and still untested."

He glares at his older brother, who takes the hostility without comment.

Despite my exhaustion, I get off the floor and move to hold Gareth's hand. The moment our palms meet, the fury in the air dissipates, and he shrinks to his human size.

"We just want to be left in peace." I meet Zissa's gaze. "Repeatedly coming at us has done nothing but hurt our families. Can we please stop?"

Zissa sneers at me. "I tell you what. When you bring Draven and Lamech here and tell them you want peace, I'll consider it."

I stiffen. "As soon as you bring both sets of my parents back from the dead, biological and adoptive."

Rance places his hands on our shoulders and backs us up. "I think that's Jules' point proven, Zissa. The suffering isn't one-sided and perpetuating it is doing no one any good. It's time to break the cycle."

Zissa looks at Sasobek lying unconscious on the floor and back at Gareth. "You really think she's worth all this?"

Gareth squeezes my hand. "And so much more. I will raze the fucking world to keep her. Maybe it's selfish, but no one will take her from me. If anyone ever does…I will spend every breath for the rest of my days hunting them down to spill their blood and the blood of anyone they ever cared about."

Rance sighs. "There we have it. Gareth is very committed to

his stance, and I think he's made his expectations crystal clear to all of us."

Zissa frowns at Rance. "You're going to let this slide? Raz threatens us, and we have to back down and play nice?"

Rance drops his chin to his chest and closes his eyes. "I'm not letting anything slide. I'm trying to keep my siblings from killing one another. Respecting *Gareth's* feelings doesn't put you in a position of weakness. It simply shows that we value his feelings."

"But I don't, and after he choked out Sas, I'm sure she won't either."

Gareth rolls his eyes, marches over to where Sasobek is lying on the floor, picks her up with one hand, and navigates the carnage of his apartment. When he opens the door, he tosses his sister into the hall like a rag doll and points at the corridor.

"Get out, Zissa. I'm tired, and I've had enough. Despite every instinct I possess, I allowed Rance to convince me Sasobek should live. If I find either of you in my life, Jules' life, or cross paths with you anywhere other than Rance's place or Poreskoro Industries, I will end what Sas started here tonight."

Rance sighs and gestures at the door. "Nod and take your fucking leave, Zissa."

Gareth's sister lifts her chin and looks down her nose at me. "You always were an idiot, little brother."

"Go!" Rance shoves her toward the door. When he looks back at me, his gaze softens. "I'm sorry our dysfunction is affecting your life again, Jules. For what it's worth, I like you and think you're a lovely pair. I wish you much happiness and good fortune. You both deserve it."

"Thanks, Rance."

He looks at Gareth, but my guy is done peopling. Rance nods and frowns at the apartment. "Go to bed and take the hounds in with you. I'll take care of the cleanup. Tomorrow will be a better day."

Given that Sasobek is alive and will wake up—I doubt it.

CHAPTER TWENTY-SIX

I sigh as I gently try to disentangle myself from Gareth's arms without waking him. No easy feat, considering the man is built like a tank and has a grip that can crush bones.

The warmth of his body is comforting, but I can't shake the nagging worry that Sasobek will be back on her feet today and out for blood.

Why did she come at us so hard for the little nest?

Is it jealousy about her little brother getting their mother's keepsake? Would she trash his life and start a war over a meditation nest?

That seems totally counterintuitive.

I finally free myself and roll to sit on the edge of the bed. Onyx is still snoring contentedly on the floor beside where I slept, and I ease off the mattress, careful not to disturb him.

Jinx isn't a concern. She's sitting up like the Sphinx in front of the bedroom door, on high alert, exactly as she was last night when we retired.

All our sexy intentions got wiped away by the home invasion. Other than a few grumbles and a couple of grunts, Gareth said nothing as we got ready for bed and crashed onto the mattress.

I pad around barefoot and gather my clothes. Gareth's master bedroom is filled with soft morning light, making everything seem peaceful and calm.

A stark contrast to the chaos beyond this door.

After pulling on my yoga pants under his T-shirt that I wore to bed, I stretch my arms above my head. The series of soft *pops* in my joints and neck are satisfying.

I bend straight-legged and hook my arms around the backs of my knees.

"May I wake up every day of my life to this view," Gareth comments behind me.

I shift to the side of my leg to look at him upside-down. "I'm stretching in your old T-shirt with morning hair and no makeup. I'm sure you can aim higher."

He rolls onto his side and props his head on his raised palm. "You underestimate the appeal of your ass in stretch pants and the 'just got out of my bed' look."

I chuckle, straighten, and bring my right arm across my chest to twist and stretch out my shoulder. "It's going to be a long day. I thought a jog and a good dose of fresh air might clear my head."

"I'll join you. Give me two minutes to piss and pull on some clothes."

I'm about to argue that clearing my head goes better if I'm alone, but watching his naked ass cross the room is distracting.

"You don't have to come, you know? I'm a big girl."

The low rumble of his laughter echoes off the hard surfaces of the washroom, followed by the toilet flushing, then the faucet turning on. "No, you're a tiny girl, and alone you're too easily outnumbered and taken down."

"Not every jogger gets mugged, broody."

He exits the bathroom and heads to his dresser. "You're not just any jogger. One of our first encounters was me stepping in to save you from being killed while jogging."

True story.

Skinheads hopped up on Second Sight and aiming to take out a few fae freaks targeted Backup and me. They didn't count on a demon prince coming to my rescue.

"What are the odds that would happen again? Like, next to nothing."

He chuckles, pulls on a pair of boxers, and threads his arms into a clean T-shirt. When his head pops through the neck opening, he winks at me. "With you, there's no telling."

I laugh, and since he's awake now, I take my turn in the bathroom before we go. "That was at the beginning of my transition, though. I'm much tougher now, and I was going to take Jinx with me."

"That's good to hear. You get five good girl points for planning to take her with you."

I finish washing my hands and rejoin him in the bedroom. "What are good girl points?"

He grins. "They're like sexual currency. You collect them for taking care of yourself and fighting the urge to be reckless and make me worry. In return, you can cash them in."

I sit on the edge of the bed and prop my heel on the frame to pull my socks on. "Is there a menu of offerings and what they cost?"

He grins. "Invested in this, are you?"

"How could I not be?"

He blinks. "Honestly, I was joking. I didn't realize there were things you'd like us to do that we're not already doing."

I wave away the concern slipping into his eyes. "There is nothing we do or don't do that leaves me wanting more."

"All right, then you tell me your wish list, and I'll assign the points."

I laugh. "Yeah? Do you trust me enough to let me take the reins?"

One eyebrow arches. "I did until you started cackling maniacally."

I laugh harder. "I am not cackling maniacally, and I promise I'll come up with some great menu items."

He shrugs. "Whatever you want—as long as I get a veto if I hate it."

I push up and kiss his cheek. "Done deal."

My mind reels with ideas as we lead the dogs up the hall and get our first glimpse of Gareth's apartment.

I stop, and my mouth falls open. "Hubba wha? How…"

There's no sign of the destruction Sasobek and her asshole skoro wrought. There's no sign of the shredded skoro either.

"Your brother did this?" I run my hand over the sofa's soft leather cushions. The same cushions that were slashed with a blade and hemorrhaging stuffing last night. "Wow. He's good."

Gareth chuckles and heads over to make us coffee. One of the many life changes I've adapted to since dating Gareth is the indulgent succulence of coffee made with a French press.

Me likey.

"My brother is definitely at the top of this game, but his success is largely due to him having talented people at his fingertips. The witch who did this was likely Aimelee, a Cajun hoodoo priestess from New Orleans. She's very expensive, and he'll likely owe her a favor for coming here and restoring my home in such a rush, but there's no one better."

"No kidding. Aimelee is da bomb."

He hands me my mug of java bliss, and I take a careful sip of the steaming liquid before wandering around.

Nothing is out of place. No damage. No bodies. No evidence of there ever having been a ransacking and battle to the death in here.

"You realize why Rance pulled out the stops to make this right for you, right?"

Gareth glances over the edge of his mug and swallows. "Because Sasobek is a bitch, and he didn't want me hunting her down and killing her—again."

I shake my head. "He made this perfect for you—got you the best and put a rush on it—to prove that you can count on him. He's showing you he has no intention of letting you down."

He takes his coffee and sips it, staring out the window for a few minutes in silence. "I don't know how to trust him again—any of them."

"That's completely understandable. They negated your feelings and silenced your opposition by tossing you into a dungeon in hell and leaving you there. It's reprehensible, but more than that, it was hurtful."

He shrugs. "Life with my siblings was always more nature than nurture."

"What about with your parents?"

"Yeah, well, the thing with figureheads is that they always have more important things to deal with. They loved us in their way, but that didn't translate into much of a life with them."

I set my coffee down and wrap my arms around him, pressing my cheek against his chest. "I'm sorry you missed out on all the laughter and warm fuzzies of loving and being loved by family. But if toughing it out is what made you the man you are today, I won't wish it was any different."

He chuckles. "Thanks?"

I ease back and smile at him. "I will, however, fill your life now with as much laughter and warm fuzziness as you can take."

He drops his head and meets my lips for a kiss. "You want to skip the jog and start right now? I can think of a few ways to get your endorphins rushing and your muscles stretched without us leaving the apartment."

"All right, but I'll warn you, I was looking forward to quite a workout to burn off the past few days."

Gareth leans to the side and sets his coffee on the table. "Challenge accepted."

It must be almost lunch when I wake, wrapped in Gareth's arms. We're naked and stretched out in his custom fireplace's blue flames. With only a couple of sips of coffee in my belly, there's no way I can loaf and lounge any longer.

As they say, one cannot live on love alone.

I think about that as I extricate myself and sit on the edge of the hearth, cooling off. *Love.* Is that where we are? Am I in love with Gareth Poreskoro?

I'm not sure because I've never been this into a guy, but if I'm not in love yet, I'm love adjacent.

After hearing what he said to Zissa and Rance last night, it's obvious that Gareth's right there with me. "She *is my family, my home, my heart, my confessor, and my love. I will not only kill anyone who comes after her, I will destroy them.*"

Those are some pretty definitive declarations. I run them over in my mind and gauge how I feel about them. It probably shouldn't please me so much that he vowed to kill anyone who threatens me or my family.

Logically, that's a bit over the top.

In his life and with the people we have coming at us, I like him being an alpha protector. Who am I kidding? I would kill anyone who comes after him.

Yeah, this is what love looks like—at least for us.

I stride into the bedroom and reach into my duffle to fish out my purse. After I make quick work of the chewy granola bar I have in there, I take out his mother's meditation nest.

How could this beautiful piece, intricately woven and adorned with shimmering crystals, cause so much trouble? Taking it to the chair by the window, I sit in the midday sun, cross my legs in front of me, and cradle it in my cupped palms.

Gareth said this is how his mother used it, so who knows, maybe I can share a little Zen and see what all the fuss is about.

With it resting in my palms, I run my fingers along the soft silver fibers, taking in the craftsmanship.

There must be something more to it, something hidden within its enchanting design. I close my eyes and focus my energy on the nest, trying to sense any lingering magic or hidden secrets.

The room grows warmer, and I sense a faint pulsing energy building around me. It's subtle and would be easy to miss if I weren't actively searching for it.

I concentrate harder, hoping to uncover the truth behind this mysterious keepsake.

A sudden surge of power courses through me as I delve deeper, nearly knocking me off balance. The nest glows with a soft, golden light, and I feel a connection to something ancient, something powerful.

It's as if I've tapped into the very essence of the fae kingdom of Lasair—no, not only Lasair.

I feel the power of the fire kingdom, but I also feel earth, wind, water…and magic.

It dawns on me then. How did Gareth's mother give birth to six children and all end up with distinct elements? Lamech was earth, as is Zissa, Rance commands the power of lightning storms, Gareth is fire… I'm not sure what Draven was. Is Sasobek magic?

I think about her attacks on us, and I'm not sure I've ever seen her use an element. Rance and Gareth have both mentioned she takes after their father the most.

Did she get passed over on the elemental gene? Is she more demon than fae?

While those questions swirl languidly in my mind, I enjoy the strength and clarity the little nest affords me. It's like a prism focusing on the realm's natural energies and giving me access to them.

It's amazing.

As I relax and give in to the majesty of the magical energy, my cells fire to life, feeding off the elemental magic available.

"Jules?" I hear Gareth call my name, but it doesn't feel like he says it from the same room. His voice feels distant, like a void of space separates us. "Jules, if you can hear me, I need you to come back to me."

If I can hear him? It strikes me as an afterthought that there's an edge to his voice, concern maybe.

I slowly pull away from the magical wonder of his mother's little nest, rejuvenated by the intensity of the connection. It's clear this keepsake is more than a meditation tool—it's like an elemental conductor.

After blinking to refocus my vision, the first thing I realize is Gareth is kneeling in front of the chair. His dark hair is tousled from sleep, and concern etches his face.

The second thing is that I'm on fire and his leather club chair is burning around me.

"Oh, shit. I'm sorry." I hop out of the chair and point my palm at the fire. I intend to absorb the flames, but a stream of water exits my palm, and I douse the chair.

Gareth's eyes widen, and his mouth drops open. "Where the fuck did that come from?"

CHAPTER TWENTY-SEVEN

We shower quickly and dress, making ourselves presentable before calling in the brain trust. Tad portals Azland and my siblings over and Dionysus brings Sloan from Toronto.

"First off, are ye all right?" Sloan looks me over. "Would ye feel better if we popped over to my father's clinic and he had a look at ye?"

I wave that away. "I feel fine, and I'm pretty sure I know what happened, even though I don't know *how* it happened."

I sit on the hearth's ledge and try to explain it as well as I can—the meditation nest, the energy it filled me with, and waking up to find the chair on fire and putting the flames out with water.

"May I examine the keepsake?" Sloan gestures at the silver nest.

Gareth nods. "If it helps us figure out how Jules suddenly had command over another element, by all means."

Sloan, Azland, and Dionysus shift to the kitchen to have a confab, and my siblings and Tad stick with Gareth and me.

"I know Sloan asked you, but are you really okay?" Kenzie is sitting on the coffee table opposite me, looking like she wants to lay her healing hands on me.

I smile. "I promise I'm okay. It was more overwhelming than anything, but not in a bad way. I wouldn't exactly call it meditation. When I connected with the keepsake's power, it felt like I could collect and store the elemental energy around me."

"You were consuming it," Gareth interjects. He's sitting on the arm of the leather sofa.

I meet his gaze. "What? Why do you say that?"

"Because that's why I woke up. I felt you drawing my fire energy away from me."

I look him over, the horror of that hitting me hard. I've been caught in that kind of connection twice and had my essence drained. It was terrible. "I'm so sorry." I move to stand before him, checking him over. "I didn't mean to. I would never knowingly do that to you."

He captures my hands and kisses my knuckles. "I know that. It wasn't the horrible essence siphoning that my siblings and their skoro inflict."

"Are you sure?"

"Positive. It was more like..." He glances up as if trying to picture the right way to describe it. "It was like taking a paper fan and sweeping through smoke. It tugged at my fire in gentle, swirling wisps, coaxing it toward you."

Okay, that doesn't sound as horrible as I feared.

"What about now?" Tad watches us. "Do you feel drained now, Gareth?"

He shakes his head. "No. I'm fine."

"Would you be fine if you hadn't called me out of it? If I intentionally went into a meditative state to consume power from around me, would it have stolen your essence and left you drained?"

"I have no way of answering that." Gareth pulls me to stand between his knees. "No harm done, spitfire. I'm good."

I hug him, trembling at the thought of draining his fire and not being aware of it.

Kenzie pats the stone hearth beside her, beckoning me back to my place. "Gareth is fine. Now, explain it to us so we can help figure it out. What did you feel?"

I reclaim my spot, draw a deep breath, and cast my mind back to the moment I was deep within the meditation. "It was like I was at the center of this immense web. Instead of feeling only the warmth and strength of my fire connection, I felt everything. The firmness of earth, the gentle touch of the wind, the cool embrace of water, and the ethereal pulse of air. It was like the meditation nest became a conduit, channeling all the fae elements into me."

Azland glances up from the silver nest across the room. "You felt a connection to all the elements? Simultaneously?"

"Yes, and it wasn't only a passive feeling. It was energizing, like my cells were fueling and firing with the power of all the elements."

Dionysus arches a brow. "That's unexpected. Fae have their specific connections, but for one to channel all the elements... that's unusual."

"Obviously, the nest is a powerful enchanted object," Tad observes. "It amplifies or changes a person's connection to the elements and somehow draws power to feed it."

Gareth frowns. "In Jules' case, she didn't mean to, but I can see it potentially being dangerous if the wrong person got hold of it."

I hear the subtext of his thought. *Sasobek.*

Maybe she learned what her mother's ancestral keepsake could do, and that's why she wanted it so badly. I shudder, thinking about the implications. "Thankfully, we have it and will keep it safely out of the hands of people who might use it unwisely."

Sloan moves into the window's light and raises his hand with the nest cradled in his palm. "There's definitely potent magic within this item. Ancient, too."

Azland has a hand up to assess the little silver troublemaker and turns to fix his gaze on Gareth. "What do you know of your mother's heritage? Before becoming a fae queen?"

Gareth rubs his fingers over his stubbled jaw. "She was the daughter of a daughter of a daughter of a queen back many generations, but when she fell in love with my father, she was cast out of her queendom."

"You never went there?"

"No."

"Did you know any of your fae family on her side?"

"No. All I remember is that she was beautiful, kind, and graceful—a queen in every sense."

"Was she an elemental queen?" Azland asks.

His ebony brow pinches. "I never saw her command an element, at least not the way we do. She was a powerful fae, so she could affect nature and breezes and make water sparkle to amuse us as children."

"But not in an offensive power type of way," Sloan clarifies.

"Not that I recall."

Dionysus leans back against the edge of the kitchen counter, his eyes narrowed. "If she didn't command elements, how could she birth children who did, each with a different affinity?"

Kenzie chimes in, her eyes bright. "Maybe it wasn't her innate power, but something she accessed through the meditation nest."

Zephyr frowns. "You think she was holding the nest and meditating during sex with the demon king?"

Gareth makes a face and holds up his hand. "Let's not envision my parents procreating in any frame of the imagination. Our question is about the nest."

Azland carefully examines the nest in Sloan's hands, his fingers tracing its intricate design. "Then let's postulate this nest is imbued with ancient magic, one that empowers the holder to consume and command elemental energies."

I absorb the implications of that. "Maybe it wasn't a during sex thing, but a during pregnancy thing. Rance said he remembers their mother sitting on the balcony in the sun, holding the nest for hours. If she was accessing the power of the nest while pregnant, maybe it affected the unborn children she carried."

"Then each child might be imprinted with a different elemental affinity," Sloan concludes.

Azland frowns. "That might explain why The Six and their spawn consume elemental energy for power."

Gareth looks horrified by that revelation. "I always thought that vile affliction could only have come from my father's lineage. My mother would never have preyed upon others."

"Maybe she didn't realize." I try to make sense of it all and think of a way to make this right for him. "Maybe she thought she was imbuing her children with power and making you all even more special."

"If her family's legacy was so deeply intertwined with this nest, wouldn't she have known that?" he asks.

"Adding demon genes into the mix is likely what did it," Dionysus observes. "By your account, your mother fell in love with a demon, which was forbidden and rejected. If no one before her paired up with someone from hell, maybe she didn't know the implications."

The room quiets down, and I focus on Gareth. "What element was Sasobek born with?"

Gareth exhales slowly, looking a tad uncomfortable. "Sas has never possessed an element. We assumed it was because she inherited more from our father's side—the demon king lineage. It's a big part of why she's always so angry and violent."

I swallow, the truth unfolding in my mind. "What if it's not about your father? What if she's more like your mother?"

Sloan frowns. "Yer thinkin' that because Gareth's mother

never had a direct elemental affinity, Sasobek might've inherited that trait?"

"Yeah. They assumed Sasobek has no elemental power because she's tied more directly to their father's demonic heritage. But their mother, like Sasobek, never commanded an element."

"Maybe that's why she hates elementals so much," Kenzie adds.

Makes sense. "She felt left out. Her five siblings had elemental abilities, and she was the odd one out. If she knew or suspected the reason lay in her being too much like their mother, her frustration would've been compounded."

Gareth runs a hand through his hair, looking thoughtful. "Sas always had a complicated relationship with our mother. Maybe you're onto something."

"It could also explain what Sasobek was doing in Toronto." I raise my gaze to meet the eyes of the others in the room.

Briar frowns. "What do you mean?"

"Think about it. She had Belvedere testing and draining the elemental street kids," I state, my mind whirring as puzzle pieces snap into place. "We also found a bunch of ancient objects in his workshop."

Gareth's gaze narrows on me. "You think she figured out the power of the nest and was trying to create a similar object that would afford her elemental power as the nest did for our mother?"

"That's exactly what I think. Then, when she saw us with the OG nest, she went full psycho, attacked you, and ransacked your home."

"What's that now?" Zephyr frowns.

I wave away his curiosity. "It was a long, hellish night with a lot of bloodshed, but she didn't get what she was looking for."

Gareth sighs and extends his hand toward Azland to reclaim his property. "We can't allow her to find it or wield it. As much as

I treasure the connection with my mother, we'll have to find somewhere safe where she can't get hold of it."

Sloan steps forward. "I have access to several vaults and guarded shrines of enchanted objects. If you want help to secure your mother's treasure, I'm happy to take responsibility for it."

Gareth runs his fingers over the fine weaving of the silver strands and frowns. "I'll consider that, thank you."

"Let's assume we get the nest tucked away before Sasobek gets her hands on it," Azland continues. "She still might be far enough along in her experimenting to craft an empowered object that could absorb and control the power of the elements. How do we stop that?"

No one seems to know the answer.

"We need to remove her opportunity to drain elementals," Briar declares. "We're scattered here, and more than half of our number don't understand their element or how to control it. I say we stop talking about the next steps and move everyone to the elemental kingdoms to regroup and reestablish our race."

My head spins as all the blood rushes to my pounding heart. "Move? For how long?"

"However long it takes. That's our home."

"No, Montréal is our home."

Briar meets my gaze, and his expression tells me this isn't something he spouted off from the top of his head. "Hannah and I have been talking about it since we rescued Payton. Then, with what happened with Ryan, and now the earth elementals... Yeah, I think we need to consider what's best for everyone, not just us."

The look he spears me with pierces straight through my heart. He wants to break up the band. He found out he's the king of a ruined land and wants to rebuild.

That's commendable, but...*seriously?*

"That's a conversation for another time," Kenzie interjects. Her gaze mirrors the hurt and shock I feel. "Right now, we need to figure out how close Sasobek got to her goal and how to stop her. Where are the boxes of information and the enchanted objects you found in the candy factory's basement?"

"At our Toronto office," Sloan answers. "Calum's been inventoryin' them and makin' copies."

"Okay, Jules, why don't you, Gareth, and Azland go with Dionysus to Toronto? We'll talk to the kids and see if they know anything about the experiments Belvedere did on them. Maybe now that we know what they were trying to do, we can figure out how close they were to succeeding."

I nod, my chest still tight from Briar's emotional bomb drop. "Yeah, okay."

"Aye then, to Toronto you go." Tad motions us toward the Greek god.

Dionysus grins. "To the Batcave!"

Portaling under Dionysus' god power leaves me a little lightheaded. The world blurs for a second before I stand in the middle of the Toronto guild office. If I didn't know it was the headquarters for the empowered policing agency, I'd never suspect it was anything other than a normal workplace.

There are three private desk areas behind glass walls to the left of the door, a large conference table in the main room, a wall of mounted television monitors, and a couple of stand-up computer terminals.

Nothing remotely magical about it.

Not like Bakkali's crystal palace.

When we've got our feet fully under us, Dionysus stretches out his arms theatrically and bows. "Welcome to the heart of our operations!"

Sloan chuckles and gestures at the table. "We've gone through most of the paperwork ye found. A great deal of it is encrypted and unreadable."

"Now that we know what it's all about, maybe you can break the encryption," I comment.

"That's certainly possible."

"What about the objects you found?" Gareth asks. "Do any of them resemble the nest or give off a similar energy signature?"

Dionysus moves to one of the side tables, revealing a large box. "All the baubles and trinkets are in here."

As he opens the box, a myriad of shimmering auras washes over me. The magical potency of some of these items is strong enough to make the hair on my arms stand on end.

Sloan carefully pulls out a tarnished silver pendant shaped like a labyrinth. "None of these gave off any discernable energy, but now I wonder if it only responds to elementals. Do ye want to hold it and see if ye sense anything?"

"Sure. I can try." I reach out, letting my fingertips graze the pendant's surface. There's nothing at first, but when I take it to a window, sit on the floor, and settle in, it doesn't take long before a rush of mixed energy pulses through me.

It's not exactly like the nest, but it's close. "This is powerful. Definitely something Sasobek would be interested in."

Gareth lifts a dark crystal shard from the box and brings it over to sit with me. He holds it for a moment and frowns. "This resonates with a deep, primal magic. Almost demonic in nature."

I swallow. "Could that be a part of her experiment?"

Gareth frowns at the crystal in his hands and shakes his head. "With Sas, there's no telling. One thing is for certain, though. No good can come of this thing. Sloan, you said you could secure my mother's keepsake. Can you also dispose of things like this?"

Sloan nods. "I have a very effective spell that will drain the dark energy from the crystal and render it harmless."

"Good, then I suggest taking this one off the board sooner rather than later." Gareth sets the crystal on the long conference table, away from the other objects. "All right. Let's see what other nightmares she and her witch doctor have come up with."

"Then what?" I ask. "Do you have any idea how to rein her in?"

Gareth shakes his head. "Other than our father, there's only ever been one person Sas fears enough to listen to."

I think about that, and the answer is obvious. "Rance."

CHAPTER TWENTY-EIGHT

We work diligently with Sloan and the others in Toronto, sifting through the objects and sorting them based on their energies and potential uses. Azland and Dionysus track the descriptions in the notebooks, and we try to determine if all the magical artifacts are accounted for.

They're not.

Two hours after we began, Gareth and I stand in Rance's office at Poreskoro Industries. We're pointing out the drawings of three objects covered in symbols and incantations that were not among the treasures we confiscated.

"These are the most recent experiment notes." Gareth frowns. "I recognize some symbols from our family's archives, but you've always been more of a historian than me."

Rance leans over his desk, scanning the notes. "This is a procedure to transfer elemental energy. By the way they arranged the symbols in this sequence, it wouldn't be a pleasant process."

I shake my head. "The elemental kids we rescued said it was torture. It took days and weeks for them to recover after a session with Belvedere."

Rance frowns and meets our gaze. "I still don't understand. Why would Sasobek be going to all this trouble? Not to sound indelicate, but if she had the teens captured, why not simply consume them?"

"Because we don't think this is about consumption," Gareth replies. "We think it's about wielding elemental power."

Rance frowns. "Sas doesn't have an element."

We spend the next fifteen minutes catching Rance up about what happened with me this morning when I tried the nest and our theories about their mother imbibing them during pregnancy.

Then we move on to our thoughts that Sasobek might be more fae than demon, and that's why she didn't inherit an elemental gene.

Rance grunts. "Well, if that's true, she'll be even more irate than she was growing up without an element. She based her entire personality on being just like our father."

Gareth nods. "It's clear she's trying to create something monumental. Something to not only consume elemental power but also to wield it."

Rance's gaze fills with frustration and concern. "She's always been cunning and dominant, but this... I'm not sure I understand what's gotten into her."

"You think there's more to it?" Gareth asks.

"There has to be." He strides over to the wet bar and removes the crystal stopper from the decanter. "Let's say she succeeds or has already succeeded in recreating an object with the same magical effect as the nest."

He extends his hand toward me, offering me a tumbler of amber liquid. I decline, and he holds it out to Gareth, who accepts. Then he pours himself one. "So, she has her object, can draw elemental power into her cells, and can wield the five elements. What then?"

Gareth sips from the glass. "She'll have an end goal...likely something violent that puts her in a position of supremacy."

"Right, so what is it? We'll know better how to stop her if we know what she wants."

I look between them, feeling the weight of protecting the elementals who are unknowingly caught in this intricate web of family dysfunction. "Does it matter why? We need to stop her before she kills the few elementals left in existence."

Gareth tips his tumbler back and swallows the contents of his glass in two quick gulps. "I don't suppose you're keeping tabs on her movements and know where we can find her?"

Rance's eyebrows arch. "What kind of brother do you take me for? Tracking Sas would be an invasion of privacy and tantamount to me saying I don't trust her."

Gareth sets his empty glass on the corner of Rance's desk. "Which you don't, so where is she?"

He sips and shrugs. "She's been frequenting the underground circuits while here in Montréal. It seems she's using the dark network as a base to gather information and possibly recruit ne'er-do-wells to build an empowered following."

I love that Rance is the kind of guy who uses words like ne'er-do-wells. "When you say the underground circuits, do you mean the black market?"

Rance tips his head from side to side as if considering. "The black market is one facet of it."

Gareth meets my gaze. "Then add empowered dealings, secret meetings, and a network of thugs for hire that offer their powers to the highest bidders."

"Seriously? And this is in my city?"

"In almost every city," Rance adds.

"It's the perfect place for Sasobek to find a witch who can empower rare and powerful magical objects or create her version of the nest."

I'm still stunned there's a dark web of empowered people

working within my city, and I didn't know about it. "Fine. It's a starting point. I say we infiltrate the underground circuit, gather intel, and hopefully find your sister before she does any more harm."

Rance's lips quirk in a sly smile. "Infiltrate, shall we?"

Gareth chuckles. "Jules, you forget who you're talking to. Think of the underground circuit as a tight-knit community of empowered criminals—a city within the city—and Rance as their beloved mayor."

I meet Rance's amused smirk, and my cheeks grow hot. "Right. I forgot. You've seemed so professional and legitimate lately."

Rance winks. "I admit I've been on my best behavior since you became part of the family. Still, my business dealings cover a broad range of endeavors and often take me into the dark waters of the violent and vile. We are demons, after all."

"Half demon," I remind him. "I don't think you're as violent and vile as you let on."

His smile fades as his pupils flare gold and electricity snaps in the air between us. The hair on my entire body stands on end, and a chill runs the length of my spine. "Then you'd be wrong, Jules. I'll never lie to you about who I am but don't mistake me for my brother. I might dress in a tailored suit and value manners and chivalry, but I am definitely my father's son."

I swallow and give myself an inward shake. "Consider me reminded."

Guided by Rance's steady steps, our descent into the underground is a stark contrast to the vibrant city above. The clamor of Montréal's streets is muted as we navigate a series of abandoned access tunnels and concealed doorways.

The air is thick, tinged with an electric charge, and my senses are alert to every shadow and sound.

We stop briefly in front of a heavily graffitied patch of concrete wall, and Rance trails his index finger from the ground, straight up seven feet, over three, and back down to the ground.

After tracing the large rectangle, he presses on a painted symbol halfway up the right boundary line he drew, and a door appears and opens behind his force.

Huh. Cool trick.

Stepping over the threshold, I wonder about calling for backup. As a cop, going into a place like this without calling it in would be a death sentence. Even with two of the Poreskoro Six, I'm not sure it's a great idea.

Not that I have much say in the matter.

I'm not sure what Gareth sees in my expression, but his hand slides against my side and he laces his fingers with mine. When he squeezes, I relax somewhat. He's telling me he's right here and won't let anything happen.

Not that I need a protector. I'm quite capable of rescuing myself. Still, it's comforting to have him here.

As we go deeper, the world transforms.

Dimly lit passages give way to an expansive cavern. Intricate arches and structures of an unknown mineral glow with a soft, bioluminescent hue. The hum of activity is palpable. Stalls and makeshift shops line the pathways, their merchants selling everything from enchanted artifacts to muscle for hire.

It's an entire city beneath my city.

"How did I not know this was down here?"

Rance glances at me sidelong and smiles. "You're not the type who runs in these circles, Jules. Don't feel slighted for not being on the invite list."

I don't feel slighted. I'm just…dazzled.

People with glimmering eyes and auras of various shades

pass, some whispering deals, others showcasing the lethality or subtlety of the powers they offer to potential clients.

Everywhere I look, there's an exchange—of goods, power, or secrets.

"Mind blown. I had no idea."

"That's a good thing, spitfire." Gareth releases my hand to wrap his arm around my shoulders and pull me close to his side.

Rance guides us, greeting various individuals with a nod or a grunt, a handshake here, and a glare there. His reputation precedes him, and seeing how comfortably he navigates this underworld is an important reminder of who he is.

Who he *really* is.

Gareth stays close, his presence a grounding force amid the overwhelming swirl of energies.

A haunting melody draws our attention as we venture deeper into the cavern. It emanates from a lounge area ahead, and I crane my neck to see who is singing.

"It's a siren," Gareth tells me.

I blink. "Seriously?"

He chuckles. "What? You don't believe me?"

The siren's song echoes throughout the space and makes me feel loose-limbed and dopey. Patrons sit on cushioned seats, entranced by her performance. Their drinks shimmer in hues of a neon rainbow.

"Wait here a moment." Rance lifts his chin and catches the attention of a man in black fatigues with small potion bottles strapped to his thigh.

Gareth nods, and the two of us step off to the side. With our backs against the stone wall, I take it all in. "It's like walking into a twisted fairy tale."

"You sound surprised."

"I guess I expected a bit more blood and grime."

He kisses the top of my head. "Dark doesn't always mean evil. Sometimes the underworld is simply about people getting what they need when there's no other option. Does that make them a criminal? Possibly, but not always."

Before I can process that, Rance returns. His gaze fixes on the far corner of the lounge. "Sasobek hasn't been here for a few days, but someone came looking for her a couple of days ago."

Following his line of sight, I spot a portly man chatting with his server in the lounge. His complexion is pale, contrasting sharply with his dark attire. As we sidle closer, notes of a British accent drift toward us, breaking through the din of the underground chatter.

"Mr. Belvedere, I presume."

Gareth waggles his brow at me and offers me his elbow. "Shall we go introduce ourselves to my sister's witch doctor?"

I accept his elbow and smile. "Why, yes. Let's."

The electric charge in the air thickens as we close the distance between us and the answers we seek.

I've always been a bit of an adrenaline junkie and learning about magical races and the beasts of the empowered world only raised the stakes to make things more exciting.

The underground crowd must pick up on the tension in the air because those who were previously engrossed in their conversations or distracted by trinkets shift their focus to telegraph our target.

As we draw nearer, Mr. Belvedere glances up. A flicker of recognition crosses his features. His bravado falters, replaced by a moment of indecision.

I've seen that same look in the eyes of perps a hundred times. He's wondering if he should run and his odds of getting away.

Not good, pudgy. Just sit your ass down.

The loud scrape of chair legs against the hard floor catches the attention of everyone in the vicinity. He bolts, trying to lose himself in the shadows of the lounge while seeking a back exit.

Gareth and Rance are off like a shot and the patrons part for them like the Red Sea.

Despite the tailored suit, Rance has legs. He races forward, cuts off Mr. Belvedere's escape route with a bolt of lighting, and singes off his eyebrows based on the yelp and how the man cups his forehead.

He veers right, but it's a feeble attempt, and Gareth is already there.

There's a brief struggle. Belvedere is surprisingly strong for his build and lashes out with magic and physical force.

His efforts are no match for the combined might of Gareth and Rance, and they quickly overpower him.

Rance grabs him by his buttoned vest and throws him against a wall, pinning him with a force that causes cracks to spread outward from the impact.

The entire underground goes quiet.

Rance seizes one of the man's wrists in a swift motion, twisting it until the bones snap.

"Enough," Gareth growls, his eyes flashing scarlet with the rise of his demon side.

Rance releases Mr. Belvedere. They steer the dazed man to the closest chair and plunk him down.

Having gotten their entertainment for the evening, the underground crowd buzzes with whispered conversations, turning their attention back to their dealings.

Rance flags down a server with a wave. "Two dragon slayers and whatever he was having, if you will. Jules? Would you like anything?"

"No, thanks." I wave the attention away and sit at the table with the others.

Rance continues as if this is merely another day in the office. Leaning close, he pushes into the man's personal space and grins. "Now, Mr. Belvedere, let's have a chat about your dealings with our sister. From what I've heard, the two of you have been rather busy. What have you crazy kids been up to?"

Mr. Belvedere is visibly uneasy. His lips are tight, but he's attempting to put on a brave face. "I'm not sure what you're going on about."

Rance accepts his drink from the server and takes a sip while she passes one to Gareth and our hostage. "Let's not play games. This will be immeasurably more enjoyable if you simply tell us what we want to know."

Mr. Belvedere shifts uncomfortably and takes three long gulps from his glass. When he swallows, he winces, and I wonder what kind of empowered concoction he's drinking tonight. "I'm afraid I can't help you. I don't know what you're talking about."

"Oh, come now," Rance continues. "We've studied your workbooks, the objects, and the enchantments. We know you recreated something powerful, something that can channel the elements. We also know there are three objects unaccounted for. What we want to know is why. What's our sister up to?"

Mr. Belvedere's gaze darts between the three of us. I can practically hear the gears turning in his mind as he weighs his options.

Still, he remains silent.

Gareth lets out an exasperated sigh. "Don't make this more difficult than it needs to be. We'll find out one way or another, and if you don't tell him, he'll get violent. You know who we are, yes?"

The British warlock weighs his options, his pride battling with his desire to avoid further harm. "I do, but I can't help you."

"So loyal." Rance grins.

"It's admirable," Gareth adds.

Rance chuckles. "However misguided. I think Mr. Belvedere here has fallen for Sasobek's charms. He thinks that protecting her agenda will win her favor."

Gareth laughs. "The moment she finds out we cornered you and had a private chat, she'll slit your throat. Our sister isn't known for trust. She'll assume you let something slip and will discard you."

The man still says nothing, and Rance's smile drops. "A smart man would be much more afraid of me than he is of her."

With a swift motion, he presses his palm to Belvedere's chest and releases his power. Electrical current passes into the man, causing him to convulse as he's electrocuted in front of us.

Gareth rolls his eyes, looking bored. "You're going to make him shit himself, and we're not ready to leave."

Rance releases the current, and Mr. Belvedere quakes for a few moments longer, his skin smoking. "All right, my brother wants me to go easy on you, so I'll give you one last chance to speak willingly."

I laugh. "That was going *easy* on him?"

Rance winks at me. "Like I said to you earlier, Jules. I'm always on my best behavior in front of you."

Yeah, well, it's hard to equate electrocuting this man with "best behavior." Still, he's an evil man, and he tortured a lot of innocent kids.

I add my two cents. "Rance is right about one thing, for sure. You being loyal to Sasobek makes no sense. If you're afraid of what one Poreskoro will do to you for talking, imagine what two of The Six will do to you for failing to respect their authority."

Rance nods. "She's got you there, old boy."

"Do you think Poreskoro men will accept failure in front of all these people? They have a reputation to uphold. You don't get to be mayor of the underworld if you don't have the balls to tear a man down to a sniveling shitty mess."

Gareth wrinkles his nose. "I'd prefer to avoid that."

"You would too, wouldn't you, Mr. Belvedere?"

The three of us wait for all that to sink in. When it doesn't look like he gets the gist of how this will play out, Rance sets his drink down and reaches for his chest again.

Gareth curses. "For fuck's sake. Tell him before he liquifies your insides."

Despite the threat of physical discomfort, Belvedere doesn't look like he's going to spill anything. Why?

"He hasn't delivered the objects to her," I reveal, reading his body language. "He's waiting around here, staying off the grid, hoping to show her what he came up with, but he hasn't given them to her yet."

Gareth takes another look at the man and grins. "Well, they'll be close at hand."

Yep, now the pudgy jerk is starting to squirm.

"You're not so stupid that you kept them on you, are you, Mr. Belvedere?"

The sweat beading on his brow is a very good sign.

Gareth chuckles and leans sideways in his chair, patting him down. He comes away with a patterned silk kerchief-wrapped bundle from his jacket pocket, and my adrenaline spikes.

Please let it be three enchanted objects.

Gareth reclaims his seat and sets the kerchief in his lap. When he unfolds the fabric, I lean over to see what we've got.

It's a copper pendant with a polished gemstone—a flat, oval green stone with white veining. Very pretty, but it's only one magical object.

"Where are the other two?" I ask.

"I don't know what you're talking about." A blotchy red mottling creeps up Belvedere's neck from the rim of his starched collar.

Rance lifts two fingers and beckons the server back.

"Sir?"

Rance smiles at the woman, who looks nervous about being called into the middle of this. "Mr. Belvedere has been loitering around town for several days. Has he met with anyone recently?"

She swallows. "A few of the locals."

He turns his head, and the man in the black fatigues with the potions strapped to his thigh rushes over. "Boss?"

"Mr. Belvedere was contracted to make something for my

sister. It seems he made three somethings and thought to improve his good fortune by selling two of them. You will find the other two items and bring them to me. Whatever the cost and whoever needs to be dealt with. There will be no side hustles on a Poreskoro contract, is that clear?"

"Yes, Boss."

Belvedere looks green.

"That completes our business. Unless you wish to tell me what you know of my sister's plans."

"Why would I? You'll kill me either way."

Rance clucks his tongue and sips his drink. "I'm not a thug. I wouldn't kill you in front of a lady. No, if you tell me, you'll still be breathing when I leave."

He hesitates, and Rance presses his hand against the man's chest. Belvedere bucks and jerks in his chair, the scent of burning skin growing stronger by the moment.

"I'm not a patient man. You die if you keep quiet. You live if you speak. That's the deal."

Belvedere thrashes a little longer, then grunts and starts to drool. "She's s-s-s-searching for a necromancer…Needs him… S'all I know…"

Rance ends the electrocution, and I exchange glances with Gareth as the man sags and doubles over in his chair, panting.

A necromancer?

Rance stands, pulls a billfold from his pocket, and drops a hundred-dollar bill. "Thank you, Mr. Belvedere. You've been very helpful."

I sit up straighter. "Wait. He doesn't get to go free. He tortured kids. He killed elementals. He can tell us where the other two objects are."

Rance offers me a patient smile. "My man will find the objects, and when my sister hears about how accommodating her man has been, she'll take care of any punishment he deserves. Trust me, Jules. Mr. Belvedere won't live out the week."

It's alarming how nonchalant Rance is about it. Then again, as he reminded me earlier, he's half demon.

After a nod from Gareth, we rise, and the interrogation is over. The puzzle pieces are falling on the table, but the picture of what they'll form is still a mystery.

CHAPTER TWENTY-NINE

Stepping through the truck bay, the sounds of home melt the day away. By the time we climb the stairs to the living area of the firehouse, the warmth and familiar smells wash over me, and the tension of the underground circuit is all but forgotten.

As always in my home, Gareth falls back and lets me take the lead. I wish he didn't feel the need to isolate himself, but I understand why he does.

Maybe one day he'll feel as welcome with my siblings as he does with me.

Zephyr, Briar, and Kenzie are huddled around the kitchen island, snacking and animatedly chatting when we crest the landing at the top of the stairs.

The atmosphere is light despite everything that's been happening. It's a testament to the resilience of my family...and of youth.

"Hey." I flash them a tired smile.

Kenzie steps forward, studying me with concern and relief. "How did it go?"

"Informational but intense." I reach for an apple from the fruit bowl.

Zephyr raises an eyebrow. A smirk plays on his lips. "Intense how? Did something happen?"

I laugh. "A lot happened, but I'm tired, and it can wait until tomorrow. How are the kids?"

I glance toward the archway that leads into our living room. There are a dozen kids sacked out on cots and in sleeping bags.

"Wait. Are they multiplying?"

Kenzie shrugs. "Our six elemental kids wanted the other fae kids, and since they had nowhere to go, Tad went and got them. They've been through a lot together and formed a bond."

I shrug. "Whatever makes them happy, I guess."

One of the best things about renovating a working firehouse into a private residence is that a building designed to hold twenty-two men in two bunk rooms and a man cave leaves a lot of floor space for us four.

"They're eager to hear about your hunt for the man who tortured them. No doubt the minute they hear your voice, they'll be flooding out here," Zephyr warns.

I close my eyes and draw a deep breath. "I haven't got the energy to go through it right now. Just tell them we found him, interrogated him, and when Sasobek finds out he spilled his guts, she'll take him out. They don't have to worry about him again."

Kenzie nods. "Good enough. We'll get the full account tomorrow."

"With that said, I really need to get horizontal. Is Tad around? Would he mind popping us to Gareth's? We wanted to check in, but I don't think I'll make it back to his apartment."

"Sure." Kenzie points her thumb toward her suite. "He's chatting online with the Heirs of the Druid Order. They've got a big Samhain celebration coming up, and he's clarifying his part in the ceremony."

"Oh, then if he's busy..."

Kenzie laughs and waves that away. "He can pop you home

and be back in the blink. He won't care. Give me a sec to ask him and for him to throw on some pants."

"Or you could stay here," Zephyr suggests. "We can clear the girls out of your bed."

"Nah, Onyx has been alone with Jinx all day, and I want to give him a quick walk and sack out."

"You can bring him home. We're cool if Gareth stays over, aren't we, Briar?"

Briar's fingers tap a restless rhythm on the countertop. "Yeah. It's fine."

I frown. "You're really selling it, B."

He looks up, and for a split second, a flicker of something—pain, anxiety—crosses his features. "Sorry. Can we talk?"

My heart sinks. "I'm really not up for a fight tonight."

He shakes his head and looks at Gareth. "It's not about you. Zephyr's right. We're working through the whole Poreskoro baggage. You've proven yourself and obviously care for Jules, so we're giving you the benefit of the doubt and moving on."

Gareth stands a little straighter. "I appreciate it."

Briar swings his gaze back to me. "Two minutes? Please?"

I nod, trying to keep my expression neutral. "Of course."

Gareth squeezes my hand in reassurance, and I follow Briar into his suite, wondering what could be on his mind. As we step inside, he closes the door softly behind us and runs a hand through his blond hair.

It's gotten long over the past weeks, turning up in curls over his ears and off the back of his neck. "Jules, I'm sorry. What I said earlier...I shouldn't have. It wasn't right. Not there, not like that."

I watch him, trying to focus on what he means. "You're going to have to give me more, Briar. It's been a sucktastic few days, and I'm wiped."

"My announcement about moving with the elementals to the earth kingdom."

"Temporarily," I clarify. "Until the elemental thing is worked out and everyone is in control of their powers, right?"

He shakes his head. "No. I want it to be more than that. I should've talked to you, Zephyr, and Kenzie privately before blurting it out…especially in front of everyone."

I cross my arms, my initial surprise giving way to understanding. "I admit, it rocked my foundation. It's always been us four against the world. Then you and Hannah talk about something so monumental, and we get brought in as an afterthought? That hurt."

Briar's eyes, usually so lively and warm, look pained. "I know. And I'm sorry." He draws a deep breath. "It's just…since I found out who I am, I feel like it all makes sense. I've always felt like I was meant for something big, that the four of us finding one another was destined. Now I'm sure of it."

"Yeah, we're elementals drawn together as a quartet, and sure, if you want to count Azland, a quint."

"True, but it's more than that. I was born into a position of responsibility—"

"Which no one expects you to assume. You're of noble birth, and if you want to learn about your parents, that's great, but you don't have to leave your family to move to the earth kingdom to unite the races. That's over and above."

"That's what a calling is, Jules. It's going over and above to follow your heart's call."

A calling? "Do you *want* to be king?"

He lifts a heavy shoulder. "It's not about the title. It's about the responsibility of having people counting on me. It's hard to explain, but when I assumed my true form, I could *feel* what the feral earth elementals felt. They were hopeless. They have nothing and no one to believe in."

"Does it have to be you?"

"I honestly think it does."

The idea of Briar leaving us to live in the fae realm breaks my heart. It steals the breath from my lungs, and I'm not sure I'll survive it.

I understand people grow up and they're supposed to move on, but we built our private spaces specifically so we could all have our area and stay together.

That was the plan.

It wasn't that he'd become the king of an elemental land and leave us.

"Is it a done deal?" My chest is so tight I can hardly breathe.

"I wouldn't make the final decision without the three of you, but it's what I want. I hope when you think about it, you can get behind the idea—maybe consider the four of us starting over there together."

My mind blanks out on that. He wants all of us to leave Montréal? Leave Charlie and the kids, my family at the Twenty-Third Precinct, and my job with Bakkali...and what about Gareth?

"Just think about it." Briar holds up his hands. "Get some sleep. We'll see what happens with the kids once we tell them about Mr. Belvedere, and we'll take it as things come. No rush. No pressure."

A knock on the door has Kenzie popping her head inside. "Everything all right in here?"

"Uh...yeah, we were talking about the king thing," Briar replies.

Kenzie comes into the room fully and squeezes both my arms. "Jules? Are you okay?"

I don't know how to answer that. On the one hand, my brother wants me to give up my entire life and identity to reclaim a heritage we know nothing about. On the other, I could stay here while he goes and faces the battles of five races alone.

Or maybe not alone.

If he asked me, he's likely asked Zephyr and Kenzie, too. What if they go? What if I'm the only one who stays? What if I lose all three of them with one decision?

"You broke her." Kenzie frowns at Briar. "What did you say?"

I tune out their conversation and move toward the kitchen. Gareth stands where I left him, and I bury my face against his chest. "Please, take me home."

The morning light filters through the gap in the blackout curtains, casting a soft glow across the room. It feels like the world outside has continued turning, although I've come to a complete stop. I'm acutely aware of the weight of the charcoal gray duvet, the silky soft pillow cradling my head, and the lingering remnants of my most recent bout of tears.

The scent of freshly brewed coffee and the tantalizing aroma of buttery cinnamon toast fill the air before I see Gareth. The *creak* of the bedroom door pulls me from my haze of self-imposed isolation.

His silhouette fills the doorway, holding a tray adorned with a carefully arranged breakfast spread.

"Morning, beautiful," he murmurs, his voice a comforting balm. Gareth moves with a graceful ease, setting the tray on the bed beside me.

I peek from beneath my covers, taking in the lovingly prepared breakfast. "You didn't have to."

Gareth settles on the edge of the bed. His fingers brush the hair away from my face. "Maybe, but I wanted to. I enjoy having you to take care of."

My heart clenches. For the past two days, he's allowed me to wallow in my pain and uncertainty, offering silent support, never pushing.

Today feels different.

"Jules," he starts, his gaze searching mine. "I get it. The weight of Briar's announcement and the decision he asked you to make is immense. But shutting out the world won't make it any easier. Your siblings love you, and they're worried."

"I don't know what to do. The thought of a future separated by realms...of potentially losing them..." My voice breaks. The weight of my emotions is too much.

He captures my hand, squeezing gently. "You don't have to figure it out right now. But hiding in here isn't the answer, either."

My gaze drifts to the tray. "But here I get to ogle you naked, and you bring me breakfast in bed."

He chuckles, the sound easing some of the tension in the room. "One has nothing to do with the other. If you showered and came for a dog walk, I'd still let you ogle me naked."

"And make me cinnamon toast?"

"Definitely."

I can't help but smile at that. I sit up, the duvet pooling around my waist. "Fine, but only because of the cinnamon toast. And because I miss my puppers."

He grins and nudges the tray closer. "He's a pureblood hellhound sired from Demon's Breath, the fiercest hound of the hell realm. He's not a pupper."

I roll my eyes and take a tentative bite. "You've never said what you would do...if I go. Would I lose you?"

Gareth bends forward and takes a bite of my toast. "Are you asking?"

"Yes."

He gives me a soul-searing look. "I'm with you however this plays out. Montréal, the earth realm, it doesn't matter. Where you go, I go because you *are* my home, Jules Gagne. I love you."

Like that, the cracks in my soul begin to heal.

Gareth gives Onyx and me a ride home, and I let him return to his life while I spend some time with my family. Zephyr's comments about not wanting me to leave the other night hit home. He's been going through a lot with Ryan and the trip to Gailleann, so if he needs me to be present for a while, I'm here.

I wait until Gareth's truck turns at the bottom of the long driveway, then take Onyx around the side of the firehouse and into the backyard. My boy always likes to do a perimeter check on his yard if we've been away.

There's no telling what the squirrels and bunnies might get up to without him here to keep them in line.

As we step around the back corner of the building, I button my lapel and fish my leather gloves out of the pockets of my trench.

It feels like frost is on its way.

I find Zephyr seated on the patio, staring at the worn wooden chest he brought back from Gailleann.

"Hey, there." I step under the overhang of the back patio and drop into the chair next to him. "I get the need for fresh air, but it's more than fresh out here. It's downright nippy. Everything okay?"

He gestures at the chest with its intricate carvings and fae design. "It's a lot, you know?"

"True story."

"I mean, I want to know about my parents, but I'm afraid too. What if they weren't good people? If they were amazing people, is it disloyal to *Maman* and Papa if I consider them my parents?"

I let out a long sigh, and air condenses before my lips. "I like to think *Maman* intended for us to find our biological parents and learn about our origins. In that vein, I think she and Papa are watching over us, pleased that we finally found out who we really are."

"You think?"

"Yeah, I think." I stand and run my hand over the top of the chest. "So, are we doing this, or what?"

He stands and studies my resolve. "You don't mind hanging out with me while I rummage through this?"

"That's what big sisters are for, Z. I'm dying to know about your father. Come on, he has to be amazing to have sired such an awesome son."

"Yeah, I guess that's true." Zephyr laughs and opens the chest, revealing the objects we barely had time to look at back in Gailleann.

The first thing that catches my eye is a dagger in a leather sheath. Its hilt is embedded with sapphires that shimmer in the sun's light, and when I draw it free, the blade looks sharp enough to cut the air.

"Wicked." I tilt it in the light so Zephyr gets the full effect.

He only glances at it, focusing on the journal Gareth found for him while searching for a spell to help Ryan. "I've been dying to go through this."

"Then sit and enjoy. I'm happy to dig through the treasure chest to see what loot you've got."

"No. The journal can wait. Once I sit and start reading, I doubt I'll be able to stop. Let's treasure hunt first." He sets the journals aside, and his fingers brush over a small collection of photographs.

Carefully, almost reverently, he picks up one and stares at it. Then he offers it to me.

It's a black-and-white image of a young couple. The woman with wavy black curls cascading over her shoulders cradles a newborn baby. The man beside her with sharp, elegant features looks on with unmistakable pride and affection.

"You come from two very pretty people, Z."

Zephyr nods, swallowing hard. "My mom was really beautiful, don't you think?"

"Yeah, she was."

For a long moment, the two of us are silent, lost in the weight of a life taken from us.

"Look how they loved you. That has to mean a lot…I mean, for you to see it with your own eyes."

He smiles wistfully. "It really does."

It fills me with sorrow and joy. Although I hate the idea of Briar wanting to leave and us being separated, I get it.

We're all searching for our roots, wanting the sacrifices of our parents to mean something, hoping to find some peace to anchor us to our lives now.

CHAPTER THIRTY

After an hour to ourselves, Zephyr and I climb the stairs with Onyx racing past us. Our minds and hearts are filled with more questions about our pasts, and our bodies are chilled to the bone.

Our plan is simple. Hot chocolates with a healthy dose of Baileys Irish cream.

The drink of the fireside Canadian crowd.

Alas, it's not meant to be. Our quiet reprieve from life is over before we have a mug in our hands.

By the top step, chatter, laughter, and a chaotic mix of animated conversations from a dozen teenagers fill the space.

Bodies are sprawled on the couches, sitting on the floor, some leaning against the walls, and each one has a story that brought them here.

To our living room.

They're safe here, and we don't know where else they can go. Sasobek is still out there. There are two objects unaccounted for. Although Rance and Gareth are both trying, we have no idea what a necromancer has to do with Sasobek's endgame.

I let out a low whistle. "Man, we have a full house."

Zephyr nods. "And have had for a while now."

I suppose I missed the implications of all that by choosing to stay at Gareth's. "Sorry. I haven't been pulling my weight. I should've been around more."

"You were missed. I'm not going to say you weren't, but we understand and are happy you're happy. I've been thinking about it, and yeah, it makes sense your perfect man is half demon."

I laugh and slide my attention sideways to hear this. "Oh? Why is that?"

"Because a guy has to have an edge and a bit of a death wish to take you on."

I smack his arm. "Harsh."

He winks and strikes off toward his suite with his father's chest under his arm.

I stride to the counter, open the cupboard, and pull out two mugs. "I'm making hot chocolate for Z and me. Do you guys want one?"

Kenzie and Tad look up from their game of Scrabble. "No, thanks. We just finished brunch."

I fill the kettle and pull out the chocolate mix while listening to Briar chatting with a group of kids, telling them about things we saw in the fae realm.

When Zephyr returns from putting away his mementos, he joins me behind the kitchen island. "He makes it sound a lot less unnerving than it was."

I chuckle and reach for the kettle's handle when it clicks off, and the water is hot. "Hindsight, right?"

Because while things in the fae realm were amazing, it was less fun and more overwhelming than Briar's story portrays. Still, they eat it up.

"Do you really think we'll go there?" the girl with the curly blonde hair asks.

Briar's expression brightens as he answers. "Yeah, Macy, I do."

"Your palace is big enough for all of us?" another kid asks.

Briar laughs. "The palace of the earth kingdom can house all of us, and you wouldn't have to share rooms."

"But we could if we wanted, right?"

"If you wanted, sure."

Briar has always been great with kids, but as he talks to the kids we rescued, I realize it's more than him being a good guy. He's already taken his role of king and is caring for his people.

Here, they can't be out, living their best lives. They're confined within the walls of our house, waiting for Sasobek to send her army here to consume them.

Helping them means more than getting them off the street. It's about providing them with the opportunity to live a meaningful and safe life.

They deserve more than this and whether it's temporary or permanent can be decided later.

"Jules?" Zephyr's voice pulls me from my thoughts. Concern is evident in his eyes. "Everything all right?"

I shake my head. "If we don't go, what happens to them? Social services? Foster care? That won't work. It's too dangerous for them to be out in the world while Sasobek is plotting."

His gaze is heavy as he watches them laugh with our brother. "What does drawing elemental power have to do with necromancy, anyway?"

"I've been asking myself that same question for two days. Rance and Gareth are searching for her or Zissa to find out, but they've both fallen off the map."

"Maybe Gareth crushed Sasobek's windpipe, and she *is* dead. Maybe our problem isn't a problem anymore."

I laugh. "We couldn't be so lucky. No, she's out there. Sasobek has something in mind, and she'll come at us to get to these kids sooner rather than later."

"What do you think we should do?"

I draw a deep breath and exhale. "Briar's right. I think we have the best chance of survival if we reunite the elementals and rebuild a community."

Zephyr's brow arches. "Yeah? You're sure?"

I snort. "I'm not sure of anything, but at the palace, we'd have the room and the elemental resources to fortify our defenses. These kids need to learn to control their elements and discover their power. It's their best chance at living through this."

Briar and Kenzie must sense the importance of the conversation because they drift into the kitchen. The four of us lean on the top of the kitchen island, and I meet their gazes. "You're right, B. We should move to the earth palace and reclaim our ancestral power. If these kids have any chance of a long and healthy life, they need us to step up for them."

Briar straightens and meets my gaze with excitement and concern. "Are you sure, Jules?"

I nod. "If we go, we go together. It's all of us or none."

Briar reaches forward, pressing his palm against the counter. "I'm in. You all know how I feel."

Zephyr sets his hand on Briar's. "They'll learn to control their elements way faster in the fae realm than here."

Kenzie sets her hand on the pile. "I still haven't seen my home kingdom, and I'm certainly not going to let you have all the fun."

I cap the pile with my hand. "Then it's settled. We'll contact all the elementals we know. We'll figure out what we need to make this work. Then we're moving to the fae realm."

ENDNOTE

Thank you for reading *Intellectus: Origins Discovered,* book five in the Chronicles of an Urban Elemental series. While the story is fresh in your mind, and as a favor to Michael and me, please click HERE and tell other readers what you thought.

A quick star rating and/or one sentence can mean so much to readers deciding whether to try a book, series, or a new-to-them author.

Thank you.

If you want to continue with the Quebec Quint, you can find book six in the series, *Regeneratus: Races Rekindled,* on Amazon.

THE STORY CONTINUES

The story continues with book six, *Regeneratus: Races Rekindled*, available at Amazon.

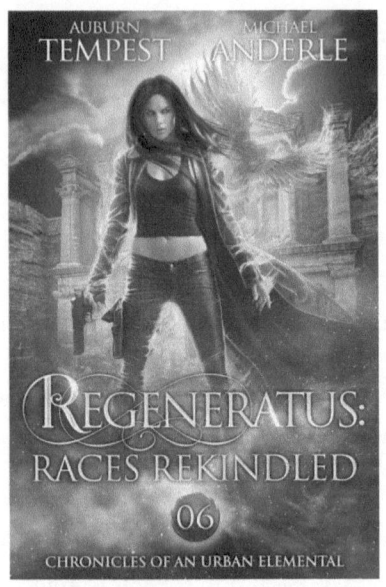

Claim your copy today!

AUTHOR NOTES - AUBURN TEMPEST

SEPTEMBER 6, 2023

I love stories. You might have gathered that by now, but it's true. When I talk to people about what I do, I invariably start encouraging everyone to write. My hubby laughs and shakes his head, telling me that not everyone needs to be a writer.

Maybe that's true, but why wouldn't they want to be?

I make up worlds and adventures and people laugh and fall in love, they fail and triumph, and in the end, everything works out and everyone is happy.

It's amazeballs!

And now my brother is writing. I know—proud sister here. For thirteen years it's been Mom and me writing, and then Dave finally caved to the peer pressure...lol.

Over the past year, I've had the pleasure of working with him through the journey of writing the first three books in his Stonecrusher Legacy series and it's renewed my conviction that I am blessed to do what I love every day, with people I love, and the characters I love.

I've also been working on some new stories. I know, many of you would love me to write Fiona forever, but I'm excited to bring you new adventures: Carry On, the first book in the Chronicles of a Hidden City, a new Paranormal Women's Fiction series I'm writing with Mom, <u>Supernatural Disaster</u>, the first book in a collaboration with my friend Ava, and two new titles for my JL romance books.

Lots happening and I hope you enjoy them all.

Thank you for reading. Thank you for loving my characters and stories and my quirky, of off-beat sense of humor. And in this busy time, when the demands on our time are many, I'm honored you spend your valuable time on my books.

Blessed be,
Auburn Tempest

If you want to keep your finger on the pulse of what is happening with the series, feel free to join the Chronicles of an Urban Druid Facebook Fan page.

Or drop us a line: UrbanDruid@lmbpn.com

If you enjoyed it and want to keep your finger on the pulse, feel free to join the Facebook Fan page.

Or drop us a line: UrbanDruid@lmbpn.com

Blessed be,
Auburn Tempest

AUTHOR NOTES - MICHAEL ANDERLE

SEPTEMBER 11, 2023

First of all, thank you for not only diving into this story but also taking the time to read these author notes at the back!

A Trip Down Memory Lane

Recently, I decided to revisit the Cryptid Assassin Series, and it brought back a flood of memories from late 2019/early 2020, just before the world went upside down due to Covid. At that time, I was frequently dining at Il Fornaio restaurant at the NY-NY Hotel and Casino. The characters in the series developed a love affair with the restaurant, and it's no secret that their fondness for it mirrored my own.

Real-Life Inspirations

In fact, I was eating breakfast at Il Fornaio *ALL THE TIME* while writing the series. I even went the extra mile to get permission to use real people's names in the storyline. Remember Marcelo? He's a real person (the manager for the morning shift). I'm not sure if he still works there, but the stories remind me of the delicious breakfasts I used to enjoy at the restaurant. Unfortunately, they no longer serve breakfast after Covid hit. Sonofabitch!

The Connection Between Stories and Reality

One thing absolutely true (I need ideas, folks) is that my stories often contain elements of my real life. Sometimes, the creative brain is on strike, and I use real life instead.

Whether it's a particular location I've visited or something I'm currently experiencing, these details often make their way into my narratives. This effort has become a fascinating way for me to remember what I was up to when writing each story, and it adds a touch of authenticity to the worlds I create.

My Present Italian Ice Love Affair

As for my latest obsession, there's an Italian Ice dessert place on S. Eastern here in Henderson (a little South of the Las Vegas Airport) called CJ's Italian Ice and Custard (website: https://www.cjsitalianice.com/) that has captivated both Judith and me. We recently bought some of their treats to go, thinking it would last us a week. Well, we seemed to get rid of them in one evening after dinner.

There went my diet weigh-in the next morning.

So, as I continue to weave my stories, I hope you'll enjoy the glimpses into my life and the real-world inspirations that make their way into the pages. Who knows? You might even discover a new favorite restaurant or dessert along the way from time to time.

Talk to you again in the next book.

Ad Aeternitatem,

Michael Anderle

MORE STORIES with Michael newsletter HERE: https://michael.beehiiv.com/

BOOKS BY AUBURN TEMPEST

Find Me
  Amazon, Facebook, Newsletter,
  Web page – www.auburntempest.com
  Email – AuburnTempestWrites@gmail.com

Auburn Tempest - Urban Fantasy Action/Adventure
  Chronicles of an Urban Elemental
  Book 1 – Incendio: Flame Born
  Book 2 – Magicae: Power Dawning
  Book 3 – Potentia: Bonds Forged
  Book 4 - Fidelitas: Trust Realized
  Book 5 - Intellectus: Origins Discovered
  Book 6 - Regeneratus: Races Rekindled

  Chronicles of an Urban Druid
  Book 1 – A Gilded Cage
  Book 2 – A Sacred Grove
  Book 3 – A Family Oath
  Book 4 – A Witch's Revenge
  Book 5 – A Broken Vow

Book 6 – A Druid Hexed
Book 7 – An Immortal's Pain
Book 8 – A Shaman's Power
Book 9 – A Fated Bond
Book 10 – A Dragon's Dare
Book 11 – A God's Mistake
Book 12 – A Destiny Unlocked
Book 13 – A United Front
Book 14 – A Culling Tide
Book 15 – A Danger Destroyed

Case Files of an Urban Druid
Book 1 – Mayhem in Montreal
Book 2 – Sorcery in San Francisco
Book 3 – Necromancy in New Orleans
Book 4 – Hazards in the Hidden City
Book 5 – Hexes in Texas
Book 6 – Wendigos in Washington
Book 7 – Gods at Odds

If you enjoy my writing and read sexy/steamy romance, my pen name for the books I write in Paranormal and Fantasy Romance is JL Madore.

You can find my JL books on Amazon.

BOOKS BY MICHAEL ANDERLE

Sign up for the LMBPN email list to be notified of new releases and special deals!

https://lmbpn.com/email/

For a complete list of books by Michael Anderle, please visit:

www.lmbpn.com/ma-books/

CONNECT WITH THE AUTHORS

Connect with Auburn

Amazon, Facebook, Newsletter

Web page – www.jlmadore.com

Email – AuburnTempestWrites@gmail.com

Connect with Michael Anderle and sign up for his email list here:

Website: http://lmbpn.com

Email List: https://michael.beehiiv.com/

https://www.facebook.com/LMBPNPublishing

https://twitter.com/lmbpn

https://www.instagram.com/lmbpn_publishing/

https://www.bookbub.com/authors/michael-anderle

www.ingramcontent.com/pod-product-compliance
Lightning Source LLC
LaVergne TN
LVHW041755060526
838201LV00046B/1016